Kit & Basie

Tales from Long Lily, 1

Tess Carletta

Cover Illustration © 2023 by Brittany Jones (Bidiza)
Cover design by Brittany Jones and Tess Carletta
Editing by Keir Editing & Writing Services
Author Photograph by Monica Gustin

ISBN 9798988101529 (paperback), 9798988101512 (hardcover), 9798988101505 (eBook)

To all the LGBTQIA+ folks that long for quiet love stories and safe places to call home. We will make this world safer for you.

And to my father, who has read everything I've written since before I could spell — even the kissing books.

Content Warnings

Kit & Basie is first, and foremost, a cozy fantasy romance. You can expect characters to earn their happily-ever-after. However, the book does feature…

- Strong themes of grief

- Death of a parent via physician assisted suicide

- Moderate descriptions of an anxiety attack

- Explicit cursing

- Mentions of sex

- Mentions of a healthy pregnancy

- Mentions of war

Please take care of yourself!

Contents

When it was morning, Cian the Huntsman draped her in a cloak.
He took her to the yard where she would rest beneath the oak.
All the woodland beasts were there, creatures big and small.
They used their claws and hooves to dig her earthy forest pall.
"Why do you dig her grave so true, oh creatures of the wood?"
The boar, the fox, the hare, the deer with eyes of cherry wood
said, "You brought your wife into your house and there you loved her thus,
distracted by her tender heart, you were not hunting us."
Cian laid her body in the grave the animals had dug.
And while he wept, the promise he forgot began to tug.
He would not love a mortal fair, no woman kind or blunt.
He swore the promise once again and then began to hunt.

— Ríordán Mac Carthaigh,
Household Fairytales for House Held Faeries

CHAPTER 1

The cottage at 6163 Annadale Drive was the only place in Long Lily that could guard impossible things. It was home to oddities that were probably magic—anomalies that shouldn't be, but *were* because they'd existed long before anyone had been around to tell them they shouldn't. Most folks couldn't make it past the barriers of their limited imagination to see what was really there. A garden that didn't die in seasons of drought. Bees that never stopped working. A willow tree that never shed its warm weather clothes.

And Basie Yeats, the town electrician who looked twenty-five, but wasn't.

The magic was easy to miss. Any sense of ethereal strangeness about the property could be explained away, mistaken as the nostalgic feeling that comes when a person stands in a place where history happened. In this case, the cottage was built on the very ground where some English fellow in 1811 dug his hands into the soil and said, *"Here. This is where I'll build my kingdom."* Back then, it was two for the price of one, both church and town hall, built to last with Long Lily oak trees and the creek-scented sweat of the village men.

It was the sort of place that made people who shouldn't settle down want to — people like Basie's mother, Adella.

The train platform was busy the day Della arrived at Long Lily. It wasn't the best weather Pennsylvania had to offer, but in 1945, a few blistering breezes were better than anything the wartime sky had given her. She stuck out in her butterscotch dress and scuffed shoes, three months pregnant, hoisting her suitcase up like a man to get a better hold. Every pair of eyes followed her like a hammered sore thumb even as a half dozen soldiers filed out from the train behind her.

Before the villagers could spot their returned loved ones, they watched the empty air beside Della as she swept her way across the platform. Everyone heard the silent question none were brave enough to ask: *Where is this woman's husband?* But all Della had brought with her was a single suitcase, her unborn son, and plenty of years to fill in the gaps of what she didn't have.

On her way off the platform, she passed a lanky fellow sitting on a spare bench, smoking a cigar. She barely paid him enough mind to notice his existence, curving around the woody smoke to avoid inhaling it. Since she'd gotten pregnant, the smell always made her head ache.

"Ms. Yeats," the man called, rising to his feet. The words appeared in a cloud of smoke enveloping his face. Upon a fresh glance, Della found that he matched the appearance of the man found in the packet she'd received via mail some months ago: Mr. Leonard Simon, a freshly certified real estate agent, who might have been handsome if only his glasses were smaller. He wore a fine tweed suit that he'd referred to in his letters as his *Number 7 Getup* because it was lucky. If he wore it the day she arrived, he promised Della would like the house he picked out for her.

"Mr. Simon," she addressed, clicking her heels to clear the snow. They were practically the first words she'd spoken since she left her husband in Mexico. "We weren't due to meet until tomorrow."

A more polite woman would've pretended the mistake was hers, but Della wasn't known for being spineless. Only honest.

Mr. Simon took another huff of his cigar. Della crinkled her nose, already feeling her temple grow tense.

"I'm afraid I've got some bad news," Mr. Simon said. His face was smooth with youth, but he spoke the way older men did over a table of cards—with an age worth of wisdom, and just as much tobacco. Della bolstered herself up against the news just in time for a particularly frigid breeze to sweep across the platform. "Someone outbid you. The townhouse sold this morning."

The news should have vexed Della, but she hadn't seen the house in person before putting an offer on it. Mr. Simon had only described it in his letters and he wasn't a very imaginative writer. Maybe once she passed it for the first time, she'd feel the loss more profoundly. For now, she asked, "What else is available in town?"

Mr. Simon worried at the mouthpiece of his cigar. Surely money couldn't have been the cause of his hesitance. She'd been contributing to a sizable savings account for what felt like an eternity, and her husband had insisted on contributing when he decided to remain in Mexico—like the bleeding bastard he was. Mr. Simon knew about the money, and had promised in his letters that she'd be able to pick the Long Lily house of her dreams.

"The thing is, I'm sure you're aware of all the young soldiers returning from overseas. Most of them are moving closer to Harrisburg where they're building those fancy new developments, but enough are staying here to marry their sweethearts and start their families," Mr. Simon explained. "To put it frankly, they're buying up the houses quick. It may be a while before more properties enter the market."

"You mean to tell me there's *nowhere?*" Della supposed she could stay with Lottie for a while, but the imposition would be as inconvenient for her as it would be for her friend. She wondered if there were any attics to rent or widows in need of companionship.

"I didn't say that. There's one place. Only—Well, maybe it's better if you see it for yourself."

Mr. Simon offered to carry her luggage, but his arms were practically as skinny as her wrist. She nudged his hands aside and carried her own things.

It was too far to walk to the property, which was further from downtown than Della had been planning, so she let Mr. Simon drive her. On the short drive, he told her all about how beautiful the trees looked in autumn. How friendly her neighbors would be when she met them.

The car came to a halt on the side of the road, skidding in a patch of icy slush. The windows had fogged, so Della ran her glove over the glass and peered into the yard. All at once, she understood what the dilemma had been.

It was a church. Its white paneling tricked her mind into believing it was disappearing into the snowy hillside, but the stained-glass window at the base of its steeple stood out to Della like the first rainbow did to Noah. Tall windows lined the sides, though even from the road Della could see several of them had been cracked open with stone-sized holes. Its front porch would need to be repaired before anyone could safely walk up to the door, which had begun to chip from disuse.

"It's not a home," Mr. Simon said. "But it could be."

Della rested her head against the window, trying to imagine raising her child here, but from inside the car, it felt as though she was looking at a photograph. She opened the door and slipped back out into the winter air. Walking through the snow made her toes feel like they were about to break off from the chill seeping through her socks and boots.

Yet, as soon as she stepped across the property line, her sideways soul stood upright.

There were flowers—real *live* flowers—dozens of them in mismatched patches in the yard, peeking strongly through the snow as if the cold was only imaginary to them. Della traced the sight of them to a tremendous willow tree, leaves still vibrant and green even as they billowed among the midwinter snowfall. The only thing that kept Della from discounting it as a trick of the eye was her own existence. If she could live forever, why should it be impossible that this house or this land could live just as long?

She had the feeling that now that she'd arrived, she could not leave. It didn't matter that the plan was just to stay here for a year and then find someplace new. She *belonged* here, and she didn't think she'd ever felt that before.

When she turned to address Mr. Simon, he was already leaning on the front of his car, arms crossed over his chest.

"I'll take it," she said.

Leonard smiled.

When Della asked to see the inside of the home, he tramped through the snow, wrestling with his key ring to find the church's match. Having never been a woman of lasting patience, Della tried the door herself with a confident twist of the handle. To her delight, it swung open with a mighty *CREAK*.

A first look inside revealed the miraculous preservation in the yard did not extend to the church's interior. It was, in fact, falling apart, blanketed in enough dust that the air was difficult to breathe.

Della purchased the house anyway and, before the end of the week, had gotten to work. She donated the pews to the local Presbyterians and thought it wise to leave the chipped-nose Madonna to the Catholics. However, it seemed to Della like the spirit of her home would wane if she removed *all* the sacred furnishings. The first to stay was the communion table, which she sanded by hand, buffing away the essence of Latin prayer with oily, golden stain, until nothing was left but a plain kitchen counter. Della kept the votive candles she'd found in a cabinet too, some with burned wicks from long-forgotten flames. Then a burgundy rug that was a few hard months away from utter mildew destruction, but only an hour of tender care away from rejuvenation.

When spring bloomed, the Long Lily folks grew curious of the strange woman they saw tending to the old headstones in the burial ground across the road. Some of the local widows had made a point to pass slowly by the church just to watch Della kneel in the churchyard and scrape away lichen from between the letters spelling *Dearest* and *Friend* or *In God's care.* Della gave them the courtesy of pretending she didn't notice, until one day the youngest of the women knelt beside her and offered to help.

Then it wasn't just the mending of the church, but the mending of war-broken hearts of her neighbors who knew the weight of an endless grief. With as much care as she painted her walls, she held the hands of mothers and wives when they wept over empty graves of men lost in muddy trenches. She received their tears, washed their hair, and kept them from tugging it out.

But soon the mourning period was over and all those mothers, sisters, and wives returned the debt of their grief to the cottage: the walls, the floors, the window panes. They helped Della Yeats cover her age-stained walls in pale honey-colored paint. They soiled the knees of their trousers by planting irises with Della by the road and taught her to raise bees near the flowers richest in pollen. They did not speak of the war-shaped crater in their chests, and instead dedicated long hours into creating a place that war could not touch.

In spring of 1945, when the repairs were complete, all of the single and widowed women gave the cottage a name—*Wellhead*.

On paper, the cottage had passed in ownership from Della Yeats down several generations of daughters. In truth, in all those years, the property had only ever passed once: from Della Yeats—mother—to Basie Yeats—son.

Because Della, for all her many names and many years, knew that you could only give gifts like family homes and immortality once.

Some months after the naming of Wellhead, when the garden's soil was tangled with roots and the tree saplings grew strong, it was time for the cottage to welcome the final piece of missing magic: a baby with open hands and a head of curly brown hair. Sweet Basie Yeats.

Basie grew up at Wellhead and lived there even when his

growing stopped—happy, cared for, and eternally twenty-five. Della almost hadn't believed Basie when he claimed he'd stopped growing. Most immortal folks didn't peak for at least another decade. Della herself was a late bloomer, aging until a few weeks after her thirty-seventh birthday. But when Basie crept slowly down the stairs to tell his mother that he *felt* the aging stop, there was no denying it. Sensing the standstill was different for everyone, but always rather curious in nature. For Della, she'd felt like a flock of birds had come to rest at the base of her feet.

For Basie, there were no birds. He only shrugged and said, "My bones are at peace."

Because she was the only person he could ask, he learned many lessons about his own immortality from his mother. Discovered some for himself. Knew some without having to be told.

Of the last variety, the most important was this: immortality was a dangerous affair when it wasn't done right.

Done right, people like Basie kept their lives in duffle bags until they were worn into threads from use. They learned a dozen languages and let the thrill of *existing* make them forget how many years they had been alive.

They did *not,* however, hang pictures on their walls. They didn't leave things in their fridge long enough to grow fuzzy, white trees. And they certainly didn't embrace the sort of commitments that might tempt a person to stay put—like Della's bees. Or a successful produce stand that the locals relied on. Or a house over two hundred years old and *constantly* in need of repair.

In short, Basie was doing immortality all wrong.

The only problem was, admitting so would also mean admitting Della was doing immortality wrong too, which was absolutely, positively out of the question. Because even if Basie could convince his mom that she might've been wrong about something—*ha!*—then they'd have to *do something* about it. Something unpalatable, like leaving Long Lily and overhauling the lifestyle that suited them fine. Willful ignorance was by far the easier option. Still, it didn't mean it was right.

When he asked his mother her opinion on the matter, she argued that he had it all twisted up. There weren't any official rules for their condition, she said, so she could live in the same damn house for her entire endless existence if she wanted. She would make her pies and drink her magnolia tea every blessed day—world without end, Amen—if that's what made her happy.

"Won't the people in town notice?" Basie asked, the night of his twenty-fifth birthday. The night he instinctively knew he stopped aging.

"Oh, they'll notice. Some already do," Della replied. His eyes were glued to her hands, the pie dough hugging around her fingers as she kneaded it into the counter. Flour sprinkled over the edge, powdering white across the old wooden inlay that read *In Remembrance of Me.* "Folks realize that if they've been watching us, we've been watching *them* for a lot longer, and that puts us right in the center of knowing all their business."

"What about the folks with nothing to hide?" Basie asked, biting into a fresh strawberry. He plucked another one out of her bowl, flicking off some of the seeds with his fingernail.

"Everyone's got business, Basie. Some people just mind theirs. 'Sides, our neighbors believe anything can happen in Appalachia."

"That's 'cause anything *can*," he replied. He should know.

Basie caught his own reflection in the window above the sink. It was a good thing he liked his face, because it wasn't going anywhere.

On those warm, summer days, it was easy to believe that when Della said her stubborn *Amens* and laughed without crow's feet, she wasn't going anywhere either.

But then, Della was Basie's mother, and she did immortality all wrong too.

THE PHONE CALL CAME years later, the day Basie took down the 2022 calendar hanging on the refrigerator. It was outdated by a few months, but Della liked its pictures of Van Gogh's paintings so much that she'd let it outstay its welcome. She wouldn't have even kept a calendar if it wasn't for her son, who insisted on tracking the days.

He was halfway through cutting out Van Gogh's *Sunflowers* to hang in a frame on the wall when the phone began to ring.

Sometimes, when Basie had trouble untangling the years of his life in his head, he would think of things as *Pre-sunflowers* and *Post-sunflowers*.

Pre-sunflowers Basie thought his mother was still in bed, sleeping past noon.

Post-sunflowers Basie picked up the receiver, held it between his chin and shoulder, and said, "Hello, this is Basie."

The person on the other line identified herself in simple, basic terms, though she never gave her name. She was one of Della's old friends, an American nurse who had moved to Canada to retire with her husband.

"And," she said, "I know your secret."

Basie, who was halfway to the stairs to wake his mother, paused.

"I'm not sure I know what you mean," he said slowly, the way he was taught.

"The thing is, Basie…" She swallowed so hard the sound passed through the speaker. "The thing is, your mother is here with me. In Ontario. She drove all night to get here."

"Why?" Basie said, frowning.

"You know she's been around a long time. And well, some things just aren't legal in the States."

They were just words—very vague ones, at that. But Basie distrusted the sound of them.

"I'm sorry, but you're mistaken. My mother's here. Hold on just a minute, I'll get her for you," Basie interrupted. But even as he took the steps to Della's room two at a time, he could feel the *wrongness* of the phone call. As if there was no possible reality in which the words spoken over the line could end in a desirable outcome. Basie turned over the facts in his mind. Della wouldn't take a trip and leave Basie without telling him. "Maybe you have her confused with someone else."

"I don't think so," the woman answered gently.

He should ask her name. Ask where exactly she was calling from. Ask her to mind her goddamn business and leave his family alone.

"Are you sitting down?" the nameless woman continued. "You should sit down."

Basie would not sit down. She couldn't say whatever she was about to if he was still standing. There was still time. He could still work out the solution to whatever bizarre twist of events had disturbed Wellhead's peace.

"My mom doesn't even have a valid passport anymore. How could she—" Basie was all frayed edges, but the woman was fortified by unrelenting patience.

"I made arrangements for her so she could drive across the Buffalo-Ontario border. She took your truck, I think. I'm looking right at her."

Basie swung Della's door open. It smelled like her, the maple of her four-poster bed and the perfume on her dresser that was a few decades too old. On the wall, Della's latest passion project went unfinished—a mural of hyper realistic, human sized flowers against a sky of mossy green. Cans of paint waited at the foot of the perfectly made bed.

But Della was nowhere in sight.

She should've been sleeping. Or painting. She should've—

"You've got the wrong number," Basie said sternly.

"Would you like the news of your mother or not, Basie?" replied the woman.

Basie tapped the wireless receiver to his forehead, gaze drifting to the empty bed.

"Can she tell me the news herself, please?" he asked.

There was another gaping pause.

"She can't. Your mother passed away this morning."

That was—But—

Basie turned his burning eyes back to his mom's empty room.

Then, he began to crash. He crashed down the stairs. Down

the valley road. Down the entire goddamn mountain.

"What did you just say to me?" he hissed dangerously. "Is this your idea of a sick joke? Because if it is, congratulations. It's pretty fucking sick. You said you knew our secret. Remember? My mom *can't. Die.*"

This was objectively not true. Having seventy-seven years of immortality up his sleeve, Basie's understanding of the rules of immortality was just as thorough as his ability to write and read. Immortal people could, feasibly, live forever. The same ancient forces that kept them from aging also strengthened their bodies from disease and quickened their healing. It meant that immortals often got out of scrapes that would've doomed anyone else. Immortality did not, however, provide protection against gunshots. Or freak accidents involving sharp objects.

Or euthanasia, apparently.

"We don't expect you to understand entirely, alright? It was—Well, it was something she'd been planning for a while. You've heard the term euthanasia before, right?"

"You *euthanized* my *mother?*"

"Because she asked to be!"

"Then she wasn't in her right mind!"

"She had a psychological assessment, just to be certain."

"Oh, I'm sure that shrink thought she was *so* mentally sound when she told them how old she was. Who even are you, any-ways?"

"Someone from your mom's hometown."

"Give me a name."

"I know you're upset, but—"

"*Tell me your fucking name.*"

"Rita," the woman replied, voice trembling. Not in fear, though. Maybe from having to own up to being a cold-hearted bitch.

"Well, guess what, Rita? You're a murderer. A goddamned murderer. You murdered my mother. You *murdered*—"

Basie was crashing. Crashing. Crashing.

He was suddenly the only immortal he knew.

His knee crumbled and he fell onto the hardwood floor. If he'd been able to find the breath, he might've spoken, but there wasn't anything to say.

He wasn't aware of much except that he was weeping. Or something close to weeping, because he could not breathe. He choked and wheezed and clung to sparse gasps, but his lungs never filled.

"She was happy," he heard himself say, though the words were nothing but a rasp. Rita made a pitying noise that made Basie feel sick.

"Even happy people don't want to live forever."

Does anyone? Do I? Basie sneered in his mind. He hadn't asked to drag around the weight of forever on his ankle. He never took his mother for a coward, either. Never considered that she'd be the one to make him the way he was, then leave him to be the *only* one stuck in time.

"It was *her* choice," Rita finished.

This Basie could not tolerate.

"You're crazy. Absolutely deranged. She'd never leave like that. Not without me there. Not without saying goodbye. You don't know her like I do. You're not family."

"If it's any consolation, she told me she left a note for you."

Basie shook his head over and over and over. *Consolation.* God, he still couldn't breathe. Why couldn't he breathe? "She said you'd know where to find it."

Basie dropped his head to his knees.

When he didn't answer her, the stranger—fucking *Rita*—explained that they would be handling the arrangements for the funeral, but he could write the obituary if he wanted. They'd bury her in the small backwater town where she'd stopped aging hundreds of years ago and, no, it wasn't possible to send her home to be buried in Long Lily. It would just bring up a nasty slew of questions and she didn't want Basie to have to keep track of so many lies. This way he could stay where he was; didn't he understand? He should come up for the service, she said. Take a bus across the US line and then drive his truck home.

Basie didn't care about the truck. He tried to tell her as much, but found he was crying too hard—hard enough that it seemed unlikely he would ever be able to stop. It was possible that no human had ever been so angry before. The sheer weight of it circled back around past ire, past rage, and right into ice cold sadness.

"Will you be alright?" the woman asked.

"Oh, *fuck you*," he snapped. He threw the phone at the wall. Shards of plastic exploded against the unfinished mural and the batteries rolled over to his feet. He wanted to hit something else until everything he owned was in small, broken bits and his hands were covered in cuts. But that meant accepting that the phone call was real. Even in this magical house, that was the one impossible thing he could not allow.

Basie slowly circled the cottage, the sheds, and the gardens in search of his mother. Della was not weeding in the flower beds, hiding behind the beehives, or reading in some nook of the house.

Because the thing about Wellhead Cottage was that it could guard any impossible thing. But if those impossible things left, so did Wellhead's protection. And Della had left, so now she was gone.

He went around once more, this time in search of the final goodbye letter that he was promised. He circled her empty bedroom, then his messy one, then the kitchen, and Della's desk. There was no letter. Maybe it was in Canada.

Then, Basie's gaze lingered on the shed. It'd be easy to look through the side window for the note. Della always kept them clean. But when Basie urged himself to step forward, to use the key in his pocket and unlock the whining door, he found his body would not move.

He regarded the shed for a long, long time—long enough that the sun and shadows shifted along the shed's exterior walls.

When it grew dark, Basie went back inside. He sat at the kitchen table and folded his hands, watching evening pour in through the open windows.

It was then Basie decided he was going to start doing immortality the right way.

CHAPTER 2

"YOU'RE NOT TRYING HARD ENOUGH," Basie told Lewie Simon during breakfast at the Redtop Diner one morning. Lewie only scoffed.

Basie had been putting off this breakfast since he'd called Lewie earlier that week. He could at least hide his red eyes and unwashed hair over the phone. Meeting up with his best friend in public meant he needed to look acceptable in order to be granted entry at a food establishment.

As far as phone calls went, it wasn't the worst he had. Basie choked the news out without completely unraveling, a miraculous feat in his opinion. He'd allowed Lewie one second of stunned silence before telling him to put Wellhead up for sale, along with everything in it. Lewie had tried to convince him to get out for a bit—*Why don't you come over? I'll put a pot of Folgers on and we can sit in silence on the patio*—but Basie refused.

"You need to list the house and I need to pack," Basie had said.

And he did, though *pack* was a loose term for the way he shoved all the necessities into one single bag and left Wellhead behind. He'd meant to leave Long Lily immediately, only there were some loyal customers with flickering lights and malfunctioning outlets that he promised he would fix before he left. The nice elderly man who owned the local fishing motel let Basie stay five days for free, because he somehow still remembered playing baseball with Basie as a boy. Basie repaid him by giving all the lobby lamps fresh bulbs, no charge.

In a week, when the five pity days dried up and all fifty years of debts and favors were paid in full, he would go.

Just as soon as Lewie sold the house.

"I've had four offers on the place, so I'll take none of that nonbeliever bullshit. I'm just holding out a few extra days," said Lewie, sipping on his tepid coffee.

Basie spooned up some raspberries, examined them, then poured them back into their bowl.

"Why wait? I'm ready to get out of here."

"Because if you sell the place without thinking it through, you'll regret it. At least go pack up some of your mom's things and put them in storage. Trust me, you'll want every bit of her when the worst of it wears off."

Basie set his jaw and gave Lewie a stern glare.

"I don't want the house. I don't want her things."

"Then give me time to find someone who will love it as much as you did. We can't have just anyone moving into Long Lily forever."

"It's not your job to control who comes into town. It's your job to sell the place."

Lewie lifted his coffee to his lips, smearing his finger through the brown ring left on the laminate tabletop. When he set his mug down, a waitress came round to top it off and Lewie did the whole thing all over again.

Basie let him sip once, then twice, before he pressed, *"Sell the place,* Lewie. I don't care *who* you sell it to. I just want to get the hell out of Long Lily."

Lewie still wasn't convinced, because Basie Yeats was always a bit of a liar. Or, at the very least, someone who knew how to withhold the truth.

"It feels pretty shitty when your best friend comes up to you begging because he can't get away fast enough."

"Come on, you know it's got nothing to do with you. When your parents died, you would've headed out on the first plane south if it weren't for your kid siblings. Look me in the eye and tell me you would've stayed."

Lewie did just that. "I would've stayed, Basie."

Basie stared back, hard. Lewie's shoulders slumped. At the end of the day, when Basie looked at him like that, Lewie's job as *realtor* won out over his job as *friend.* "But just because I would've stayed doesn't mean you have to hang around. If leaving is really what you want, I'll have Wellhead sold by the end of the week."

For the first time, Post-sunflower Basie relaxed into his seat.

A week. He could survive a week. In fact, he'd survived more weeks than most people he knew who looked twenty-five.

It was short lived peace, because then Lewie turned to him and asked, "What are you going to do about the shed?"

Basie stiffened.

"Nothing," he replied carefully. "It's locked. I've got the key."

"Come on, Bas. You've gotta hand over the shed key when you sell the house."

"Tell them I lost it. If the buyer ends up wanting the shed so bad, they can get a new key made. It's not my problem."

What *was* his problem was finding somewhere to stay. Any of his neighbors would jump at the opportunity to host him, because above all, Long Lily people loved two things: hosting guests and overfeeding them within an inch of their life. But the thought of being under constant attention was unbearable.

His gaze drifted over to the booths next to them, lingering on the cracks in the striped upholstery. Suddenly, he knew exactly where he'd stay.

"I gotta head out," said Basie, pushing his hands to his knees, the way that always meant *Well, would you look at the time?* "I told Love Dixie I'd fix that flickering light over her auntie's kitchen sink."

"I reckon we oughta talk this out a little more."

"I *reckon* you give good advice, but unfortunately, I'm just not in the mood. Maybe next time." Basie plucked a ten-dollar bill from his wallet before stuffing it into his back pocket. "I really do want *you* to be the one to sell the place, Lew. Your grandfather is the one that gave the papers to my ma. It's only right."

"I said I'd do it. The advice is entirely of the friend variety."

"Then write it in a letter and I'll get it in a day or two," teased Basie, dropping the money on the table.

"And send it *where?*"

But Basie was already gone. And not to Love Dixie's aunt's house either, but to the small nook of Long Lily that would be his interim home.

The Redtop Diner, before it moved to its prime location downtown, had once welcomed guests in the middle of Crane's Nest Wood on the north side of town. Its patrons had enjoyed the mountainside route to the diner just as much as they liked the pie and the larger-than-life soft pretzels. One of Basie's only surviving memories from his youth was the absolute chaos that ensued when the Redtop Diner announced it would shut its doors after a flooding incident. The community conspired together to raise the down payment on a Main Street location, a scheme that was so successful, Basie still ate there at least once a week over sixty years later.

Redtop's owners had never gotten around to tearing down the old building. The only folks who remembered the red-roofed nook in the woods were either retired or immortal.

Basie paid no mind to the muddy forest trails as the fettering overgrowth and fallen twigs nipped at his boots. With each crunching step, his mind skirted around the things he *should* be thinking about, circumventing them from a safe distance like a half-interested buzzard. They were meaningless words on deaf ears. Della's funeral. His plan for moving. The mystery of who would buy the house.

The white noise distraction carried him all the way to the crest of the hill where a faded red roof materialized through the trees. It was only when he recognized the sight that it occurred to him that he'd been walking at least a mile in the pouring rain. The old diner might not have been a five-star hotel, but at least it would get him out of the downpour.

From the outside, the diner looked like it had been plucked apart the same way people pluck at grass—frayed along the siding, with no rhyme or reason to which boards stayed nailed in and which were cracked with age. It probably wasn't safe to stay here for long, but the roof hadn't collapsed during the last sixty years of neglect, so he imagined it would last another week.

The dark sky overhead wept fat raindrops through the trees

and into Basie's eyes. His boots sank two inches deep in the mud when he walked up to the main door. He squinted into the window, smudging a thick layer of dirt away with the meat of his fist. He was met with his own sharp brown eyes peering back, along with the brown curls stuck to his forehead. The tan skin his father had given him hadn't seen much sun since he had become Post-sunflower Basie, so there was little color to hide the dark bags under his eyes.

But past the gauzy smudges of his own reflection, Basie saw the dining room he'd visited most Fridays during his childhood, stuck in time like a scene from a snow globe, wet and faded. He gave the door a shove and it pushed open as if the lock had been broken for so long, it couldn't remember how to do its job.

Basie dropped his bag on a patch of dry floor where the rain hadn't smuggled itself in. He gave his damp head a good shake.

"*Hogar dulce hogar,*" he said, listlessly. *Home sweet home.*

That night, Basie pushed five stiff booths together, laid back across the seats, and pretended to look for pictures in the mildew stains on the ceiling. He blocked all mention of Della from his mind, ignoring the soul-deep ache to return home and lay under a mountain of his own quilts.

In the silence of the diner, his empty thoughts circled around until Basie could take the quiet no longer.

Instead, he sat up and planned. He focused and plotted and did not allow his attention to waver until everything was laid out in his mind.

It was decided.

Once Lewie sold Wellhead, Basie would take the money and hitch a ride to Snyder County. After squirreling away some of the money for his savings, he'd sign the first lease he could get his hands on. He would *not* purchase a house, but he would buy a real nice truck. As soon as the keys were in his hands, he'd stomp on the gas and—*westward.* To places where he wouldn't learn anyone's names or stick around long enough to know how to get around without his GPS.

Everywhere, *everything*, would be temporary. That was the way it ought to be.

Lewie sold the house first thing the next morning. He wouldn't tell Basie anything about the man other than the fact that he looked to Lewie like he *belonged* in the house. As if it were built for him the same way it was built for Della and Basie.

Curiosity that hadn't been there before now itched behind Basie's eyes. He allowed himself one question: the man's name. Lewie offered it with little judgment—Kit Elliot.

Basie tried not to care, but the name fit snugly into an unexpected corner of his chest the second he heard it. It made him feel…He wasn't sure how it made him feel, really.

There was an irritating trail of distrust, as noticeable as a bad itch, demanding to know who this Kit Elliot was, where he was from, and what his intentions were. Yet, answering these questions probably would've made Basie tear his heart out. The only thing he knew about Kit was his name and the fact that they had kindred tastes in living arrangements, and even that was too much. The similarity would've meant the world to Della, but didn't matter a bit to Basie.

"He'll be over tomorrow morning to sign the paperwork if you want to meet him," Lewie said.

"I don't."

"He asked me to tell you that he promises to take good care of Wellhead."

"Doesn't matter to me whether he does or not."

"Sure, alright," Lewie sighed, handing him a pen. "Go ahead and sign your life away."

For once, Basie did as he was told.

And, with a final swirling of the 's' in Yeats, he was no longer Post-sunflower Basie, or the Long Lily electrician. He was just Basie. No roots, no home, and many, many years to live.

Wellhead Cottage—its grounds, its memories—was someone else's problem now.

CHAPTER 3

Kit Elliot had been in Long Lily for all of thirty minutes and the locals had already sniffed out fresh blood. They were like vultures—albeit friendly, neighborly vultures—slowing their cars to an ominous creep as they passed Wellhead Cottage. The most unnerving part had to be the drivers' faces plastered at their windows, gaping as if Kit were some prized pig at the county fair. Not that he'd ever been to a county fair, but it wasn't hard to guess how the pigs felt: overly hot, scrutinized, and hungry. The only difference between Kit and his blue-ribbon counterparts was that he was wearing dress pants and a button up. Pigs got to lay in the mud. This mild discomfort did not, however, prevent Kit from waving politely at every spectator who passed.

One brave man hand-cranked the window of his bright yellow truck and called out, "Who're you, there?"

"Kit Elliot, sir," Kit called back.

Maybe he'd just hang a banner up over the porch and save everyone the trouble of wondering who he was. *NEWLY MOVED IN: CHRISTOPHER MYRON ELLIOT OF BALTIMORE. PLEASE REFER TO AS KIT.*

"You one of Basie's friends?" the truck driver pressed.

"I'm afraid I don't know anyone named Basie, sir."

"Well, that's a right shame," the man said. "They'll sell a house to anyone these days."

Before Kit could wonder what that was supposed to mean, the man drove off, cranking the window up as he disappeared in a cloud of dirt and gravel.

Kit wasn't sure what was so strange about a man sitting in nice clothes on his own porch. Of course, most folks didn't know that the cottage was his now. (Well, the cottage wouldn't actually be his until the real estate agent, a man named Lewis Simon, arrived to sign the papers and give him the keys.) Kit hadn't expected the semantics to matter to the locals. Where he was from, people minded their own business.

Eventually, a vehicle that was more van than truck pulled into the driveway and parked behind Kit's U-Haul. He almost expected half a dozen children to pop out the back doors, given the extended passenger cab and all the booster seats that filled it. The man who exited circled around the front of the truck, a time-worn briefcase tucked under his arm. This was Kit's only indication that the man was the Realtor he was waiting for. The other clues, his business casual jeans and plain button down, were hiding underneath a large Carhartt jacket. Lewis Simon must've been crazy to be wearing a coat in this early summer heat.

Besides his strange clothing choice, Mr. Simon was handsome in a small-town way. All his features were made of straight edges, except for his eyes, which were two lopsided moons. He wore his long, midnight-black hair in a frantic bun and his skin was just as pale as Kit's, without the freckles.

"Sorry I'm late. Raising six kids under the age of eighteen pretty much guarantees I'm chronically running behind," the Realtor rambled. He shoved a hand between them and offered Kit a firm shake. "I'm Lewie Simon. Thanks for waiting."

"Kit Elliot. It's no trouble at all. I'm partial to taking my time."

"That's a relief. You've got your work cut out for you with this house. Not that it's falling apart. The Yeats family kept it in top-notch shape. It's only that…Well, you'll see."

The front door groaned open. Lewie led him down a short hallway into the main space, then stepped out of the way so Kit could see for himself.

Wellhead Cottage was a sight. The pictures online were enough to have Kit emailing Lewie instantly, but there was something about stepping past the threshold that could not be captured in pixels and polarized glass. Kit attributed the feeling to the very air in the house, the all-consuming atmosphere that made him feel like he'd met his match.

But the thing Lewie was referring to surrounded him in a different way. Because whoever the previous owner was, they had left all of their belongings. All their coats, hanging in the entryway. All their dishes, waiting on the drying rack to be put away. Pictures on the walls, books lining every shelf, real life flowers on the windows. The evidence and history of an entirely different existence was everywhere.

When Kit turned to Lewie, he found him squinting up at one of the family portraits on the wall. Lewie caught his curious look and answered the unspoken question with a sigh.

"The man who lived here before, Basie—Well, his mother passed away earlier this week unexpectedly. Shook him up real bad, as you can probably guess. He was eager to get out of the house.”

“Won’t he come back for any of his things?”

“Definitely not. He just wants to get out of town.” Lewie scratched the back of his head. “A little hard to explain to someone who isn’t used to small town living.”

It was true that Kit hadn't lived anywhere but a city in a long time, but that did not mean that he had never lost anyone or that he did not know the shape of grief. Sometimes sadness was even worse in Baltimore, where the streets never slept or ceased their babbling. Looking around this quiet house, sitting on even quieter property, Kit could see how *this* silence could be hard too.

“And here I thought the listing online was just to show what the cottage would look like completely lived in,” Kit said. “The house in its current condition makes me expect the previous owner—Basie, you said?—to walk right through the door.”

“If it makes you feel better, he can’t anymore. He doesn’t have the keys.” To prove his point, Lewie tossed the key ring onto the kitchen table. “Everything inside the house is yours to do with what you wish. I would just wait a few days before you throw it all out or something. Just to give Basie some time to leave town before he sees everything on the side of the road.”

“He doesn’t want it thrown out?”

“If he did, he would’ve done it himself. I can get you the names of some cleaning companies. I know it’d be a lot to take care of all on your own.”

Kit stuffed his hands in his pockets, examining the house around him. The kitchen was cozy, made lighter by the white cabinetry. An open window over the sink spilled light onto the surrounding counters, where hand-painted canisters and a few parched plants added some color. He spared an interested glance at the oven, which seemed to be in good enough condition to keep up with his baking habits.

Ambling across the open floor into the living room, Kit found the walls were half bookshelves, half pictures. It felt like an intrusion to examine the pictures too closely, but the shelves were beautiful. They wrapped around the living room and continued into the entry hallway that Kit had passed through on his way in. Books, in his opinion, were an excellent welcoming committee. There were plenty of window seats and couches in the living room, too, each promising a comfortable spot to read and draw.

It was smaller than he pictured, but if he was being honest with himself, the size was perfect.

Lewie waited for him back in the kitchen, closely watching Kit drift around the space. He leaned up against one of the countertops that, to Kit's surprise, had words of prayer inlaid on the side.

"Is that a Catholic altar?" he blurted.

Lewie frowned beside him. "Huh, forgot about that. Della wanted to preserve some of the original furniture when she renovated this place from a church into the cottage it is now. Most of it is gone though, except for the bench by the door. That used to be part of a pew."

Kit remembered this little piece of Wellhead's history from the listing online. Wellhead Cottage was the first building ever built in Long Lily. Even Henry St. Anna, the town's founder, had lived here while his own house was being built. This meant the floors were original to the house, and so were the stained-glass windows in the side rooms. During an interview over the phone, Lewie had explained to Kit that Della renovated the place herself, putting up walls to give it the semblance of a real house, complete with upstairs bedrooms capped by low, vaulted ceilings.

"Am I remembering right that your offer letter mentioned you're a painter?" said Lewie, rolling one of his sheets into a tight scroll.

"Only as a hobbyist," Kit answered. He was admittedly distracted by the arching stained window, running his fingers along each piece of smooth glass and their chipped edges.

"There's something upstairs I need to show you, then."

This captured Kit's attention. He nodded good-naturedly and followed Lewie up the stairs. Each of their steps echoed out loud creaks and Kit was so charmed by it, he almost went down the steps to go back up all over it again. All his previous homes had been newly built when he moved in and never bore the charm of rickety stairs or walls that groaned in the wind.

The upstairs hallway was a trove of pictures, all hanging on the wall without any particular care for spacing or organization. An alarming number of the photographs were cabinet cards, recognizable by their sepia hues and eerie, Edwardian subjects. The rest were old nature photographs, faded snapshots of country days gone by.

The real treasure laid behind the door to the master bedroom.

A quiet gasp slipped out of Kit's lips.

Along the green vaulted walls was a mural of a patch of flowers. Marigolds, daisies, tiger lilies, and wildflowers he didn't know the name of all swayed larger than life on an invisible breeze. Easy brushstrokes betrayed the trained, meticulous hand that laid the paint down. Perhaps the only thing that was peculiar about the piece was that it wasn't finished. Only half of the wall was complete, the other half a mess of sketched pencil markings. He followed the graphite outline to the floor where paint cans and rolled tubes waited along the baseboards.

There was something about the painting. The more Kit examined the wall, the more he was certain he'd seen the mural before. Possibly it was a copy of a famous piece he might've seen in a museum. Or maybe it was just that Kit liked looking at flowers and these ones were so realistic, they exuded familiarity.

"What do you think?" Lewie called out behind him.

"It's hard to believe no one else placed an offer on the house. For its size, it is deceptively full. It almost feels…" Kit didn't know how to tell Lewie it felt too good to be true. In any other case, Kit would be suspicious that a house of this price, and this quality, would last on the market long enough for him to find it nearly a week later. But he'd grown a sort of sixth-sense at telling which people were worth his time and which could not be trusted.

Lewie Simon could be trusted. Therefore, the house was exactly as Kit perceived it— perfect.

"For what it's worth, I did have a few offers before yours. But I had a good feeling about you," said Lewie. "Though what I was actually asking about was the mural. Do you think you'll be able to finish it?"

Kit turned back to the wall. Whoever completed the piece would have to have masterful skill and plenty of time on their hands.

"I'm curious. Why does it matter?" he asked.

"It was in Ms. Yeats' will. I'm sure you could hire someone to do it for you if you don't want to commit to it, but— "

"I can finish it," Kit declared, holding back a small smile.

Lewie nodded, eyes bright.

"Thank you for not disappointing, Mr. Elliot. If you'll follow me back downstairs, we'll get the paperwork signed. Then Wellhead will be yours."

The last of the papers Kit had to sign were waiting on the dining room table with two pens: one blue, one black.

This was it. All the moving around and leaving people behind would come to an end right here. He'd paid the down payment and signed most of the papers at the bank. This was just a formality. With a few important flourishes of ink on paper, this cottage would be his.

Just as Kit uncapped the pen, his phone started to chime with the awful ringtone he used in Baltimore. He'd originally chosen it because it was the only preloaded option that could get his attention. Now, the chiming seemed too grating against the quiet of this cottage.

A name was displayed across the screen: Lara Tom.

Lara was a walking hurricane with no rescue relief. She had lived next to Kit for nearly the entirety of his stay at his old townhouse, which was to say, a few years. In that time, she proved to be the loudest and most loyal individual Kit had ever met, fixing her relentless protection over three things: her parents, their downtown Asian Market, and Kit Elliot, even when he was more than capable of taking care of himself.

He sighed.

"I'm sorry, I have to take this. It's my old neighbor. I'm worried something might be wrong with my previous apartment."

Lewie offered an understanding smile and waved at him to

answer it.

When the call connected, Lara was already off to the races.

"You need to get here now, Kit. Maris is here squeezing all your books into cardboard boxes. I don't know what he intends to do with them. Worst case scenario, he's taking them right back to the dumpster. And he won't answer my questions—" she said pointedly to someone Kit could only assume was Mr. Maris, his old landlord. "That's right, old man. I'm talking about you. When Kit gets here, he's going to—"

"Do nothing. Lara, this isn't a good time. Could I call you back?"

"Did you not hear me? I said Maris is boxing up your books to throw out to the wolves! I'm staring at empty bookshelves right now and it's a deeply alarming sight."

"One I'm sure you'll recover from. I'm hanging up now."

He did. Lara called back immediately.

"Listen," he said before she could venture into another frenzy. "It wasn't feasible to bring them all with me. There was no space in the moving truck and the moving boxes were expensive. Besides, this new house is really quite small and the bookshelves are already filled. I told Mr. Maris that he could donate my books."

"But you've been collecting them for—"

"I know."

"Kit…" Lara faltered. "They're your books."

Eye's falling shut, Kit tipped his head back. He'd been shoving the memory of his prized collection as far from his mind as possible. This call was nearly enough to send him out the door and back to Baltimore. But the mortgage was signed, the pen was uncapped, and this was happening.

There would always be more books.

"If that's all, I have to go. And leave Mr. Maris alone."

"No promises," she deadpanned. Then, a smile soaked through her voice as she added, "Happy Move-In Day."

The line went dead. Kit could feel Lewie's curious gaze track him as he shifted to sit straighter and picked up the pen.

"My apologies," said Kit thickly. "Now, where were we?"

He opened the packet, dropped the pen to the line, and signed.

Skidding across the table, a ring of keys fell into Kit's lap. Lewie's smile blossomed.

"Welcome to Long Lily, neighbor."

CHAPTER 4

THE ONLY BRIGHT SIDE to the Yeats family truck being stuck in Ontario was that Basie really liked to walk. Knowing Long Lily like the back of his hand, Basie knew just how long it would take him to arrive at the gas station on foot where Ed Nougat filled his tank every Monday before driving to Snyder County to buy lumber. If he was lucky, there'd be room for Basie, too.

The stiff, uneven bed he'd made in the diner had stolen his sleep, making him wake up later than he had in mind. If he was going to make it before Ed hit the road, he'd have to take the route past Wellhead.

The modification went against his own strict resolution to avoid Wellhead at all costs, under threat of…Well, he hadn't come up with a punishment, yet. But *something* lousy.

It wasn't the view of the house itself he wanted to avoid. It was the sight of the things *in* the house that he could see from the road—the photographs on the wall, his mother's paintings, the Amish quilt folded over the couch. He still had a secret spare key. If he wanted them— which he *didn't*—he could go in, take the heirlooms before Kit Elliot threw them all away, and be gone before anyone knew he'd been there.

The only problem was, Kit Elliot was already outside.

A moving van swallowed half of him up, but he appeared out the back with an arm full of boxes a second later. From the road, Kit looked tall, though Basie had a feeling that they'd stand eye-to-eye up close. In the shade, his hair was the color of ground nutmeg, but melted into auburn gold when he stepped into the sun.

Basie hated himself for it, because he could not explain why, but he understood what Lewie had meant about Kit looking like he belonged at Wellhead. Maybe it was something about the way everything was just a little bit more vibrant where Kit stood. It made a traitorous part of Basie want to draw nearer.

It was Kit's attire that stood out against the Maryland U-Haul—brown dress pants, a striped button down, and (good God) a *tie*. Dry dirt kicked up around his dress loafers, sullying the expensive leather with a typical Long Lily welcome. Unaware or unconcerned with the dust storm at his feet, Kit dropped the boxes on the front steps and snuck a peek inside the top.

Basie appraised the grace with which the man moved, assured but gentle, like there was no cause in the world to rush. He wondered what sort of things a man like this brought with him when he moved and if he'd play nice with all the things Basie had left behind.

"Need a ride into town, Basie?"

Basie practically jumped out of his skin. Jed Donlevy was just behind him, grinning like a long-tongued dog from the window of his bright truck—locally known as the Submarine for its Beatle-like yellow hue. A wide grin showed off the cracked tooth he'd gotten from a bar fight last January. Basie knew Jed was otherwise harmless, but he still jolted. All at once, it occurred to Basie that if he had heard Jed, then…

Kit was already looking at Basie, staring the way people look at lions in a zoo—hands in his pocket, a safe distance away in case the unknowable creature decided to lash out. Understanding lit his eyes, as if he was calculating with perfect accuracy just how long Basie had been standing there watching him.

In short, Basie needed to get the hell out of there.

"Uh, yeah. A ride would be great. Thanks," he said.

As soon as Basie slammed the truck door, Jed had questions about how he wanted to relocate some wires in his attic, but a bee's nest had built itself around them, and would Basie please help him because he was an electrician *and* good with bees. Basie probably answered. He wasn't sure. He couldn't remember—not when he was still watching Kit Elliot in the side mirror. Not when Kit Elliot was still watching back.

"Hey, since I've got you in the car," Jed began when they had reached town. "Jaime was asking me about getting the aluminum wires in his shop redone. I told him he'd probably have to run the copper himself, but since you're still around, think you could have a look at it yourself?"

The truck chugged, nose dipped a little too far into the intersection as they waited at a red light. Across the street, Ed Nougat was at the gas station pumping diesel into his pickup. If Basie hopped out of the Submarine now, he could still catch Ed before he took off. He could still be out of Long Lily *today*. He just had to get out of the truck.

The light flashed green and the Submarine rolled forward.

"Jaime'll kill himself if he tries to do it. He never wears gloves,"

Basie said, knowing full well he was the intended audience of his own statement. He twisted in his seat to face Jed, the seat belt cutting into his collarbone. "Might as well drop me off at his place."

"You sure you got the time? Don't want to pester you if you're trying to hit the road."

In the rearview mirror, Ed Nougat turned north up Main Street and disappeared over the hill. Basie heaved a sigh, weighty with the cab's stale scent of hay and mud.

"No, I've got time. I'll be in town for a few more days."

New plan, Basie thought. Spend the week making sure no one in Long Lily had *any* electrical issues in need of resolution and try to catch Ed Nougat again next Monday.

What was another seven days avoiding Wellhead?

WHEN BASIE RESOLVED TO his new plan, the townspeople saw an invitation and the universe saw an opportunity to say, *careful what you wish for*. Because for a week straight, he squatted into attics and ducked into basements, fixing every last electrical problem his neighbors in a five-mile radius could come up with. The sheer volume of requests nearly outnumbered hours in the day, resigning Basie to work into the late evening. It kept him out of his damp squatting nook in Crane's Nest, and for that, he could not be sour.

Monday came just when Basie felt that he would surrender his last threads of sanity if he saw another wire or breaker panel. His things were packed, bundled up much messier than when he first arrived. All he had to do was zip the pack shut to finally head west and away, when his phone gave a cheerful little ring.

Jed started speaking before Basie could even say, *Hello, this is Basie.*

"Are you coming over or not, Basie? It's been a week."

Basie leaned his forehead against the diner wall to keep from sighing. How Jed had known to call precisely when he did, Basie could not fathom. He *could* just tell Jed to call any of the neighboring electricians outside of town, that *I'm not the only shitting electrician in the state.* But Della would turn over in her grave and haunt him for the rest of eternity if he talked to a Long Lily local that way.

"Uh, yeah Jed. I'm just packing up to walk over now. I'm nearby, so it won't be long."

"Good, 'cause I've been living with bees in my attic for a week, and they're starting to get into the vents. Stung Elise just last night while she was sleeping."

"Sorry, sir. I'll get them cleared out right away."

Jed hung up and Basie tapped the phone against his forehead.

Bees. He'd forgotten there were bees. A whole nest of them if he remembered correctly. The supplies in his tool belt wouldn't be enough. He needed his beekeeping suit and veil, which were…

His heart dropped. They were in a storage box in his old yard. *Dammit.*

Basie let his pack fall to the floor with a defeated *thump* and wrapped his tool belt around his waist. A deal was a deal.

Wellhead came into view the way it always did, cresting over the hill, steeple eclipsing the sun. Basie slowed his pace as he passed the cottage, checking the flowers in the front yard to make sure they were still alive. He let his gaze wander through the window, peering in to see if his mother's paintings were still hung on the wall. They were, and to Basie's surprise, so were most of his baby pictures.

Possibly Kit hadn't had a chance to properly unpack yet. But what did it matter? It was his house now. He could spend the next decade settling in, if he wanted to. If he liked someone else's family pictures on the wall, Basie wasn't going to be the one to tell him it was odd.

Basie kept walking. His objective was clear—get to the storage box, "steal" his bee suit, finish his very last task as Long Lily's electrician, and get the hell out of town. His shoulders relaxed when the storage crate was unlocked, giving him extra time to snatch his things and gain a few extra miles on the road.

He'd just folded the suit under his arm when a voice behind him drawled, "What the hell are you doing?"

For a blood-chilling moment, Basie thought the voice be-longed to Kit. He nearly tripped over his own feet spinning around, an apology ready on his lips. His heart gave a few relieved punches when it was only Lewie, hands on his hips, wearing his best, *I'm a legal guardian and you better listen to me* face.

"What's it look like? I'm getting my bee suit," stated Basie sensibly.

"I didn't mean right this second, though I'm pretty sure this counts as stealing. I meant what are you doing *here,* in Long Lily. You were supposed to be gone days ago."

Basie shifted the suit under his arm, uncomfortably.

"I missed my ride with Ed."

"And today?"

"Jed's got bees in his attic."

Lewie threw up his arms, eyes rolling so far into his head it had to have hurt.

"Great day in the morning, Bas. If you didn't want to leave Long Lily, you should've just said so. Now your house is sold and you don't have anywhere to be."

"I *do* want to leave Long Lily," Basie insisted fiercely. "But apparently I didn't give our neighbors the two-week notice they wanted, so I've been running all over town fixing every last flickering light this side of the Susquehanna River." It then occurred to Basie that perhaps it wasn't appropriate to start yelling outside someone's place of living, so he stuffed his free hand in his pocket and took a breath. "Is Kit home?"

Lewie stared at him, hard, for a long moment.

"No. I don't know where he's at. And you're damn lucky he's not here, either, because I wouldn't help you explain this to him if he was."

Basie waited for the relief to set in, but his nerves kept racing, electrified by something he could not put a name to. He shifted his weight.

"What's he like?"

"Well-mannered, quiet, polite," Lewie answered, looking Basie up and down. "Whatever the opposite of *reckless* is. Why?"

"Can't a man be curious?"

"Not if he's sworn it off like a Lenten sacrifice."

Basie squinted up at the sun so Lewie couldn't see his face, which would surely betray the jumble of confusing thoughts that were turning his head into a swamp. He might not have known what he was feeling, but Lewie always had a habit of guessing just what Basie was ignoring inside and calling him out on it.

"How's this for a Lenten sacrifice: I'm giving up Long Lily, starting tomorrow. You can come see me off in the morning if you want."

"My goodbye gift to you will be pretending like I actually believe you. Be sure to write when you're gone, oh headstrong youth. Don't get swept up in those western winds."

Basie didn't know how to get tangled up in the winds, but he wanted to. Possibly he could never be the sort to get the air kicked up beneath him, to let chance sail him to unknown places. All he knew were age-old roots—the kind that weren't easily tugged from their home soil.

Perhaps this was why, in the midst of bees and wires, Basie asked Jed if the dollar store on the corner still had flickering lights over the bread aisle. Or why he walked past Wellhead on the way back to the forest diner to see if Kit would be standing outside (he wasn't).

It wasn't a healthy routine, but Basie was powerless to change it. In the days after his bee suit heist, it went like this: Wake up. Empty the rain buckets by the rusty coffee machine. Walk past Wellhead on the way into Long Lily for one odd electricity fix or another. Confirm that the unkillable irises on the side of the house were still alive. Check to see if Kit was visible from the road. Not dwell on the disappointment when he wasn't. Untangle wires. Let his neighbors feed him homemade meals as appreciation for his help. Go back to Crane's Nest. Rinse, repeat. Rinse, repeat.

If you asked Basie how long he'd been doing this, he'd lie.

If you asked Lewie Simon how long Basie'd been doing this, he'd tell you it'd been seventeen days.

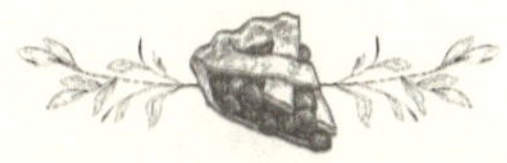

THINGS CHANGED THE MORNING Kit Elliot put out a sign that said in pointy cursive, "*ESTATE SALE! THIS WAY → 8AM TO 3PM.*"

Basie noticed the sign from his usual spot up the road where he watched the house. He allowed himself a few extra moments to stand there, a little dumbfounded, hidden out of sight by the cars in the driveway.

Since he promised to start doing immortality right, he *should've* continued up the road toward the grocery store and pretended that he hadn't seen anything. But at this rate, Basie was only doing immortality marginally better than he had been when he lived at Wellhead—which was to say, his progress was piss poor at best—so he supposed one more lapse in judgment wasn't the end of the world. Barely looking both ways, Basie jogged across the street and over the Wellhead property line.

He took one step into Wellhead and regretted it immediately.

Kit Elliot had turned his childhood home into a goddamn Walmart.

Okay. That wasn't exactly fair. But it *felt* like it!

In reality, all Kit had done was mark the odds and ends around the house with neon price stickers. He hadn't moved anything from where Basie had left it when he fled the cottage, but made things more *open*. Drawers were pulled out to reveal Della's stamp collection from her scrapbooking days. Her salt and pepper shaker collection from the 20s filled the bureau top. The closet door was propped aside so buyers could browse her old coat collection.

Basie bumped shoulders with familiar faces as they ambled through the tiny cottage. He didn't look up to see if they'd reacted to his presence there. It was too much—all of his childhood exactly how he remembered it, now just…up for sale.

"Anything good in that shed out back? The one by the bees?" someone asked.

"I imagine there might be, with all the treasures inside the house," came the reply. Basie looked up from a box of his mother's bandanas to find Kit Elliot counting change in a cash box. He wore one of Della's baking aprons, having stuffed the pockets with pens and more stickers. Red curls poked into his eye, so he flicked his head back and nudged around the pennies in his palms.

"Don't you know what's back there yet?" the woman paying pressed. Kit politely shook his head, then handed the lady her change. The key in Basie's pocket felt like a sack of stones.

"Thanks for stopping by," Kit said, leaving no room for any more questions. The woman didn't seem to care.

"I bet there's good gardening supplies back there. I'd be interested if you were willing to take a look."

"You don't want anything from inside there," cut in Lewie Simon. Basie ducked behind a corner, knowing that if Lewie saw him here, he'd never hear the end of it. "Basie didn't take very good care of his tools. It's just a bunch of old rakes and rusty nails. Not worth bustin' the lock over."

Basie frowned. Was Lewie covering for him or insulting him?

Either way, the lady wasn't buying it.

"That doesn't sound like him. He loved his mother's things."

"Really? It's a wonder then that he left so many of her belongings here," Kit cut in, though not unkindly. It sounded to Basie like the man was genuinely curious—which made it worse.

"Maybe he's not the boy we thought he was," conceded the woman—who apparently knew all about him, without Basie having a first name to match to her face.

He had enough of this. Not caring who he bumped into, he stumbled toward the front door, knocking into a rack of—of *his* hats!

Coming here was a mistake. A stupid, selfish mistake. Sure, it was easy to plan to do the right thing, but the actual execution of said *right thing* was a thousand times harder and Basie was only one single, imperfect person. A small town guy.

Alright, an *immortal* small town guy. You'd think that in all seven decades of his infinite wisdom, he'd know better than to—

Oh. *Oh.*

Basie's eyes fell on a cluster of ceramic pie plates hanging on the wall and all at once, he couldn't move. *Well shit,* he thought.

No matter what his neighbors said, he didn't care about anything in this house. Not the stamps, not the bandanas, or the weird salt and pepper shakers.

But these? These were different.

There were five altogether, one for each decade he didn't age. There weren't pie plates for the first two decades of his existence, because Della didn't usually reward something as simple and easy as aging. She had wanted something practical to commemorate the occasion of Basie's immortality, something that captured exactly where they'd been in that moment in time without taking up space they didn't have. So, she painted flowers on the pie plates, food-safe glaze bouquets that were exact replicas of whatever flowers Della had picked out for his birthday that year. The most recent plate, the one Della had painted earlier that spring because they'd almost forgotten the fifth decade, was a bouquet of sunflowers.

He wanted them.

"Mr. Elliot," Basie called behind him. Kit, who'd been politely laughing at some joke the Catholic priest was telling him, looked up and froze. If he recognized Basie as the man who had stared at him from the street, or even from the pictures on his walls, Basie couldn't tell. "How much for the pie plates?"

Kit's eyes traveled behind Basie, lingering on the stoneware for a long second.

"Oh, sorry. Those aren't for sale," replied Kit. His voice was as smooth as raindrops down a windowpane.

Basie couldn't quite comprehend that he'd been told no. He straightened his back, a scowl on his face.

"And why not?"

It was Kit's turn to straighten up.

"Because I like to bake, and they're high-quality pie tins."

"I could pay you for even better pie tins."

"That's very generous, but I'm afraid I have to decline."

Basie dug the toe of his boot into the carpet, gritting his teeth. He'd sold this house for a mere fraction of what it was worth, left all his earthly belongings behind, and didn't ask for a single thing in return. Who was Kit Elliot to come in and decide that Basie could not have the one thing he wanted of his mother's? Maybe this was what Lewie had meant when he practically begged Basie to take some of his mother's things. At the time though, it seemed like if he couldn't have all of his mother, he didn't want the inconsequential pieces of her, either.

As if reading the expression on Basie's face, Kit offered an apologetic smile and said, "I'm sorry."

It was the wrong thing to say.

"You know what I think?" Basie snapped. Kit's face dropped, as if he'd been slapped—like he already knew what was coming. "I think you're not sorry at all. I think you bought this house because it was cheap and you knew you could sell all the things inside, without any regard for their value to anyone else."

Kit drew in a quiet, controlled sigh.

"You're…entitled to that opinion, certainly." Basie scoffed, but Kit pressed on patiently. "You may not know, but the person who owned this house before me left all his belongings behind. It would've been easier to just throw everything away. But out of respect for the previous homeowner, I didn't want to be so thoughtless with his or his late mother's belongings. It took almost a month and quite a bit of effort to get everything ready for the sale on my own. I didn't have to do that." Kit wiped his hands on his apron, as if the argument had made his hands sweat. "If what you said was true, if I *really* didn't care for this house or the things in it, I would've just sold you the pie plates."

"Then sell me the fucking pie plates!" Basie was entirely aware that Kit's logic was too sound to argue with. Even to his own ears, Basie's rationale sounded like the ravings of a mad man, but his blood was boiling too much for him to care.

"That doesn't—" Kit sighed. "Please don't swear at me in my

home."

"It's *my*—" Basie snapped his lips shut. The back of his throat burned.

Kit said nothing as Basie crossed the room and snatched a picture off the wall. He presented it to Kit, holding it where the frame splintered on the left side. In the photograph, Della was smearing a piece of pie against the mouth of sixty-seven-year-old Basie. His face was stained purple from blueberries and crust.

"How much for this?" he demanded flatly. Sarcastically.

Kit looked down at the picture. Then, back up at Basie.

"Oh, you're…" Kit said to him, to the man with blueberries staining his lips. "Basie, I—"

"Enjoy my fucking house, pal."

Basie spun on his heels and left.

CHAPTER 5

**From, The Diary of Adella Moore.
Vol. 8. November 4th, 1937.**

There is a man on my couch.

Before he was on my couch, he was hunched over on the street corner staring out at the southern expanse of our New Mexico desert skyline. He seemed like the sort of fellow who did not want to be hunched over by himself, so I squatted beside him and tried to find whatever he was staring at. There was only one cactus, tumbleweeds, and sand, sand, sand.

When I asked him what he was searching for, he told me that he was sorry, but he did not speak English. I didn't answer, because people always lie to get what they want, and in this case, he wanted silence. When that wasn't what he wanted anymore, he said, "My brother is supposed to cross that horizon."

"When?" I asked him.

"Three weeks ago."

I told him that I knew what it was like to wait for your family. I asked him to come and stay with me.

His name is Basilio Olmeda-Silva. He is twenty-nine years old. He is a strange sort of man, I think. He likes to count the lines of wood grain on my dining room table to compare the quantity to the number on the floorboard beneath his chair. He only drinks room temperature water. And sometimes in the early morning, I catch him looking to see if the door is still locked. He unlocks it, locks it, pulls it, unlocks it, locks it again.

But he likes to paint. And oh, the things this man pulls from his mind. He insists that they are much more vibrant in his own head, rifer with color and life. It is my hope that if he stays long enough, I will get to see them as he does. Sometimes he looks at me, and I think he wants me to find those things too.

So, there is a man on my couch. And we agree that, by tomorrow, he won't be there anymore. He says it is because the hospitality of strangers should only live a lifespan of a few days. I say it is because he will have moved onto the pillow next to mine.

CHAPTER 6

"You shouldn't have done that, Basie."

Based on the words alone, Basie knew it was Lewie. No one else would be brave enough to accost him in the canned goods aisle so soon after his mother's death. For this interaction to be happening so late at night, it meant that Lewie had finally wrangled all nine thousand of his kid siblings and decided to sacrifice his precious relaxation time in favor of reaming Basie with whatever speech he had planned.

Basie would not give him the satisfaction easily, if at all. He plucked a can of chicken noodle soup off a high shelf, appraising the label as if it were a rare artifact.

"I'm in the middle of something," he grumbled.

"Come on, you really expect me to believe you don't know what's in *chicken noodle soup?* I'm talking to you," Lewie pressed. Grabbing Basie by the shoulder, he added, "You shouldn't have yelled at Kit like that."

Basie put the soup back on the shelf a little too hard.

"He's the one that shouldn't have been so stingy with my mother's things."

"You know damn well it wasn't like that. He didn't—Jesus Christ! Basie, don't you walk away from me—he didn't know who you were. For all he knew, you were some wack job that likes to put vintage stuff on eBay just to watch strangers tear each other's teeth out in violent bid wars."

"There are plenty of respectable people who earn necessary secondary income that way. Plus it's very sustainable. Do you know about—"

"This isn't one of your liberal tirades, Bas. This is you being a dickhead over something stupid and ruining a reputation you've spent—" Lewie glanced around. "*Seventy-seven years* building. I shouldn't have to remind you that you were the one that said you didn't want any of your mom's things. You insisted left and right that I could sell all of it with the house, so I did, and now you're acting like he stole everything. If I were you, I'd think about giving that man an apology."

Basie crossed his arms tight over his chest.

"I wasn't aware that when my mom died, you became my legal guardian. I know you're used to parenting your siblings around—"

"Hey now," Lewie warned, jaw tight.

"—but I'm not your personal orphan that you can boss around. And I won't be another one of your *golden children* to brag about at town hall meetings. I'm a lot older than you are," Basie concluded. He yanked a bunch of soup off the shelf, not bothering to worry how many there were or what kind he'd shoved into his basket.

Before he could disappear into the check-out lines, Lewie grabbed Basie's wrist, crashing the red basket into an endcap of boxed potatoes. He was lucky the display hadn't toppled over, because Basie would've left him there to pick it up by himself.

"Then act like it. You're not the only one who's lost your parents," he said. Basie twisted his hand free.

"I never said you had it easier, either. But you know why it's different."

Lewie frowned. He *did* know why it was different. Sure, they both had become orphans in unfair circumstances. But unlike Basie, Lewie had siblings. He had aunts and uncles, cousins, second-cousins—a tremendous bloodline that only knew how to grow in leaps and bounds. Anyone who might've shared Basie's blood was long gone now, and even if some of his distant relatives were still alive, he couldn't reach out to them. What would he say? *Hi, I'm your long-lost cousin. I know I look like I'm young but I'm actually pushing eighty.*

Christ.

Della's choice might've been made out of a pain and desperation so deep that Basie hadn't been able to detect or understand it. But that didn't change the fact that it left him alone. His life as it should've been was no longer possible. There was no point in spending eternity chasing some twisted sense of belonging in a world where all the people and places he fit into were ancient history.

The tortured guilt on Lewie's face was enough to make even Basie squirm. The fluorescent lights made them look like gaunt spirits with unfinished business—one stuck in time, the other impossible to keep pace with, both staring back at each other.

Basie was the one to break the silence.

"Look, I appreciate you watching out for me. But the truth is, I'm gearing up to hit the road in the morning, so it doesn't matter what people are saying about me. And you can uh— you can tell

Kit that I was having a bad day."

"No, if you want him to know, you can tell him yourself." Lewie checked his watch, frowning. Apparently, he'd surpassed the *Scold Basie* allotment in his schedule. "Listen, I didn't come here to yell at you." Basie scoffed. "I just wanted to tell you that the folks down at Mallory Farm have some stuff of your mother's that you might like to pick up before you leave town for good. And this time, you might swallow your pride and follow my goddamn advice."

Basie added one more soup can to his basket to occupy his hands. His nose wrinkled when he caught a glance at it—low-fat split pea. Gross.

"Thanks," he said finally. Lewie tried to catch his eye, but Basie refused to look away from the label; smushy little ham chunks floating in their green pool. "I mean it. For everything. You know—thanks."

Lewie stared at Basie for a long moment, then took the liberty of returning the split pea soup in Basie's basket back to the shelf where it belonged. He clapped Basie three times on the shoulder and turned back down the aisle.

"Listen here, kid. If you don't call to check in every now and again, we'll be exchanging some strong words," Lewie promised.

Basie rolled his eyes with a begrudging smile. *Kid.*

T HE NEXT MORNING, BASIE moved all the booths in the old eatery back from their "bed" position to a state of, "Ready for ghost diners." He emptied out the rain buckets one last time and made sure none of his socks had blown under the milkshake counter.

The best thing about leaving Long Lily, he thought, would be sleeping in a real bed again. He didn't care if it was too firm, so long as it didn't have stripes or foam filling bursting out of the seams.

A dull ache rang down Basie's shoulder as he carried the pack of his earthly belongings down the oil and chip road. The weight seemed to disappear as he passed Wellhead, the reminder of what he left behind far outweighing the burden of what he carried. But to his credit, he did not peek into the windows or listen to hear if the bees were buzzing outside their hive. For once, he just walked.

He was half a mile away from the gas station where he planned to hitch a ride with Ed Nougat when a sky blue sign came into view on his right— *Mallory Farm: Berries and dairies since 1920.* Basie ambled to a halt.

His bag was heavy, but there was still *a little* room left. Maybe whatever Lynn Mallory had of Della's would fit in his pack. Hell, he'd carry it under his arm if he had to. He wasn't making the mistake of leaving behind his mother's things twice.

Wiping away sweat with the back of his hand, Basie turned right.

All it took was three steps into the barn and one look behind the cash counter for him to question if he *really* wanted whatever silly thing Della had left behind.

"Basie?" Kit Elliot called out.

Basie turned stiff as death. *Busted.*

Through the dense line of shoppers, Basie saw Kit was halfway through weighing a quart of strawberries for some extraordinarily short old woman. He loomed over the checkout counter in his work apron and a red sun visor that made his face look sun-bleached.

Basie could run now. It would only take a few days before everyone forgot both of his embarrassing displays. Not that he'd be around to hear the gossip anyway.

"Basie!—Excuse me, ma'am. This is really quite urgent—*Basil Yeats*!"

The barn went quiet.

It was a well-known fact throughout all of Long Lily that you never, *ever* called Basie by his full name. Why? Because he hated it and he would not spend his immortality being called a name he didn't like.

Gritting his teeth, Basie trudged past the line of berry pickers waiting to check out and approached the counter.

"You're a hard man to find," said Kit by way of greeting.

"You've been looking for me?" replied Basie. He was dumbfounded, apparently enough to make Kit crack a sideways smile. He was a strange sight, in his office pants and apron combo, but comely enough that Basie didn't mind looking.

"Not actively," Kit admitted. "I wanted to give you some space. But I really, truly owe you an apology. It's been difficult living at Wellhead comfortably without giving you one."

Basie pressed his lips together. *Of course* the city slicker didn't actually care about apologizing. He just wanted to assuage his own guilt.

Basie still hadn't decided if he was going to permit Kit his atonement when he replied, "I'm really just here to grab something my mom left behind. Lewie said I could find it here."

For a second, Basie was certain Kit had no idea what he was talking about. But then understanding crossed across all five million of his freckles and he nodded.

"Right, well, if you wait off to the side there a minute, I'll just finish up what I'm doing and uh, get it for you."

Basie gave a nod of his own, aware of the dozen pairs of eyes watching him—all expecting him to make amends with the outsider. Stuffing his hands in his pockets, it occurred to Basie that maybe he'd been exaggerating when said he wouldn't mind if his neighbors thought poorly of him. But the heaviest gaze of the room came from Kit, who didn't look away even as he bagged and cashed out baskets of fruit. It made Basie squirm.

When Kit was finished, he wiped his palms on his green apron. Somehow, he'd gotten strawberry juice all over his palms and under his fingernails.

"So uh…the apology," said Kit, flicking a tiny black seed off his knuckle. Basie cocked a brow.

"That's really not necessary."

"No, I insist!" A bolstering breath. A half-slanted frown. He scrubbed a hand over his face, then turned to his customers and said, "I'll be with you all in just a moment. This really can't wait." When he faced Basie, he was all determination. Gently, he pulled Basie out of earshot from the line, and to Basie's own astonishment, he let himself be dragged. Ignoring the glares from the overheated visitors, Kit began to speak.

"When I left Baltimore to come live here, my friends told me that living in a small town would be unlike anything I'd ever done before. They warned me to be *ready*. I didn't believe them at first, because I've done just about all there is to do. But they didn't budge. The city is full of distractions, they said. You're always focused on things that never really stop. I agree, too. Baltimore *is* full. My friends said that because places like Long Lily don't have the tall buildings or the sleepless nightlife, there's more room for other things—like…well, like love."

"Love," Basie parroted back, uneasy.

"Yes. Not that there isn't love in the city. There's plenty. But in Baltimore, the entire city is full of strangers. Some people know each other, but not for long. Here, the whole town knows each other well enough to know that the worst thing anyone could do to you, Basie, is sell your mother's things and call you by your full name. The people here love you enough to tuck that information away and whisper it to ignorant newcomers when they mess up." Kit ran a hand through his hair. "Sorry. I'm rambling."

"It's okay," Basie found himself saying. "Clearly you've been thinking about this."

"I have! I have and it's—I was told to be *careful*. To make good first impressions. To love the land and people just as much as everyone else that lives here. The truth is I'm not used to knowing everyone's business and them knowing mine. There's still a lot left for me to learn. But that doesn't excuse me from being insensitive at your expense. For that, I'm really sorry."

The apology rang out the way a firework lies in the sky for miles. Kit's red stained hands were clenched around a wooden quart of strawberries, so Basie plucked one of the berries out and threw the whole thing into his mouth. Kit tracked the movement with an interest that made Basie believe he expected him to do it again—*wanted* it.

"They're sweet," Basie commented lightly.

"They are," was Kit's nervous reply. "That's why I like to bake with them. They— they're good in a pie."

Basie, who had been eating Mallory Farm strawberry pies for as long as he could remember, already knew this—it was Della's recipe for Christ's sake. But he made a sound of agreement and flicked the strawberry leaves to the dirt by his feet.

"So you're working here, then?" Basie asked.

"Yeah! I applied because it's close to the house. Of course, you knew that. At first, they had me harvesting strawberries for the shop. Then, they had me helping families do their own picking. That was the best part for me, getting to know people. I baked Lynn a pie as a *'thanks for hiring me'* present and she practically threw me into the kitchen." Basie sucked his lip between his teeth. Lynn didn't let just anyone into her kitchen. "Now I get to do both—the neighborly stuff and the baking."

"I'd say that works out mighty well," said Basie. What he really meant was, *I'm starting to worry you'll fit into Long Lily better than I ever did.*

"Thank you." It was so unbearably sincere, all soft edged consonants and warm eyes, that the back of Basie's neck tickled.

A beat of silence.

"It's nice that my mom's position got filled so quickly. And by someone who enjoys it so much. She was the baker before you."

"Right! I remember; Lynn did tell me that. What esteemed shoes I have the privilege of filling."

Basie blinked. Did people *talk* like that?

"Ye-up. They're all yours." Even to his own ears, Basie knew that he sounded like he'd literally rather be drowning in the creek out back than having this conversation.

Another beat of silence. This one was so long Basie really did consider drowning. He found that the quiet was not caused by a lack of things to say, but an overabundance of possibility. Because, if this were a different situation and a different day, Basie strongly suspected that he and Kit had the capacity to talk…forever probably. But forever couldn't start until Basie got his head out of his ass.

"Listen, Kit, you don't owe me an apology."

"That isn't—!"

"—I let you have your moment, now you gotta share the talking stick," Basie said with a sideways smile, which was curiously effective at shutting Kit up. A rosy flush warmed his freckled cheeks, but he sucked his lips and nodded for Basie to continue.

"When I sold the house, I signed a contract stating that you would be entitled to everything in it," explained Basie. "All of it was yours to do with what you wanted, even the damn pie plates. I made my choice. Then I crashed your estate sale and treated you like you'd cheated me out of my livelihood. I was unfair. And loud."

Someone in the fruit line scoffed. Basie tossed a glare in their direction.

"For what it's worth," he continued. "I don't think you need to worry about not loving the town enough, or whatever. I can tell you already do. And hey, it takes more than three weeks to learn the life stories of every neighbor on your block." He met Kit's eyes. They were warm brown, like clay in a creek. "So yeah. Sorry."

The corner of Kit's lips twitched, and though it wasn't the best apology in the world, it seemed that it was enough. He seemed to be struggling for something to say.

Basie wasn't struggling at all. In fact, now that he'd gotten the worst part out of the way, he had too many things to say. *Have you scraped the honey out of the hives lately?* And, *Careful of the rocking chair in the living room, sometimes the nail comes loose and you don't want the leg to break off.* And, *My god, you're gorgeous. How is it possible for someone to have such soft hair and a jawline that might as well have been carved from Olympian marble?* And, *Have you broken into the shed yet? I still have the key but I would sooner burn the whole thing down than have you see what's inside.*

Instead, Basie said, "I'm glad we got that out of the way now."

"Oh, yeah? Why?"

"Because I'm leaving Long Lily for good, and it would've been a shame to take off before you could get your groveling in."

A rosy flush turned Kit's cheeks to ripe apples, dark against the paleness of his skin.

"You're—" He swallowed. "You're leaving?"

Basie nodded. "This place was all my mom's. It can't be mine without her."

"Oh, I see." There was no judgment in Kit's face. Basie wondered, for the first time, what exactly had driven Kit out of Baltimore. What had he left behind? Kit wiped his berry-stained hands on the fabric of his apron. "Then will you allow me to give you a parting gift?"

Basie held back a cringe. If it wasn't a birthday or Christmas, Long Lily folks didn't really give presents. They were more inclined towards favors.

"I don't suppose you'll let me say no."

"Of course you can't say no," Kit asserted. "It's just in the back. I'll go grab it," Kit said. At the last second, Basie remembered the reason he'd originally come, but Kit disappeared into the kitchen before Basie could call out a reminder.

When Kit returned, he was fumbling to hold something behind his back. Basie tried to crane his neck and get a peek at it, but Kit twisted to keep it out of sight. The aroma of hot cinnamon and nutmeg wafted into the air, masking the dry scent of hay and musty barn, so Basie had a guess about the surprise.

Kit appeared wound up like someone was cranking a gear in his back and Basie bolstered himself against hearing what would surely be an awkward, canned version of *Goodbye forever, have a good life.*

"Lewie lied to you," was what Kit wound up saying. "At least, I think he did. I mentioned I wanted to see you, and he promised he would get you here one way or another."

Disappointment fell hard from Basie's chest to his stomach, but something kept it from crashing into an angry temper. Maybe it was the way Kit said *I wanted to see you.*

"Oh. So nothing of my mom's, then?" he said.

"That's not *quite* true." Kit placed a steaming apple pie on the counter between them. "It's her recipe, isn't it?"

Basie only had to take one look to know for sure. He knew the recipe. The lattice of golden crust across the top gave it away, but Basie had eaten enough slices of this particular recipe to recognize the pinch of cinnamon and the sweet smell of Granny Smith.

"Yep," Basie replied, voice thick. "That's hers, alright."

"Take it."

Basie smiled. "Alright, thanks."

Kit mirrored the soft smile, though didn't meet Basie's eyes when he said, "Best of luck to you, Mr. Yeats."

The inside of Basie's mouth went dry, too many words on the tip of his tongue to possibly be spoken at once. *Take care of that house, Kit. I mean it. Let the grass grow tall and leave the wild berries out for the rabbits. Don't worry when the creek runs high. Have wood ready for the winter months. Don't open the shed. Don't sell all of my mother's things to hipsters, they were meant to be used at Wellhead. If you see something magical, something that seems impossible, leave it be. It was there before you were.*

Basie picked up the pie, hot in his hands.

"You too."

BASIE MISSED HIS RIDE with Ed Nougat (*again*), so he walked back to Crane's Nest, shielding the pie from the forest rain with his jacket. Inside the diner, he set out the old bucket under a leak, positioned the pie next to it, and took his seat at the bar.

It wasn't until he gobbled down the first slice with his plastic fork that Basie could see a familiar painted bouquet of sunflowers. He took a few more bites from the center of the pie, each one revealing more of Della's handiwork.

All at once, another transformation occurred. There was a new Post-sunflower Basie now, only this time, he didn't know it.

He ate nearly the whole pie himself and smiled when it made his stomach hurt. Maybe in the morning, he'd be too full to go anywhere.

He polished off the rest, just to be sure.

CHAPTER 7

L EWIE SIMON HAD AN UNCANNY WAY of knowing things. If you were halfway through baking a cake and needed two eggs, he appeared like an angel on your doorstep. If you were pulled over on the side of the road with a flat tire, Lewie would ride up a few minutes later, the perfect spare in tow, sometimes with the kids. If you had slipped, he was offering a hand. If you were lost, he was already leading the way.

In Long Lily, it meant having a volunteer at the fire department who was always on the way before anyone could yell *"Fire!"*

For Basie, it meant that there was always someone thinking about what he needed even when he couldn't. He knew better than to question it. He was, after all, a man with his own brand of strange magic. If his best friend had some talent to divine exactly what he needed, then he would do nothing about it except say, "Thanks, Lew" and try his best to return the favor.

In this case, Basie needed a better place to sleep and some camping supplies. If he had to eat cold ravioli straight from a can again, he might go homicidal. But it was his own fault he'd landed in these circumstances, and thus had been prepared to suffer quietly.

So, of course, Lewie came.

The only evidence that he'd dropped by were the wheel tracks in the mud, the crate of camping supplies next to the pie plate on the counter, and the cot lined up against the wall with the fewest unbroken windows. Waiting on the cot was a note, folded in half like a tent and written in Lewie's block printing. It read, *HAPPY 30 DAYS TO LL'S FAVORITE SQUATTER.*

Basie scoffed and pulled out the battery powered hot plate from the crate to warm up his soup. As thankful as he was for a hot meal, Lewie's help was officially a sign that Basie was dangling a little too close to dangerous territory. Because Basie had plucked himself out of Wellhead like a wildflower—only, instead of re-planting himself somewhere better, he'd merely thrown himself across the yard, not nearly far enough away. And now, he was sprouting new roots.

The first testament of this was the phone call to his old supervisor at the electric company. Basie called the morning after his first night sleeping on the cot, politely asking them to switch on the diner's power for a few days under the guise of, "Remember that favor you owe me? Well, I'm doing some work for a friend out in the woods. I don't want to run such a long extension cord."

This in and of itself was not terribly damning. What *was* damning was that when his old boss asked, "How long do you want me to leave it on?" Basie had answered, "Until I call. Might be a while."

Some of it was easy, like the discovery he'd made a few weeks ago that the old diner, because of its remote location, had its own private septic and water supply: both meticulously maintained by Jed on the Donlevy property. Basie still drank out of bottled water, but it was of little consequence when the *toilet flushed* all on its own. Hallelujah.

They were all the sort of things a person did when they intended to pick a place and stay there. He could try to explain this away, but this time, Basie didn't have an excuse for staying. He just wanted to. And for a man who was currently having trouble not being positively miserable all the time, he decided he didn't mind.

But if he was going to stay, he needed real sheets. And a real towel. And more soap. And probably some more toilet paper. And, overall, a long trip to the store.

Out of all the roots Basie had sprouted, this was the longest: the impulse that made him walk slowly by Wellhead, looking for…

Well, just looking.

On this particular day, he took note of two things: Kit, walking up the road with his back to Basie, and Della's sunset purple irises, which were halfway to death. They were the same irises that Della had planted the year Basie was born, grown tall and fussy, sown with all the tender care that came with having Yeats genes in your blood. They were the same irises that, because they were planted on Wellhead property, they should not have been able to die. Yet between the wilting petals and the browning leaves, there was no doubt about it. They were decidedly *not* responding to Elliot blood.

Under normal circumstances, it would be unfair to lay the blame on Kit. Having only lived in a place where the square footage of concrete and asphalt greatly outnumbered that of grass, how could Kit be expected to keep a garden alive by himself? But these were not normal circumstances.

As he took in the suffering garden, Basie waited to feel angry. The *one* condition of Kit buying Wellhead was the sworn promise that he would take care of it. The blame never came, though. Because deep down, Basie knew someone like Kit Elliot would not—*could* not—set his wrath upon something so fragile and precious as this garden. Watching Kit pace farther up the road, Basie wondered if he could not bring himself to be resentful because he was the same.

The morning sun was hot on Basie's skin as he jogged up the road to fall in line beside Kit. To his credit, Kit did not startle. He merely glanced out of the corner of his eye as if being woken up from a nap, then gave a small smile.

"I knew a fellow like you once," Kit said lightly. "I baked him a pie and he made it seem like I would never see him again."

Basie appraised Kit's loose white button-up, lingering on the open *v* at his throat, and said, "Your baking must've been pretty bad to scare him out of town."

"Must've been," Kit laughed. "Wonder why he stayed."

Basie hummed, feigning thoughtfulness. "The weather?"

"I don't think the Pennsylvania climate can boast that effect on *anyone*." Then Kit turned to him fully and asked, "How are you, Basie?" Though the words were shaped into a common pleasantry, the sound of them was all joy, delivered with a contagious smile that Basie could not help but mirror.

They chatted, walking shoulder to shoulder past Basie's old neighbors, over the jagged railroad tracks, across the bridge connecting East and West Pearl Street, and into town. Every now and again, Kit would fall into step directly behind Basie to let a car pass. Each time, Basie could feel Kit's gaze on the back of his neck—warm, the way you can tell the sun is there even when your eyes are closed. He fought the urge to straighten out his hair, silently praying that Kit would stop looking at him with such watchful fascination. Underneath, there was another prayer that hoped he wouldn't.

"I'm sure you know more about me than you ever wanted to, but I can count the things I know about you on one hand," Basie pointed out, plucking an orange lily from the side of the road.

Kit stuffed his hands into his pocket. "And what are they?"

Basie spun, walking backwards with a palm held to the air.

"One: you're a city slicker from Baltimore who's used to the fast-paced *high life*." Kit rolled his eyes with a smirk, but nodded. Basie ticked a finger down. "Two: you're a baker with a specialty in pies. No one shuts up about them. My mom probably would've hunted you for sport over it. She was very competitive."

"That's a bit alarming."

Basie ignored this, putting another finger down.

"Three: you don't own any jeans."

"Now what on earth gives you that idea?"

Basie tossed him a flat, knowing look, then gestured with his counting hand at Kit's linen pants and shiny loafers.

"I own jeans!" Kit blurted defensively.

"Uh huh, and when was the last time you wore them?"

"*That* was not the question. Keep going."

"Four, because the last one definitely still counts: you quit your job as a fancy corporate archivist to move to Middle-of-Nowhere, Pennsylvania."

"Alright, who in town let that one slip?"

"That's not important. Emily Long. The first rule of living in Long Lily is to not tell anyone anything you don't want everyone in a ten-mile radius to know. Face it, everyone knows you're white collar."

The joke tripped and stumbled into Kit, wiping the light clean out of his eyes. Basie's heart sank. Did he know how to do anything except put his foot in it?

"Did you…not enjoy it?" he asked.

"Not terribly, no. The archival work was always gratifying, though my boss ruined it with his propensity for yelling. But I painted on the side. I enjoyed that."

Basie tried to imagine Kit sitting behind a desk scanning documents while his boss yelled profanities at him, but the image was too depressing to ponder for more than a few seconds. His feet crunched in the gravel as he stopped abruptly, holding up his last finger.

"Five: you need something hands-on and meaningful in order to take pride and satisfaction in what you do. There's nothing wrong with that. And for what it's worth, I think you made the right choice coming here."

"You think so?" asked Kit, his own humility making his voice light and airy.

Basie's heart felt like it was uprooted into a pool of direct sunlight.

"Wellhead was built for someone like you," he stated, certain.

Kit's smile returned, just by a fraction. He didn't say anything, but as he clasped his hands behind his back, Basie thought he was walking a little lighter.

Kit broke his silence when they'd almost reached Mallory Farm, saying something that was immediately swallowed away by the gust of a car speeding by. Basie might've missed it completely if he hadn't been thoroughly focused on Kit's presence behind him. He glanced over his shoulder, and the sight of Kit with his red curls sweeping into his eyes made his chest squeeze.

"What'd you say?"

"I asked why you haven't left yet."

"Trying to get rid of me?"

"Quite the opposite," Kit admitted. Basie's face transformed into bright heat. "It's just people in town thought you would've been gone ages ago. They have no idea where you've been staying."

Basie shrugged, then kicked a broken chunk of asphalt across the road and into the ditch. It'd be a cold day in hell before he admitted to anyone that he was squatting in an abandoned diner—even Lewie had just sort of figured it out on his own.

"Haven't got anywhere to go, really," Basie said.

Kit hummed, squinting at the road as if tossing the dilemma around in his mind a few times.

"Forgive me if this is rude," he began carefully. "But why sell your house in the first place if you didn't have a plan? Most people pick out their destinations before passing *Go*."

Normally, Basie would've lied, fabricated a story about some job that fell through or a friend who was supposed to have an extra room, but didn't anymore. It would've been easy, too. Lying was the red in his blood, the very thing that protected his life as a normal man from becoming a life as a government science experiment. A near century of practice had made him one of the world's greatest con men—an unapologetic one, at that.

This is why he surprised himself when he said, "When people lose someone they love, they either cling to everything that person left behind or—they run away." He trained his eyes to the passing rumble strip, bumpy under his feet. "I just had to get the hell away from that house." Kit's rueful grimace was heavy on Basie, so he added, "If I'd known some city-slicker was going to move in and kill my mother's irises, I might've stayed a little longer."

Kit sighed.

"You saw that, did you? I confess I've never been very good at keeping things alive. My old goldfish could tell you, except I overfed him a week into having him."

Basie tripped on his own feet, catching himself with very little grace.

"*Overfed*—The instructions are right on the bottle!"

"And I read them!" Kit insisted, hands flying to cover his face. "But it was cold in Baltimore that winter and I thought it'd be smart to give him a little more so he could…you know, bulk up some."

"Mr. Elliot," Basie said seriously. "Do you mean to tell me you forgot that fish are *cold blooded*. How much did you give it?"

Kit hesitated, perhaps considering how much he wanted to concede to his own humiliation, then said, "Half the bottle."

"*Half the—*"

"The poor thing was so *bloated,* bobbing on the top of the water like a pool floaty. When I moved here, I thought plants and bees had to be easier—"

"They absolutely are not. Nothing is easier than a *goldfish.*"

"But it rains a lot in the mountains! And the bees mind their own business."

Basie chuckled, shaking his head.

"You've got your work cut out for you," he said.

For a moment, Basie thought Kit might ask him for his help. For a more dangerous moment, Basie thought he might offer it. But then Kit's face twisted up and he turned his gaze to the ground. Either he could not suffer his pride to ask for help or he could not suffer Basie's pride to ask him to return to the place he'd so deliberately left. Basie thought it might be a mix of both.

He needed to change the subject—and fast—before he made offers he would regret.

"You're going to walk right past the farm," he warned mildly.

Kit stopped dead in his tracks at the foot of the Mallory Farm entrance. He looked up the drive, then back at Basie, apparently deciding whether or not to quit his job on the spot in favor of continuing their conversation.

"How long do you think you'll stay in Long Lily? Truthfully, this time," Kit asked.

"Truthfully?" Basie looked over the open pasture, the tiger lilies and cattails at its crown. He squinted at the sun's reflection on the green-tinned roofs and Wellhead's steeple peeking up over the tree line. In those slow seconds, he could not imagine ever leaving Long Lily. But he could not imagine staying either. "Truthfully, I don't know."

Kit nodded, more to himself than to Basie.

"I'll be seeing you," he said.

Basie said it back. The words sounded to his own ears like a bedtime prayer.

CHAPTER 8

K IT ELLIOT HAD LIVED in Long Lily for a month and already his neighbors knew almost everything about him there was to know. They knew his full name was Christopher Myron Elliot. They knew that he had left behind a corporate job that sucked his soul dry and a handful of friends who liked to eat his cooking but sometimes weren't good for much else. They knew that he once had a library, one he'd intricately curated over the course of his lifetime, only to leave it behind because it wouldn't fit on the moving truck. They knew that he no longer had any family to host in his new house, because his parents lived too far away to travel after moving back to Ireland. They knew that this did not hurt him. They knew that he favored sunflowers to roses. That every night before he went to bed, he had a cup of lavender tea, no matter how hot it was outside.

Elise Donlevy had even correctly stated—completely un-prompted and with unyielding confidence—that Kit's favorite time of day was during dawn and dusk, when the skies became swaths of purple and rose.

Kit did not try to guess how these personal facts had become common knowledge. It seemed that small town living meant that the world around him was an open book, and because he'd chosen to live in it, he was one too.

There were only two things his neighbors did not know about him.

They were not secrets. Kit could not lie effectively enough to make it worth the effort and was prone to blurting out the truth under pressure. They only remained unknown because no one cared to ask about them. Kit would unleash all his truths if only someone asked.

The first unknown was that he had left home for unjustifiably selfish reasons, reasons that a man of his age should have known better than to indulge. The unknown was magical in nature and Kit never allowed himself to think of it. But thinking it—articulated and concrete— was different from swimming in constant awareness of it. And Kit was *always* aware of it. Remembering it brought the feeling that a bucket of slimy, burning shame had been dumped over his head. But if he had to make the choice all over again, the outcome would've been the same.

The second unknown was that his heart had set loose on Basie Yeats the moment he saw him across the road standing in that patch of amber tiger lilies. It clawed and keened behind his ribs at the sight of him, all tan skin and wild eyes. Each breath Kit let out on Long Lily soil was heavy with the memory of it, weighed down with unspoken supplication—*please let him stay.*

Kit was surprised that his affection for Basie had yet to become common knowledge. He did not believe himself to be doing a particularly good job at keeping it under wraps. Sometimes it seemed as though it was all he was made of—not a man of blood and muscle, but of molten *want.* It seeped into the tone of everything he said, the hint of strain and smile in the simplest of exchanges. It made him latch his eyes on every empty entryway and the pictures in his living room.

Oftentimes, his two unknowns were strands of the same secret, soft colors curled around one another until they were one of those wispy dusks he liked so much. When the second strand became too laden with want, the first would check it into balance and remind him what he deserved—and what he didn't. But sometimes the yearning left behind was too strong to be swallowed down. In those cases, the balance was upended and Kit could do nothing more than *ache*.

He was up to his neck in it that morning when Basie walked him to Mallory Farm, barely able to find the air to speak in complete sentences. It seemed unreal that he'd let his elbow brush against Basie's, made him laugh, without imploding.

It wasn't until lunchtime that he parted the Basie-hued fog of his mind and discovered he'd forgotten his lunch: a bag of apple slices and turkey sandwich. There was no choice but to circle back home through the damp midsummer heat to retrieve them.

Only, when Wellhead came into sight, something was in his garden.

Someone.

It would've been easy to mistake Basie for sunlight—truthfully, Kit almost did. It took him a moment to realize that his eyes were not playing tricks on him, that there really was a person in his flowerbed.

Basie was kneeling before the irises, cotton shirt riding up far enough that the small of his back had tanned into a gilded copper. His hands were buried in the cool dirt, yanking and tearing at chickweeds until the soil was free of them. It was careful art, a task that killed, and in killing, made room for new roots. Everything about the way Basie gardened reminded Kit of the time he'd been in Ireland, watching loose haired women perform the Beltane rite. It was untamed heat and sweat, but it was also worship of the land and sacred in its labor.

Then Kit blinked, and the magic—Well, it didn't *disappear* exactly. It only faded to a level that Kit was able to see. At once, Basie went from a druidic acolyte to a young man staining his jeans with soil. He looked thirsty, dry lips framed by a crown of sweat.

Kit slipped in the back door to fill twin glasses with iced water, one for each of them. When he approached Basie, he was humming an old Appalachian folk song that Kit hadn't heard in a long, *long* time.

He placed the water glass on a flat brick beside Basie, who in turn took a greedy gulp without deigning to look up.

"It needs a little more work than I thought, Lew, but—" Basie caught one glance of Kit's leather shoes and promptly shut his mouth. He tilted his chin all the way up to take in the rest of Kit, squinting up at the cloudless sun.

"Kit," he said. He might as well have said, *Well, shit.*

Kit—very valiantly, he liked to think—fought back a pained smile. Basie Yeats had sold him this house, yet every time Basie saw Kit standing on Wellhead property, he flinched. It made Kit feel less like a homeowner and more like a very well-dressed burglar.

"Could've at least waited until the sun shifted to the other side of the house. It'd be cooler then," Kit said. *Not that I've ever known you to think anything through.* He wisely did not add this.

Basie sat back on his haunches and wiped a dirty wrist against the pool of sweat at his brow. Soil streaked across his skin in a way that would've been impressive and roguish had it been a scar and not dirt.

Kit smeared his fingers through the glass' condensation and wiped it through the filthy crow's feet at the corner of Basie's eyes. It wasn't until the dirt turned to mud that it occurred to Kit to be embarrassed—that he'd done something without regard for how Basie would react. But Basie only closed his eyes for a long second and brought his own water up to the other cheek. Kit clutched his misbehaving hand to his knee.

"If I'd waited until the sun started to set then you'd—" Basie hesitated. *You'd be home.* Kit could fill it in easily enough. "Then I'd have to walk home in the dark."

"You never did say where your new place is."

Basie chugged another long gulp, then filled the glass back up with the watering can. It was so bizarre Kit couldn't help but chuckle.

"Crane's Nest. Just on the town line," Basie replied. "Not for long, just…for now."

To the best of Kit's knowledge, Crane's Nest was a miserable, rainy patch of land that the residents of Long Lily left alone because the forest there was older than Wellhead Cottage and trees like that deserved their solitude. At first glance, it was unclear what Basie could have there that he couldn't have here at Wellhead. But solitude was very appealing when the only other things in your heart were grief and sorrow. Kit knew that well enough.

"For home, you don't spend a lot of time there," Kit noted.

Basie wiped his hands on his jeans and stood up.

"Irises don't need a lot of water, but they need *some.* If it hasn't rained in a while, you ought to water them at least once a week. But not too much, otherwise the roots will rot."

"How will I know what's too much?"

Basie's brown eyes glinted.

"You'll know."

Kit couldn't help but roll his eyes. "Do you always give such helpful answers?"

"Look, that's all I got," Basie said, tossing his hands up. "You'll just feel when it's been enough. Go ahead and Google it if you want to trust some stranger on the internet over the guy who's been taking care of this garden for a *long* time."

"You're what, twenty-five? The garden's old enough to be your grandpa," Kit teased.

A strange expression crossed over Basie's face, but it was gone as quick as it came. Kit was not well enough acquainted with Basie to guess what it meant, but trying to guess would only disservice them both.

"Alright. See for yourself," Basie said. He handed the watering can to Kit, who held it the way single adults hold squirming babies they're afraid to drop. "Pour these suckers a tall glass."

Kit surveyed the thin plot of land, looking past the flowers to the soil. Then, for no reason other than *he felt it*, Kit poured a sprinkle of water in the top corner. Then a little more all around, a little more, *aaand…* no more. It was enough.

"I accept verbal and written apologies," deadpanned Basie.

Kit chuckled, bumping the can against Basie's side so that it sprinkled water over his boots.

"What on earth are you doing here anyway?" Kit asked. "I was planning on calling a landscaper to come and help with the flowers. You didn't have to…stay in town just to help me."

"Still sounds like you're trying to get rid of me," Basie remarked. He paused just long enough to let Kit sputter out the beginning of an argument, then continued, "It's really no trouble. Part of the reason it got so bad was because I stopped taking care of the garden when…well, you know. It should be more manageable now. If you do call a landscaper, I'd sleep a lot better at night if you asked them to leave the irises alone. Take care of them yourself."

Kit nodded, the unspoken promise sweeping relief over Basie's face.

"Will you at least let me pay you for your time?"

Basie scowled.

"Absolutely not. You don't have to pay me for pulling weeds and watering the soil. I'd be offended if you did."

"But I don't know how to weed a garden. You've done me a great favor."

"News flash, Baltimore. Small towns *run* on favors. Besides, if you don't know how to weed, I can show you. It's not rocket science," Basie took Kit's wrist and tugged him to sit down on the brick ledge of the garden. "Don't worry. We won't get your fancy office pants dirty."

Kit was about to say something clumsy regarding how he didn't mind if Basie got his pants dirty, but was thankfully saved from humiliation when Basie smoothed his palms over the back of Kit's hands, rendering him speechless. The corners of his fingers were rough with callouses over Kit's knuckles, but impossibly gentle as he guided their joined hands into the dirt. Even three inches beneath the surface, the dirt was cool and damp.

"You can tug the weeds out right at the top, but if you don't pull them all the way out, they end up just coming back sooner. I like to dig in a little further and get a better hold on them." Every word Basie spoke landed against the underside of Kit's jaw and the back of his neck. If his hands weren't rooted in the ground, he might've leaned back into him. He was moving on his own, searching around for the best way to yank the chickweeds away, but his mind's focus was sharp on Basie—the musky smell of his sweat, the way his tan hands made Kit's look like snow, the heat of his body sitting so close at his side. "You got it. Now pull it out—with confidence, Mr. Elliot."

Kit flushed—How could Basie just *say* something like that?—but gave the weed one hard tug, springing it free with a shower of dirt. Basie took it, tossing it on the pile of shoots he'd already torn away and knocked their knees together.

"See, you learn something new every day," Basie said.

Kit had several perfectly appropriate responses queued up and ready to go. *Wow, that was much easier than I expected. Thank you for your help. Should've pulled my head out of my ass a week ago and just tried it myself, but I've been too busy thinking about those five freckles on your nose and how nice they make you look. And actually, I think all of you is pretty nice, which is strange considering you yelled at me when first we met and—*

"Come inside for lunch," was what Kit actually said. Then, remembering himself, he added, "As a thank you."

It could've been complicated. Asking a man to lunch was troublesome enough when you were harboring romantic feelings for him. Asking that same man to lunch should've been even more problematic when the other variables were factored in—like the fact that the last time they'd been inside the house together, Basie had hated his guts and told him so. Loudly.

But Kit got the impression that Basie didn't *do* complicated—not when he could help it.

"Sure. Beats the canned minestrone I've got waiting for me. I'll just, uh, put away the gardening tools and head inside?"

Kit nodded, worried that if he spoke, his voice would crack and expose him for all he was worth. When Basie disappeared around the corner of the house, Kit slipped into the kitchen. He leaned back against the door. The back of his hands still prickled where Basie had held them. The more he focused on the sensation, tied with the memory of Basie's teasing smile, the more the feeling crept up his arm and resonated behind his ribs.

Out the window, Basie was rinsing his hands under the old fashioned well pump. He tossed some water into his face and hair, then gave a secret smile up to the sun as if it had paid him a compliment.

Kit's head thunked against the old wooden door.

"Well," he whispered, undone. "Nothing for it."

"Can I ask you a question that might be a bit insensitive and personal?" Kit asked.

Basie wished he could see Kit's face for any sort of warning as to what the question might be. As it was, Basie could only see

Kit's back as he worked at the kitchen counter, piecing together turkey sandwiches and squeezing fresh lemonade. His shadow threw a perfect silhouette onto the tiled floor, but that was even less help.

"I probably owe you one," replied Basie. "It's the least I can offer you after I swore at you in your own home and trespassed into your yard."

Kit glanced over his shoulder, face screwed up like there was something about *your home* and *your yard* that made his mouth sour.

"There was an article in the paper last week to honor your mom. They picked a real nice picture of her and wrote about some of the stuff she'd done for the town," Kit explained carefully. Not that Basie needed him to tell him—the article was already folded up in his bag. "It's just…the house doesn't—They wrote that your mom was sick, which surprised me. Moving in here, I wouldn't have known someone battling with a long illness had died here. And Lewie said you left in a rush, so…"

Basie knew what he was trying to say. Kit was wondering where the hospice bed and empty bottles of pills were. Wondered why the air wasn't stale with sickness.

"She didn't die here," Basie said.

"Oh, I'm sorry. It's just…the article said—"

"I didn't tell the paper what really happened."

Basie met Kit's eyes then. It was another moment of that silent communication that they always seemed to favor. Whatever Kit saw in Basie's expression would determine whether or not he would ask more.

"What *did* happen?" Kit asked finally in a voice so quiet, it was a wonder Basie heard it at all.

"My mom was sick her whole life. But it wasn't….uh, terminal. She would've lived her whole life and been exactly as she'd been the day she—stopped being healthy. I didn't realize how unhappy she was. I thought she was managing it, but they always say you never know what's truly going on with someone. She took my truck and drove to Canada, because they wouldn't do what she wanted them to do here. When she got there, she asked the doctor to—" He couldn't say it, but Kit didn't need him to. "She didn't tell me she was doing it. I thought she was upstairs still asleep when I got the call."

"*God,* Basie."

"I'm sick the same way she is. But it was easy to forget until she—left. Now it's all I think about."

Kit shifted on his feet. There was a heaviness in his arms that made them dangle at his sides, unable to bear any more weight. Basie wished Kit *could* hold something, because it had been a damned long time since anyone had given him a hug.

"Do you think you're going to…I mean, do you want to—"

"No," Basie replied immediately. "Not for a long, *long* time at least. It wasn't fair of her—leaving early without warning. It wouldn't be right, even though I wouldn't be leaving anyone behind."

"That's not true."

Basie let out a thin breath. He knew if he asked Kit to expand on that truth, Kit wouldn't have lied. So Basie didn't ask.

Before the silence stretched on too long, Kit placed the sandwich on a Pyrex plate in front of Basie. His own sandwich was still where he'd forgotten it that morning, wrapped in a plastic bag and waiting at the opposite place setting. To Basie's fascination, the crust on Kit's sandwich was cut off on the long edges. Basie tore the short edges off his own sandwich so that between the two of them, they had one full set of crusts.

"You should come over more often," said Kit, pouring Basie a glass of lemonade.

A strange feeling began prodding inside Basie's chest. It seemed to Basie that the feeling had always been there, nudging and squirming, but looking at Kit now, it was *more*. It was a pair of wings stretching and growing and yearning to set loose. An imprint of desire etched harshly onto Basie's old bones, making them ache when the selfish want was unfulfilled. It dug its claws into every single plan he'd been forming for the future and tore them to ribbons, until the only plan Basie could see was the one that involved him staying in Long Lily and getting to know Kit Elliot as well as he knew himself.

"Unless you'd rather not come over," Kit rushed when Basie hadn't answered. "I wouldn't blame you if you didn't want to be here."

Seventy-seven years of immortality had given Basie the clean ability to keep his cool, but even now, he was floundering.

"As long as you wouldn't mind the company," he replied. The nudging in his chest turned to pounding when Kit smiled.

"No, I can't say I'd mind at all."

CHAPTER 9

KIT ELLIOT WAS NOT a forgetful person. This was how Basie knew the whole thing was his own fault. Later, they'd call it *The Phone Incident*.

It happened like this: Basie had shown up uninvited to Wellhead claiming he was starting to feel like those cowboys from Brokeback Mountain who only ate beans, and would Kit please feed him a home cooked meal. In true Kit fashion, he proceeded to pester Basie about where he was staying and why his hosts were only feeding him beans. Basie replied it was a metaphor and advised Kit not to take things too literally. Kit was reluctant, but he lived in Long Lily now, and therefore was incapable of turning away a hungry belly.

Dinner was nice. It was so nice that Basie had forgotten he was sitting at his own kitchen table, sharing a meal with someone it would've been best to avoid. And yet, it was nice nonetheless.

When it was time to go, Basie put his phone in his bag. Only, his phone was already in his bag and the device he'd deposited with unyielding confidence actually belonged to Kit.

As soon as he realized it happened several hours later, it was clear that explaining the situation away would be impossible without exposing what a supreme idiot he was. Because here was the kicker: Kit's phone didn't look *anything* like Basie's. Basie's phone was in one of those cases that could get thrown into an active war zone and survive. Kit's had a simple, leather wallet style. His driver's license, his credit cards, and an old photograph of a dog were tucked neatly in the back—which of course escalated the crime from stealing, to stealing *and* identity theft.

The only reason it had happened in the first place was because Kit had looked Basie dead in the eyes and said, "You look so well tonight," and Basie had to get the *fuck* out of there before he turned into a puddle of soupy affection. Or worse, said it back and otherwise made a fool of himself.

The joke was on him, apparently, because all it took was one smooth spoken compliment, and Basie had a stolen phone.

But it was fine! Because even though it was too late in the evening to bring the phone back, Kit could survive overnight without it. It didn't matter that there was no way to let Kit know Basie had it. It wasn't like Kit was prone to worrying…much. And even though Basie never did get around to having the landline phone fixed after he shattered it, it would be alright if Basie had kidnapped Kit's only method of calling 911. Completely alright.

Damn it all, he had to bring the phone back.

His shoes and coat were halfway on when Kit's phone began to ring.

It was packed safely in the front pocket of his bag, wrapped in a clean pair of socks to protect it, but the ringing was *brutal*—a sound Basie could only attribute to an alarm clock getting ruthlessly murdered by another alarm clock *with* an alarm clock.

"It's fine," Basie murmured to himself, continuing to tie his shoes. "If it's important, they'll leave a message."

They did not. Every time the phone kicked the caller to voice-mail, the ringing began anew.

Later, Basie would clarify to himself that he answered because maybe Kit was trying to locate the phone or speak to whoever had stolen—er, accidentally pocketed it. He absolutely *did not* answer the call because if he had to listen to the ringtone in the dark, raining woods all the way to Wellhead, he was going to throw himself into the raging creek.

The caller began to speak before Basie could even utter a simple, *Hello?*

"I'd like to remind you that *you* were the one who promised that you'd pay me ten dollars if you ever forgot our biweekly Kit-Calls-Lara time. Lucky for you, I accept cash and check, so I expect a crisp envelope in the mail by tomorrow," rambled a woman's voice.

"Uh, do you accept layaway?"

The answer was lightning quick.

"You're not Kit."

"No ma'am."

"Don't ma'am me. Now, you listen here." The woman—Lara?—must've brought the phone right up to her face because her voice was suddenly louder, despite coming out in a threatening whisper. "If you stole this phone, I'll warn you not to underestimate my ability to track you down and remove you from this earthly plane of existence."

Well that was something. Stifling a laugh, Basie leaned over his knees.

"Are you one of Kit's friends?" he said with a slight challenge.

"What's it to you?"

"Well, you're either one of his friends or his bodyguard, and I gotta admit, I pictured his friends with less of a warrior streak."

"Are *you* one of his friends?" she replied, not denying the allegations.

"Most days."

"What are you doing with his phone, then? Is he alright?"

"So you *are* his bodyguard."

Lara let out an indignant noise, making Basie tap the volume down.

"Alright, alright. Sorry for ribbing you, miss. My name is Basie Yeats and—"

"Oh, *you're* Basie," she hummed with a meaning Basie wasn't sure what to make of. There were an excess of things Kit could've told this woman about him, and at the moment, he couldn't come up with any that put Basie in a positive light. Maybe she'd still make good on her promise to smite him out of existence, after all.

Which is why the phone nearly dropped out of his hands when she finished, "In that case, I'll leave you both alone to your time together."

Basie had been alive a long time, but he'd never known anyone to jump to such a conclusion. It couldn't even be considered a jump. It was more like a launched rocket conclusion, complete with a NASA level propulsion system. Lara's assumption was currently landing on the moon.

"We're not—!"

"Could you to pass along a short message, though?"

Basie sighed.

"Of course," he answered, thankful she was not asking further questions. "Whatever you need."

"See, here's the situation," Lara began in a way that very much did *not* sound like a short message. "When Kit moved away, I helped him pack up all his things—which was a big feat, by the way, because the list of his personal assets is a mile long." Basie was inclined to agree. "But he left every last one of his *books*."

"His books," Basie mirrored, confused.

"A library unlike anything you've ever seen. I've never seen a person care so much about inanimate objects in my life as much as I have watching Kit fawn over his books. I called him the day he moved because our landlord started to pack them away, but Kit said to just leave them."

"That doesn't sound like him. Did he say why?"

"He said *someone* had left the bookshelves completely full."

"Oh," Basie said, sounding like someone punched his gut.

"And also because the moving truck was full and boxes are expensive. The point is, I've been keeping the books in my storage unit for safekeeping without him knowing. It's about time I fessed up, though. The longer they sit in there, the more susceptible they are to storage perils. You know—mold, theft, rats."

"*Rats?*"

"The city rats are like small cows."

Basie scrubbed his chin. If Kit tried to fit his prized library into Wellhead right now, there wouldn't be any room for it. He might be able to stack the boxes into the tiny office, Kit sometimes used that space for his sketching. There was also whatever bedroom currently laid empty, but the stairs would be a bitch to get heavy boxes up and down. The only place he could think of that might have the space to fit so many books without burden was the shed, and that was entirely out of the question.

The answer, then, was simple: don't store the books at all.

"You know what?" Basie started, his voice lighting up. "Hold onto them a little longer. I've got an idea."

THERE WAS A VIOLENT pounding behind Basie's ribs the next morning as he shifted his weight back and forth on the Wellhead porch. The restlessness was entirely his own, unable to taint the pleasant morning—the airy birdsong and refreshing breeze. It seemed impolite to worry on a day so determined to ease and abate any tribulation he faced, but Basie couldn't help it. He was beginning to feel like this every time he saw Kit—an exhausting combination of craving Kit's attention and the stomach-churning fear of being perceived in the first place by a man so devastatingly good.

All in all, it took a surprising amount of agony just to return a cell phone.

Basie rubbed a hand over his heart, trying to coax the butterflies in his chest to quiet down. Filling his lungs as much as he could, he rapped his knuckles against the door.

No answer. Basie worried at his bottom lip. Kit didn't work on Saturdays. It was possible he was somewhere else, enjoying the idyllic weather with a new friend Basie didn't know about. Was there someone Kit preferred to spend his Saturdays with?

He knocked harder, practically scraping his knuckles. Still, nothing.

Wiping his palms on his pants, Basie considered his options.

Maybe he could plant the phone in the mailbox. No, that wouldn't work. Long Lily folks did their favors in person. Leaving the phone in the mailbox would be like confessing to the crime, especially if Kit remembered where he'd last seen it. Basie could always hold onto the phone for a while longer, even if it felt like a hot brick in his pocket every second he kept it.

"To hell with it," he murmured, fishing his keys out of his pocket. Hadn't he kept his secret house key for emergencies like this?

Gingerly, Basie unlocked the door and slipped inside. He lingered in the entryway, turning an ear to the rest of the house for any noise. Complete silence, save the gentle rustling of a ceiling fan. Inching down the hallway to the kitchen, Basie slipped the contraband out of his pocket and set it carefully on the table where he'd swiped it last night. He turned around and—

"Great day in the morning!" Basie yelped.

Kit spun around with a start, nearly dropping the paintbrush balancing in his left hand. He was perched completely upright on a short stool across the open floor in the living room. An easel was situated in front of him, bearing a painting that matched a vase of flowers and apples sitting on the windowsill.

For a second, the men only stared wide-eyed at one another.

"I knocked," Basie rushed out, suddenly feeling like a burglar.

"Did you?" replied Kit, half-hysterically. A long ribbon of apple red streaked on his cheek where he skimmed himself with his brush.

"I did. I knocked twice."

"Oh. I didn't hear you."

"I can see that."

Kit placed his painting supplies on the table beside him, wiping his hands on the painter's apron knotted around his waist.

"How'd you get in? I don't remember unlocking the door."

"Really? It was open when I tried the doorknob," Basie insisted, averting his eyes. There was something about Kit Elliot that made all his lying finesse fly out the window.

Get a grip, Basie.

Kit's gaze fell to the cellphone on the table, then drifted back to the intruder frozen next to it. An amused, albeit befuddled, smile hooked his lips up.

"Is there a key hidden under a rock outside that I don't know about?" said Kit, far too delighted for the circumstances.

"No," Basie stated firmly. At Kit's raised brow, he added, "I…may have a spare key to the house that I kept just in case of emergencies."

Kit paused, as though listening to the air, which was filled with buzzing bees and the rustling of the willow.

"I don't hear any emergencies," he quipped. "Does it have anything to do with the fact that my brick disappeared last night?"

Basie's jaw dropped.

"Your…what? Kit, no one calls them that anymore."

"Sure they do."

"I can't think of a single time in the last—" *Abort, abort!* Basie bit down on the words *forty years* before they could tumble out. "How'd you know I had your phone?" he said instead.

"Why did you have it in the first place?"

The whole thing was entirely absurd. You could've tossed them into a cattle town, placed cowboy hats on their heads, called it a game of quickdraw, and it still would've looked exactly the same. In this case, Basie knew Kit was the sharpshooter. Basie's aim would have to be dead on if he wanted to keep from leaving himself exposed. When dealing with Kit Elliot, it was more lethal to give up the truth than come up with a lie—at least, in the case where the truth involved a sickening level of heart-eyes and racing pulses. Kit was too good at detecting lies for that.

That didn't mean that Basie had to give the *whole* truth. He fired the first shot.

"I accidentally packed it in with my things when I was gearing up to leave last night," stated Basie, somewhat defensively. "I didn't go through it or anything. I only talked to Lara for a bit to explain because she kept…" He shrugged, chuckling. "She kept calling and your ringtone was making my ears bleed."

It was Kit's turn to fire, but he was more the sort to lay his weapons down. He pushed the stool away from the easel, reaching behind his back to untie the apron. Basie caught a glimpse of the painting Kit was working on, fascinated that the brushstrokes had disappeared entirely, making the piece easy to mistake for the real thing.

Kit crossed to the sink to scrub patches of dried paint from his palms and under his nails, smiling over his shoulder when Basie followed close behind.

"Lara didn't give you too much trouble, did she?" he asked.

Basie leaned his hip onto the edge of the counter. It took him a second to answer, a little distracted by the sight of Kit haloed in the morning light coming through the window.

"She made a valiant play at threatening to eradicate my earthly existence, but I talked her out of it."

Kit groaned. "A near impossible feat. How did you manage it?"

Now that was a secret Basie would not give up so easily. He grabbed the dish towel hanging over the oven handle so Kit could dry his hands.

"Would you believe me if I said it was my natural charm?"

"Not a chance," asserted Kit.

The insult met its target with alarming accuracy. Basie jolted away from the counter with a disbelieving laugh.

"And why not?"

"I hate to be the bearer of bad news," began Kit with a teasing glint. "But I think *natural charm* might be an embellishment of the truth."

Under oath, Basie would not be able to tell you what came over him.

He tapped into his dusty reserves of smooth elegance from somewhere deep inside, shortening the distance between them so quickly that it sent Kit bumping into the sink. Basie peered up through his long lashes just in time to see Kit give a dumbfounded, quiet sigh. Flicking a finger beneath Kit's tie, Basie ran his finger along the underside of the fabric, grabbing it fully at the top. He tugged, drawing Kit forward until his breath fell hot against Basie's mouth.

"That's a bold statement. You willing to swear to it?" murmured Basie.

Kit fell forward, just an inch, eyes dark and wide, before he snapped back. He cleared his throat, elbowing Basie away with a strained chuckle.

"I only meant that Lara isn't affected by the charm of men," said Kit with a flushed smirk. "She's gay."

Basie didn't think about what it meant that Kit *was* affected—but he wanted to. He had a notion of trying it again to see if he could yield better results, but the immediate danger of that idea clawed its fingers around his throat in an instant. He could not spread more roots. He could not care so desperately for Kit Elliot.

"Good for her," he declared, honestly. "Her and I got to talking, though. Gave me an idea—the real reason I came over today."

He fished into his pocket, retrieving a piece of paper he'd folded at least seven times. Tugging at the corner, it unfurled into a flier reading: "MCALLISTER MEMORIAL LIBRARY ANNUAL BOOK SALE."

"If you're going to be living in Long Lily, you gotta donate to the book sale," Basie prodded. "I was thinking that I could make up for the mess you inherited by boxing up all the books I left. Then you could drop them off at the library the day of the sale and be everyone's favorite newcomer for contributing such a generous donation."

"Oh, *I* can bring them, can I?" joked Kit.

"I'd deliver 'em myself, but then you wouldn't get the credit. Besides, I don't have a car. I bought the boxes. They're out on the porch. And the book sale isn't until the end of the month, so I've got plenty of time to pack them up for you."

The teasing glimmer in Kit's brown eyes turned so truthful, Basie thought Kit might have more natural charm than he knew about.

"That is a very kind and thoughtful idea you've had, Mr. Yeats. I don't have any books of my own to donate, so—thanks."

Basie bit his lips against a bashful smile, but Kit seemed to catch it anyway.

"I'm thinking grilled cheese for lunch," suggested Kit. "Am I…making two?"

"Oh, you're making four," said Basie, flicking the breadbox up to reveal a loaf of homemade bread. Already, its sweet, fresh aroma saturated the air. "Grilled cheeses are best enjoyed in pairs. And don't even think about stopping me from breaking out the tomato soup. I'm curating the perfect experience here. You can thank me later."

In the next hour, Basie discovered that Kit's ability to craft award winning grilled cheeses was not helping him smother his affection. Possibly his first mistake was letting a man who was good at everything, from maintaining his own appearance to baking pies, cook for him. That was just asking to fall in love. When Kit told him he used three types of cheese, Basie was practically ready to propose marriage.

Kit had to be divinely favored, to be so *good*.

When the afternoon began to heat the west side of the cottage like an oven, Kit was back on his painting stool. Behind him, Basie got to work packing books, listening to the quiet guitar music Kit was playing on Della's old record player. They didn't speak—Kit was too focused for that. But Basie found himself straining his ears to make out the little brushstrokes on the canvas. All the while, Della's books disappeared into box after box.

Then, one particular book slipped from the shelf and directly into Basie's quick hands. As soon as he flipped it to read the cover, his heart tugged at all its old wounds. The title embossed into the dust jacket in old, golden letters read: *Household Fairy Tales for*

House Held Faeries.

Basie must've gotten too quiet, because Kit called out softly, "Alright there?"

"Yeah, of course," Basie answered with a sniff. "Just found an old book my mom used to read to me practically every night. Seeing it again feels…"

"Weird?"

"Very. I had no idea she kept it. I thought that she would've donated it after I grew out of it, but it's been here the whole time."

"You should take it," Kit suggested. "Or I can keep it here, if you'd like. I'm about to have *a lot* of shelf space."

Rolling his lips together, Basie nodded.

"That'd be real nice, thank you."

Kit came up behind him, so close their shoulders were pressed together. He peered down at the storybook, reaching out to spread it open. The spine cracked with age, but Basie had a feeling the archivist in Kit knew how to handle old books.

"What's it about?" asked Kit. "Doesn't seem to be the usual fairy tales."

Basie knew this book well enough he could've explained it in his sleep. Maybe even in death.

"Once upon a time, there were a group of faeries who resided in Ireland and possessed powers beyond all human comprehension. When they were overthrown from their power, it's said the faeries fled underground. Some of them, though, settled among the humans and lived simple, ordinary lives. They were able to hide from extinction there, focusing on human things—like running farms, harvesting food, making things with their hands.

This book holds the stories of those faeries. This first one is about a faerie man who turned his goats into clouds and had to wrangle them out of the sky."

Basie skipped ahead a few dozen pages. He pointed at an illustration of an orange haired man crossing a creek, three snared rabbits over his shoulder.

"My favorite is this story, the tale of Cian, a huntsman who sneaks a human woman into their faerie village because he loves her too much to let her marry a human man. It's sort of gruesome in some spots. He makes her long ears out of a rabbit's, and she wears them to trick the other faeries. By the time the rest of the villagers find out the truth, they already love her too much to drive her out. Instead, she becomes one of them for real. Without the lies."

"That's a nice ending."

A dull ache thrummed in Basie's chest.

"The ending is that she discovers the secret he never told her: faeries live forever. But still, they spend the few years she has left together, happy in their little home. Eventually, she dies an old woman and Cian goes back to hunting."

"Oh," Kit said. Basie didn't trust himself to look at his reaction. "It's still a nice ending, in a bittersweet way. But I can't imagine how terrible it would be to love someone, knowing they would die and you wouldn't. It would never seem fair to me."

Eyes suddenly burning, Basie slammed the book shut. The dull pain in his heart was growing like a flame fed by a wild wind, making it impossible to breathe.

An image began engraving itself in his mind: Kit, an old man with a century in his pocket, unable to move on his own or whisper Basie's name. When his body gave out, Basie would be left with eternity to remember what the universe was trying damned hard to tell him—he should be alone.

This is what he got for forgetting what he was.

"Is it alright if I finish this up another time?" Basie heard himself say.

"Of course. I'm not going anywhere."

Biting his tongue hard, Basie placed the storybook back on the shelf. He forced a tight smile onto his face, though it sank into something desperate and longing when he noticed the little flecks of paint over Kit's nose. His mouth tasted of iron.

"You better not."

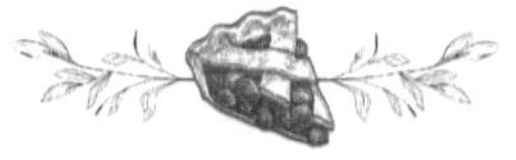

W HEN BASIE WAS TEN and still moaning through his growing pains, his mother had told him this: heartbreak was the leading cause of death in all ageless people. They could not succumb to regular sickness, nor were they particularly unlucky when it came to lethal accidents.

But heartbreak, she said, did not discriminate when it struck people down and immortals were not immune.

Basie had scrunched his nose, trying to picture what it would feel like. He imagined a cartoonish, jagged line cracking down his own heart and squirmed when imaginary blood spilled out over the rift.

If Della had corrected this belief, she would've saved Basie from several years of living in fear of dying from a literal cracked heart.

Maybe that was the intention—to keep Basie alive by helping him avoid becoming another immortal statistic.

When Basie asked how he could avoid heartbreak, Della's answer had been simple: *"Do not love people you shouldn't."*

But how was he supposed to recognize who he should and should not love, he wondered.

"It's like watering the garden. You won't have to wonder, you'll just know."

At age seventy-seven, Basie did know—because he was starting to love Kit Elliot and he knew he should not.

CHAPTER 10

Basie wanted to drive into a ravine.

Okay, that was an exaggeration—

Actually, no. It was not an exaggeration, and he did not care what greater powers eavesdropped on his thoughts and called him dramatic. Basie *did* want to drive into a ravine. He wanted to throw himself into his truck, leave the seat belt undone, and stomp on the gas pedal right until he flew over the cliff's edge. All just to feel his stomach jump into his throat so high it almost popped out of his mouth.

Anything was better than feeling…*whatever* this was—this fucked up combination of stale grief at the thought of his mom and unrelenting desire for a man he could not have. One minute he'd be smiling, remembering a joke his mother always used to tell, then get so sad that only picturing Kit's smile would allow him to breathe again. This, of course, only made him *sadder* because what sort of son tried to distract himself from grief by indulging in superficial infatuation and thinking about *boys*.

Except it wasn't superficial infatuation, was it? Whenever he remembered that he was leaving Long Lily, then it wasn't *just* that either. The pain was heartache on heartache—his own grief holding itself hostage with more impossibilities of things he'd never have.

You couldn't take medicine for this type of affliction. You could only run the hell away from it. Or drive into a ravine. Too bad Basie didn't have his truck.

Thus far, Basie had proven himself spectacularly bad at running away, but this time, he *meant it*. He was going to make himself a list, pack up his things, hit the road, and let the memories of Della and Kit settle in his mind like dust on a forgotten banister.

He scribbled the list on the back of an ATM receipt with a pen he'd swiped from the bank.

- *TOOTHBRUSH, TOOTHPASTE, AND SOAP*
- *CLOTHES (CHECK UNDER TABLES FOR SOCK STRAG-GLERS)*
- *WORK GLOVES*
- *MOM'S PIE PLATE (WRAP IN T-SHIRTS BEFORE PACK-ING AWAY)*
- *WALLET + LAUNDROMAT QUARTERS*

He tapped the butt of the pen against the side of his jaw. *What else, what else?*

Someone knocked at the door.

Basie flinched so hard the pen flew out of his hand. He peeked out the window, finding fresh tire tracks. From his cot, he couldn't see what the car looked like. It had to be Lewie, though. No one else knew he was out here.

"It's open!" called Basie, fixing the blanket over his unruly cot to at least *pretend* he didn't live in complete squalor.

The door creaked open and Basie looked in abject horror at Kit

Elliot. There was a cardboard box in his freckled hands, though Basie couldn't see inside of it. Kit had draped his jacket over the edges to protect it from the downpour breaking through the trees.

"Hi," Kit breathed, undeterred by Basie's discomposure. Rain swelled and dripped at the tips of his red hair, dropping flat onto his lashes (which, to Basie's immortal undoing, were *long*). In the stretching seconds of Basie's silence, Kit seemed to notice the pack slung over Basie's shoulders and the way his boots were laced to withstand a long distance of walking. "Where are you going?"

As far away from you as possible. To Sunday service. To go fix a dead doorbell. Nowhere at all if you tell me to stay.

"Get in here. You look like a wet mop," said Basie instead, yanking the bottom of the box to tug Kit in. He watched Kit's appraising eyes dart around the space—at the leaks, the dust encrusted on the old coffee machine, the pitiful cot in the corner.

It was impossible to guess what Kit thought just from his expression alone, but he gave himself away when he said, "You could've just stayed with me, you know."

Basie did not have the time or energy to explain all the reasons he could not do that.

"How'd you know where to find me?"

Kit's cheeks turned the color of half-ripe blackberries.

"I drove around town a while because you always seem to be walking places. I figured I'd eventually stumble into you. Then Elise Donlevy noticed that I'd passed her six times in a single hour and stopped to ask what I was looking for. When I said I had some stuff to give you, she pointed me in this direction. Said you were staying next door to her father's house here in Crane's Nest."

Basie stiffened. Technically, the diner was on Donlevy land. How long had Elise known he was trespassing? How on earth did they even find out in the first place?

The humiliation drained away when another thought took hold off his mind: Kit, driving around Long Lily for hours looking for *him*. Driving around enough times that even a teenager like Elise Donlevy took notice.

It was Basie's turn to blush.

"Well, I'm glad you found me," he said, so Kit wouldn't be alone in his vulnerability. He stepped forward, hands sliding over Kit's where they held onto the box. Kit stood as still as death, but Basie could sense no displeasure. "What'd you bring?"

Kit blinked blankly, then jolted, pulling his coat away from the package.

"Some of the things from the house that didn't sell during the estate sale. I thought you might like to look through them before I took the box to the donation facility. And there's, uh—pictures too. Of you and your mom."

Basie pressed his lips together. How thoroughly had Kit looked through the pictures, he wondered? Had he merely glanced at them long enough to recognize Basie's face in them, or did he stare at them long enough to realize how old some of them were? In a horrible way, he hoped both were true.

"I was going to pack them away in the shed for you. You know, hold on to them for as long as you needed me to, but I couldn't find the key anywhere in the house."

Hot panic sliced through Basie.

"Don't—" Basie swallowed. "Don't open the shed."

A pause.

"Do *you* have the key, Basie?"

"I do."

"Okay."

Basie could feel Kit's urban curiosity prodding at the space between them. Sometimes he wanted Kit to ask hard questions just so he'd have an excuse to talk about the things that hurt him. This was not one of those times.

Unwilling to meet Kit's eye, Basie took the box and placed it down on the cot. He settled onto the thin mattress, and something eased in his chest when Kit sat beside him. Basie reached into the cardboard box and pulled out the frame from the top. The glass had a few fresh drops of rain where the jacket had failed to protect it, but he swiped them aside with his thumb.

The photograph was, thankfully, only a few years old. It'd been one of the last ones Della had printed before she developed the tendency to let them accumulate on her cellphone's memory card. In the picture, Basie and Della were sitting side by side at the kitchen table. Della had a paintbrush between her fingers, her thin lips split apart in a wide grin. Messy dark hair was tied up on the back of her head, half of it falling out and sticking to the side of her lip. She'd always looked a little older than thirty-seven, the age she'd been when she stopped aging—a symptom of being born in The Enlightenment in her opinion. Beside Della in the picture, Basie quirked a brow at her, holding a book in one hand and a glass of iced tea in the other.

It'd been so long since Basie had seen her, that he noticed the crows feet at the corner of her eyes and the sharp creases of her smile, facial landmarks he would never have.

"Do you remember why she was laughing?" Kit asked.

Basie touched a fingertip to the glass.

"She always laughed when something brought her joy. Like she couldn't believe it was actually happening, which is strange because…because she had a very full life. Still, I don't think she ever got used to the surprise of being happy." Basie handed the picture to Kit, who received it reverently. "Here, I think one of our neighbors was asking about a bee sting remedy. He got stung right on the tip of his nose. Right here." He tapped the very point on Kit's own face. "The picture was taken right as he walked in the door. His nose was all red and swollen, and my mom asked if he was bringing Santa Claus along with him for dinner. He was not amused," Basie finished, surprised by the chuckle that bubbled out of his lips.

"Bee stings on the nose can kill you, you know," Kit pointed out, though he was chuckling too.

"I *do* know, that's why I was making this face! I couldn't believe she was laughing at him when we should've been taking him into the ER in Harrisburg. He was fine though. Mom put some homemade salve on the sting and he lived to see another day. I think there's a mole where the sting used to be, oddly enough."

"How many times have *you* been stung by a bee?"

"Plenty. Not that I have any strange moles to speak for it." Basie pulled another picture out of the box. This one was of him in his beekeeper suit, head to toe in white canvas with a mesh veil across the face. Even behind the shadowy covering, Basie's grin was still visible. He waved with a hand that was covered up to his wrist in a cluster of honeybees. "If you dress like this, though, you hardly ever get stung."

"It must be amazing to walk up to them without any fear. I

don't know that I've ever seen that many bees up close."

"I've got my bee suit here if you want it. Maybe just the veil, I think you're too tall for the suit." Basie's heart attached itself to the glint in Kit's eye. "I could help you. Lewie said he's been sending Orion—that's his sibling—over to check on the bees a few times, but it's been a week since they went. I bet there's some honey to harvest and eat."

Kit tried, and failed, to keep his amazement under wraps.

"Can you eat honey right out of the hive? It doesn't have to get…er, boiled?"

Basie laughed. The sound stemmed from a patch of warmth in the depth of his chest.

"If you did, I'd have to ship you back off to Baltimore for good. No, Mr. Elliot. You don't have to *boil* the honey." Basie kicked his foot up underneath him. Kit, on the other hand, sat like he was at a royal table, straight and polite. "You can eat the whole honeycomb just as it is. When I was a kid, my mom would give me bits of the wax to chew instead of bubble gum. She said it was good for me."

"Was it?" Kit asked with a grin.

Basie was tempted to say, *I'm fucking immortal, so I guess*—but something caught Kit's eye before he could answer.

Kit reached into the box and pulled out a wallet size photograph. Without a frame to protect it, the edges had gone soft with wrinkles and tears. The fuzzy black and white of the image had aged to sepia. Someone who didn't know better might date the photo to the fifties. But Basie, who had sat for the picture when he was only four-years-old, knew it had been taken in 1949.

"He looks just like you," Kit noted. "You must be related."

Kit was not the first person to find this picture of Basie. When others had stumbled upon it, they reacted the same way they would if they walked in on someone on the toilet—a bit embarrassed, closing their eyes and pretending they'd never seen a thing.

Kit was not from Long Lily, so he could not be expected to react in the same way. Instead of returning the image to its rightful spot in the bottom of the box, Kit held onto the frame with reverence for the history it held. He toed the line of being in the Yeats family's business without care for the secrets he was on the verge of discovering.

Basie didn't mind Kit being there, nosing into his business. For once, it was nice to pretend that his family's history wasn't something to be ignored. He'd keep lying if it kept the softness in Kit's eyes.

"That's my grandfather," Basie lied. The falsehoods came easily, as they always did, but with them came a new churning queasiness in his stomach. To abate the acid on his tongue, he offered a truth to balance the scales. "The picture was taken in Mexico, where my father's side of the family is from."

"What was he like?"

"I don't know. He died before I was born." Another truth. Marcelo Olmeda-Cruz was a mortal man who, like his son, had never met Basie. All three of them shared a resemblance—from the straight lines of their chins to their full, umber eyes. He would've turned one hundred and six that year if he was like his grandson. "He was a train conductor."

"When I was little, I used to envy people like that, always getting to see someplace new."

"I thought you liked staying in one place?"

"Now I do," Kit replied. "For most of my adult life, though, I moved a great deal. There's a certain wonder that comes with exploring the unknown for the first time. It's very appealing when you're a dreamy-eyed boy that's never left home."

He smiled up at Basie.

All at once, Basie felt like *he* was the unknown. If Kit asked, he would let him explore every bottomless inch of his mind and soul and body, until once again Kit would set his roots.

"Do you speak Spanish, then?" Kit asked.

In Spanish, Basie replied, "Of course! No thanks to my mom. I taught myself when I went on a trip to Mexico in middle school to visit my family. I practice so I never forget." He waited for the befuddled expression that always followed when he spoke his father's language to someone in Long Lily, but Kit only nodded.

"I found Rubén Darío's *Azul* on your old bookshelf," Kit confessed, to Basie's immense surprise, in his own faultless Spanish. This time, the dumbfounded expression was Basie's to wear. "I like it a lot so far. '*En las pálidas tardes yerran nubes tranquilas en el azul.*'" Then, in English, "It reminds me of being here."

In the privacy of his own mind, Basie wished his memory was an old cassette player. He'd rewind this moment over and over until the tape spit out his mouth just to hear Kit recite the soft, rolled poetry once more. He wanted to carry it with him everywhere. To know how the whole poem sounded in the fields just past dusk, by the hives when the bees were sleeping, in his bed when all the birds began to sing in the springtime.

"Do you like it here?" Basie asked, voice barely above a whisper.

"I don't know. This diner is pretty damp."

"I didn't mean *here* here," Basie laughed, elbowing Kit's side. "I meant here like Long Lily and Wellhead."

Kit's eyes drifted to the dusty window as he considered. A thoughtful expression crossed his face, like he was comparing every Long Lily street corner to the ones he was used to in Baltimore.

"Long Lily makes me want to settle down," he decided finally.

"Funny." Basie's eyes drifted back to the family portraits in the box. "My mom used to say the same thing."

"And you disagree?"

If he said no, then what the hell was the point of all of his packed bags by the door?

"I used to agree," said Basie, not willing to look at Kit straight on. "God, for the longest time I loved living here so much. The people, the clean air, the view of the town when you're really high up and you can see *everything*. There's magic here and it's hard because I just…I don't fit in it anymore. My mom died, and it turned me into an outsider in the only place I could ever call home."

There was wisdom in Kit's eyes that was much older than he was—older than Basie, maybe older than the mountains. When he spoke, it was with absolute certainty.

"That's not true. This world is full of Long Lilys." Kit placed his hand on Basie's so that his freckled skin laid on Basie's hard-earned calluses. Warmth simmered in the depth of Basie's stomach and moved behind his cheeks at Kit's touch. "But you're not an outsider. There's no shame in staying here until it *feels* like home again. If you give it time, it'll happen. I'm certain of it."

Without Della, Basie doubted this. But he turned his hand over in Kit's and gave it a long, gentle squeeze.

"It's nice of you to root for me. But I can't stay," Basie murmured, resolute. "I can't."

Kit's hold loosened, but he didn't steal back his hand completely.

"Then let me help you."

Basie looked up, finding himself closer in Kit's space than he intended.

"How?"

"I found a lot of really valuable resources while I was looking for the right place to move to," Kit explained. "We could look through them together. Create a solid plan so you aren't drifting around from place to place."

Basie swallowed—and let his hand meld against the shape of Kit's without hesitation or reservation.

"You're too good to be wasting your time on me—but okay."

The smile on Kit's face told Basie that he was not one to waste anything.

L ATER, AFTER KIT HAD left with plans to return the next day, Basie stood in the window and looked out into the forest. The expanse of towering trees looked completely different, which made Basie uneasy. For all that the view before him felt like a new world, it was untouched by people and their hand axes.

This meant one of two impossible things: either the forest had shifted itself away from perpetual *sameness* when Basie wasn't looking. Or—Basie was the thing that had changed.

Melancholy closed in on him, oozing down the windowpanes and through the crack under the door like thick, foul tar. It made his skin itch, made him recoil away from the all-impending downpour and sunless gray outside.

Behind him, Kit's cologne still lingered in the doorway, a whisper of apple and sumac. The Yeats family pictures waited face up on the cot.

Something in Basie shifted.

He took the key to his grief and unlocked the shackles.

He was *done* with it. Done being pulled in a thousand different directions until his bones ached. Done wading through each day in a lukewarm haze. Done stopping in his tracks at the first sign of something good. Done holding himself back from actually *going* somewhere.

Absolutely *fucking* done.

He wasn't foolish enough to think that the grief was gone for good—that it wouldn't come back. Some things were out of his control. But he had pried its slimy, barbed fingers off of his heart and for the first time since his mother had driven his truck across the Canadian border, he could breathe.

A line of verse came to his mind, one from the same poem Kit had recited earlier that day. When he spoke it aloud, he pretended his own voice was Kit's and let his heart make the daydream real.

"Quiero en el alma mía tener la inspiración honda, profunda, inmensa…" He let his breath fog the window and turn his view to a blurry haze. I want my soul to have deep, profound, immense inspiration.

"Luz, calor, aroma, vida."

Radiance, warmth, fragrance, life.

Only, when Basie pictured those things, it was Kit's face he saw.

He turned back around, crossed the room, and unpacked his bag.

CHAPTER 11

From, The Diary of Adella Olmeda
Vol. 13. May 14th, 1944.

Is there anything more beautiful than Mexico in the summertime? Or more <u>hot</u>?

I adore Sonora and its mountains. Sometimes I sit on our veranda and stare at the scalded peaks in hopes of seeing someone staring back from the very top. I think sometimes my mind tricks me into thinking there's someone there. Here in Sonora, it is just me, Basilio, and the imaginary man on the mountaintop. I have finally outrun the war.

Basilio has been talking of children. I think it is because we are so close to his family, but have yet to reveal ourselves to them. Silio says he cannot face them. I can't know for sure what happened, but I suspect it has something to do with his brother, who is still missing. Some nights he murmurs his brother's name—"Jesús, Jesús." I mistook the murmurings for a prayer. But in some ways, I think he is calling out for both his brother and Jesús' namesake.

There is a very serious part of him that longs to ease his loneliness with a baby.

It is hard to consider bringing a child into a world that's going to hell, but he wants one so very badly. I wonder if he'll feel the same when he finds out that the child he fathers will never die. That's the rub about immortality. It only takes one parent.

It is terrible to be immortal and surrounded by war.

While people hide for their lives, I hide in my head and picture the face of my child. He looks like Basilio, but he has at least one thing that marks him as <u>mine</u>. I don't know when I decided he would be a 'he,' but somehow, I know. Maybe this means the Almighty has already decided.

I picture both of them fighting away in Germany or France, and I find I can't breathe. I have told Basilio that I will not bear his children until the war is over. He's worried I am running out of time. How strange, when time is all I have.

Last night, Basilio brought home a fine copy of poetry by William B. Yeats. He stayed up all night reading it, *scribbling Spanish translations and notes in the margins. Then, he set his book down and told me that when we go back to America, and the fighting is finally done, I should change my surname. "I want to protect <u>our</u> legacy. Not the legacy of the Moores, or even the Olmedas. I want to protect the legacy of Basilio-and-Adella, create it with names that mean something to us."*

I decided we would keep the name Olmeda, because I knew that one day, he would regret it if he gave it up completely. I would not have such regrets.

"The name Moore means nothing to me anymore," I told him. "But what shall I replace it with?"

He pulled the poetry book into his lap and laid his finger on the cover. Yeats, he said, for his poetic soul and my Irish heritage. The name may have to grow on me, but then, I've always been partial to things I've chosen myself. And I must admit, I like the idea of letting Adella Moore die so that Della Olmeda-Yeats can open her eyes.

But here is the real legacy: Basil Olmeda-Yeats, the child of my imagination and the miracle that will let our legacy live forever.

I will tell Basilio how old I really am soon. I do not often like to think about it, but the idea of having sweet Basil Yeats in my life forever makes the thought a little less painful.

CHAPTER 12

Certificate of Death

Full Name: Basil (Basie) Olmeda-Yeats

Date of Birth: March 22, 1945

Birthplace: Gettysburg, Pennsylvania

Date of Death: July 30th, 2022

Location of Death: Smack dab in the middle of the lawn at the McAllister Memorial Public Library; Long Lily, Pennsylvania.

Cause of Death:
A. The unfortunate moment Basie happened to look up from his volunteer work at an approaching local resident, Kit Elliot—who was dressed, for once, in his casual clothes. Mr. Elliot was noted to be wearing well-fitting jeans, a white shirt, and an unbuttoned flannel, rolled to the elbows. Like an Olympic

champion, he carried a hefty box of books on either shoulder. Basie's death was immediate.

(Due to or as a consequence of:)

B. A pain in the chest, likely resulting from: Mr Elliot's squinty smile, AND Basie's continuing avoidance of his rapidly growing affection.

(Due to or as a consequence of:)

C. Mr. Yeats refusing to consider any options for his future that did not involve leaving Long Lily, even if one of the alternatives was *very* handsome and had a smile that could make the sun crack in half.

"Hello? Earth to space cadet Basie," said Orion Simon beside him. "Snap twice if I need to alert the authorities or summon medical assistance. If you need CPR, I can give it my best shot. But I gotta tell you, I did not pass that certification exam."

Basie blinked.

"What are you going on about?"

"You tell me. You were in the middle of saying something and you just—trailed off. It was real spooky. Sounded like someone turned down your volume knob or something."

The terrible thing was, it took Basie a few seconds to remember what the heck he was doing before Kit walked entered the scene, hulking out with boxes of books on his shoulders. Basie was volunteering at the library book sale, just as he had since he was a little boy. It was kind of nice, he thought, to wear the same aprons with the same worn-out library logo. The lawn was a treasure trove of books—some standing upright on the tables, some leaning on library carts. The library spent all year collecting donations and the citizens of Long Lily never disappointed in their generosity. Basie was not much of a reader, so he donated his time instead.

Orion was here too, because they needed to complete service hours for school. A book sale was not what Orion originally had in mind—printed books were worthless to the blind—but their completed service form was a week overdue. Orion had brought their sight dog, Canis, who admittedly was not very much help in sorting the books. Instead, she found a cool little spot underneath one of the tables, close enough if Orion needed to grab her harness.

Orion and Basie's task was simple—sort the boxes of donations by genre and line them up neatly on the tables. This meant Basie was the one digging though the boxes, identifying the genre, and Orion would put each book on the table.

"I'm fine," said Basie. "Just got distracted by something. Keep sorting."

"I would, except you never finished telling me where to put this. I mean I could give a guess, like a fun, little wild card in the middle of the table, but—"

"It's a mystery book," Basie said exasperated. His eyes kept darting over to Kit, who had not quite made it to Basie's table. Emily Long, the chief librarian, had accosted him at the foot of the parking lot, no doubt thanking him for all the books he was donating. She'd always wanted to pilfer through Della's books, or so Basie's mom always told him. Basie just needed to focus on the task at hand.

Basie had just bent under the table to fill up on more books, when a voice said, "Special delivery."

The top of Basie's head met the underside of the table with a teeth-rattling *slam*. He swore, books tumbling out of his grasp.

"Sorry, didn't mean to startle you," chuckled Kit sheepishly. A bead of sweat pooled on his brow and trailed to the bow of his jaw. He gestured at his legs. "Look, Basie. *Jeans.*"

Once again, Basie's faculties stopped working.

"Must be the second coming," grumbled Basie, picking the books from the dirt.

Kit ignored this and turned to Orion.

"Hi Rion. It's Kit. I've brought more books for the tables. Hope it's not too much trouble."

"'Course it's no trouble," Basie grumbled, rubbing the back of his head. "I'm the one who told you to bring them."

"Speak for yourself," Orion said, pointedly. "How many boxes are there?"

Kit adjusted his hold, nose scrunching as he thought.

"Twelve altogether."

"Unfair labor practices," Orion stated immediately. "Basie and I will be unionizing. Capitalism as you know it has finally reached its end, Mr. Elliot."

"Would you quit being a little shit?" Basie hissed through his teeth, bumping Orion's shoulder. "If you hadn't put your service project off until the last second, you wouldn't have to unionize." He rounded the table, holding out his hands to Kit. "Gimme those."

Just as Basie's fingers met the boxes, Kit swirled them out of the way, leaning his face directly in line with Basie's. In an instant, Basie couldn't breathe.

"I'm fit enough to handle these packages myself," he said with a smirk.

Basie choked on his own spit.

Letting the boxes fall gently to the ground, he wiped his brow with the sleeve of his shirt. Basie mourned that he hadn't gotten to it first.

"Guess I better go fetch the other boxes. Back in a jiff," Kit announced, then disappeared.

"I'll help you. Just—just a second," rushed Basie, dumping all of the books in his hands on the table in a heap. "Orion, would you—never mind. I'll just—"

"*Ahhh*," crooned Orion.

Basie froze. "What?"

"Nothing. I've been wondering why you stayed in Long Lily when you sold the house two months ago. Now I've got my answer."

If Orion knew how red Basie's face was, they would've teased him mercilessly for it.

"What's *that* supposed to mean?" he objected.

"That you're gay."

"Wow, Ri. They better give you the Nobel Peace Prize for that discovery. It's not like I've been out for five decades." Sometimes it was still uncomfortable to mention his immortality out loud to the Simon family, even though most of them had known his secret their whole lives. Mentioning his feelings for Kit and his immortality in the same breath felt like stripping naked and twirling around in front of all the gray-haired librarians. "Whatever you think is going on between Kit and I, you're wrong."

"You say that now, but us Simons—we *know* things."

It was true, and remembering so made every last one of Basie's hairs stand up. Lewie had never explained to Basie what the Simon "knowing" was, had said that some things were meant for family only. At the time, this pissed Basie off into next week, because Lewie had *just* learned Basie's secret by sticking his nose where it didn't belong. But over time, Basie had simply come to accept that the Simons knew things about him and they wouldn't ever use those things to betray him.

Until now.

"How about you head in and have Emily pour you a few glasses of lemonade?" Basie offered.

"So you can help your boyfriend with his *packages*?" Orion deadpanned. "Thought you'd never ask." They released their hold on a line of sideways books without a second thought, sending the rest tumbling across the table like a bunch of dominos.

Basie squeezed his eyes shut to avoid watching the damage, but Rion was already walking away.

"Later Basie-gator," they said.

Kit was rifling through the back of his van when Basie came to stand beside him. He hunched under the hatch of the trunk, a few wrong moments away from bashing his skull just like Basie did on the table. His focus, though, was adhered to a sizable glossy book with pictures of a place Basie recognized instantly: the Sonoran Desert in northwestern Mexico.

"Ever been there?" Basie asked, standing so close to Kit that their hips bumped together. Kit turned the page, revealing a dusky mesa crowned by a row of cacti, each raising their arms triumphantly to the unforgiving sun.

"I've only been to central Mexico to visit the Aztec ruins."

"How Indiana Jones of you."

"You didn't think I got to be an archivist filing papers, did you?"

Basie turned to sit on the edge of the trunk, folding his hands into his laps.

"I'm sure there's a lot I don't know about you."

"Oh please, sometimes it seems like all we ever talk about is me. You knew all sorts of incriminating information about me the first day we met, but you never let me ask questions about you," Kit said.

Ignoring the spark on his skin when they touched, Basie grabbed Kit's wrist, guiding him to sit in the empty space next to him. He spread the book out on their laps, the pages rippling as a car drove through the parking lot. The page he wanted was at the beginning of the book, a map that highlighted the desert on the southern corner of California and the northwestern tip of Mexico. He laid his finger to a point in the center of the region.

"For starters, this is where my father's side of the family is from. Right around here."

Kit followed the movement of Basie's fingers as he flicked through more pages and found a wide spread image of an amber crested mountain range. Basie wondered if Kit's eyes would track his fingers if he laid them on Kit's bottom lip.

"You want to know all the incriminating things about me? Here they are," mused Basie. "My mom and dad separated before I was born, which was complicated to begin with. Then, we found out my dad never told his side of the family that I existed. Which, of course, felt really great." Basie could sense Kit's intense gaze on his skin, making it difficult to speak without stumbling. "So, right around the time I turned twenty, I did everything I could to track them down in secret. It turned out all my father's sisters, their children, and my *abuela* were all living in the same house. I sent them a letter to ask if they would host me during a summer trip to Mexico."

"Did you tell them who you were?"

"I lied and said I was Basilio's friend, instead of his son." It was one of the only times Basie had ever lied for something that had nothing to do with his immortality. In fact, his trip to Mexico in the sixties was his one opportunity to see his family as Basilio's son—not that Basie could tell Kit that. "I always imagined my dad had this *Not worth my time* mentality about me. I thought that if I told the rest of his family the truth, they'd feel the same way."

Kit's expression fell. He moved the book until it was fully on his lap. A piece of heavy paper stuck out from underneath one of the pages. Basie flipped to it, revealing a Polaroid picture of an ivory church, as grand and beautiful as any royal palace.

"This is the church where we all met up."

He flipped the picture to see if he'd written anything on the other side, only to twist it back over when the year 1964 was scrawled in blue ink.

"I only got around to telling my mother when my bags were all packed, about five hours before my flight," continued Basie. Kit's face scrunched in on itself, a look that said, *I think that was a foolish move, but I'm too polite to say anything.* "She was so disappointed in me—but not for the reasons I expected. I thought she hated my dad and assumed she would despise his family or feel like I was betraying her by boarding with them. But she was hurt that I'd gone behind her back. If it had been up to her, she would've gone with me. Just as well, though. It was something I needed to do alone. It was the only time I've ever left Long Lily. Damn good place to get fluent in Spanish, too."

Kit laid his hand on the book beside Basie's, sending another flush crawling up Basie's neck.

"Did you ever think of staying?" asked Kit.

"Once, when I was lost in the fantasy that one day we'd be a big happy family. Got over it eventually."

Putting it like that was a massive understatement. The dreaming of *Project Live in Mexico* had been all passion. Basie had been baptized with the intention to move into his family's house like there was a Pentecostal fire over his head, giving him the power to speak his father's tongue and endure his ancestors' heat. It frightened his mother, but there wasn't any true cause for fear. His fierce wanting died the night he asked his *Tía* Cristina if she could ever consider him family and everyone at the dinner table laughed and laughed. Everyone except *Abuela*.

"Guess I was always destined for colder mountains," Basie said, in a small voice. "September rolled around and it was time to go home. Right before I left, my *abuela* told me she knew. I looked too much like my father, she said. The others didn't notice because they didn't have a mother's memory. I wrote letters to her until the day she passed away. My *tía* wouldn't host me for the funeral. She said it was a family matter."

The story rang out between them. Maybe Kit could tell the story was more complicated than Basie was letting on. The anecdote as it stood was unchained from the reality that bogged it down—like Basie's immortality and the lack of eagerness to confess, out loud, that his father turned his back on them. He hoped Kit would be able to hear just how much he loved Sonora and just how deep the cut was when he left.

Stretching his legs out in front of him, Kit said, "My parents disowned me."

Basie managed to contain a jolt, but the photo book tumbled from their laps to the ground. Kit retrieved it like it was nothing, like he hadn't just casually confessed he was estranged from his parents. This was one of those moments where Kit was handing Basie a fragile piece of himself. For once, Basie refused to bulldoze it into a thousand pieces. He would handle this matter with care.

Their eyes met, both cautiously doleful.

"My folks live their life in a very particular way," Kit explained, somewhat wearily, "and are not usually kind to those who live differently."

This new information tossed in Basie's mind, bumping into the familiar knowledge that Kit always wore dress clothes and had an old-fashioned way of speaking.

"You weren't…You weren't *Amish*, were you?"

Kit blinked blankly, then exploded with bright, effervescent laughter.

"No, Bas, I wasn't Amish," he grinned. "It is rather similar, though! I grew up in a small community where everything was done a certain way. It wasn't a bad way of doing things by any means, but it was so…simple. I suppose I got my own version of a Rumspringa, because my parents gave me the time to go off into the world and unturn all the stones I could find. They probably expected that I would find the world far too overwhelming. But I fell perfectly in love with it. The more I traveled, the more it became clear to me that I would rather be anywhere else than the little hamlet my parents wanted to confine me to."

This was something Basie had been trying desperately to relate to since his mother's passing. Though unlike Kit, who spoke of the vast world with the soft tones of a lover, Basie only felt terrified.

"That doesn't make sense." He gestured at the library sale spread out on the lawn and all the faces he knew. "*This* is a little hamlet. Like, the littlest. Why do you want to live here?"

Kit rose to his feet, stretching his arms until they touched the clouds. Basie caught himself wondering what Kit would look like against a boundless blue sky or a million stars. Even now, with Kit's arms hooked above his head, drawing his shirt away from his waist, Basie found Kit's freckles streamed all the way to his stomach in a waterfall.

"Sometimes I think the easiest thing a person can do is lie to themselves. It's like breathing. You can't help it. You just open your mouth and it's what fills you up." Kit said. "It's true that my time traveling was beyond compare—one once-in-a-lifetime experience after another. Then, one day, I was sitting alone in my Baltimore apartment, looking around at all the empty seats in my living room." His gaze traveled across the lawn, lingering on the book sale volunteers exchanging stories and smiles like they cost nothing to give. "And I realized I was very lonely."

An image appeared in Basie's mind of Wellhead Cottage during the hours after his mother's death. He squeezed his hands into fists so tightly, his nails left crescent indents on his palms.

"You had your friend. Lara?" Basie pointed out quietly.

"Her company was probably the only thing keeping me from completely cracking. When I finally got around to telling her my grand plan—the wild idea to move to a smaller town to finally *know* people and belong somewhere my parents couldn't reign over me—she said she was surprised I hadn't done it sooner."

Basie tilted his chin up just in time to catch a smooth breeze sweep all of Kit's hair across his face.

"Do you think you made the right choice?" he asked Kit, trying to keep his voice as light as possible.

The question captured Kit's full attention in an instant.

It was moments like these, when he trapped all his truth behind a single guarded smile, that Basie would trade all the years of his life for the ability to read minds. Yet underneath the heavy weight of Kit's quiet stare, there was a *wanting*. Basie wished he knew just what hungered Kit so profoundly. Basie would provide it, if only to satisfy the appetite in Kit's eyes. If only to stop wishing that need would turn to him. On him.

"I think so," Kit answered eventually. "Wellhead is where I was always meant to be."

Basie mirrored Kit's smile with tight lips.

"It has that effect."

In an attempt to shatter the tension, he hopped off the ledge of the trunk and wrenched another box from inside. The sheer bulk of it had Basie gritting his teeth. How Kit ever put these on his shoulders was a miracle.

"God damn," blurted Basie, like someone punched his gut. "Who packed these? I've got a few choice words I'd like to give him."

But Kit could not be averted. The distance between them cracked like a live wire, suddenly shortened by Kit with a few fearless steps. His hands easily slid over Basie's, sharing the burden of the weight and cupping his palms over calluses and dry knuckles.

"I'm going to help you find your own perfect place," he promised. "Who knows? Maybe you don't have to look very far at all."

Basie's mouth turned dry. With any luck, Kit wouldn't be able to feel how sweat made his grip on the box slip. A jumbled mess of questions and confessions tumbled around inside his mind, nearly slipping down his throat and out his mouth. He wasn't sure what embarrassing thing he was about to say, but was only glad that he caught it behind his teeth before it broke loose.

"Guess we ought to get back to work," Kit said, the barest trace of *something* outlining his words and drawing the vowel sounds. If Basie didn't know any better, he'd say it was affection.

Without warning, Kit stepped closer, and for a dangerous moment, Basie thought Kit might kiss him. Even worse, Basie discovered he would let him.

But then the box disappeared from Basie's grip, leaving him in a familiar state of emptiness. Kit sauntered past him with a gleam in his eye of pure knowing. Their shoulders brushed as he passed and it seemed as though for everything Kit Elliot knew, Basie knew nothing at all.

CHAPTER 13

"THIS ISN'T A VERY equitable exchange," Basie said, but Kit was delighted to find Basie grinning at the casserole dish in Kit's hands.

"I'm not sure what you mean," Kit replied. He brushed past Basie and set the shepherd's pie on the milkshake counter. The bottom was still hot enough that a foggy cloud spread onto the surface of the linoleum, as if the countertop hadn't known a fresh cooked meal in decades.

"Every time you visit, you bring something you cooked." Basie settled on a barstool, ignoring the way it squeaked as he spun and knocked knees with Kit. "You're the one crossing town to help me look at places to move to. If anything, *I* should be cooking for *you*."

Kit agreed with Basie that it wasn't an even exchange. All *he* had to offer was a mediocre amount of wisdom and a meal he'd thrown together in under an hour. But for every hot meal he brought to Crane's Nest, Kit received the tiny dimple that crowned Basie's lips when he smiled. For every trip Kit took across town, Basie gave him hours of his company and his rock-solid attention that did not roam or wane. For every *You should look into this town* or *This place is close to a national park* or

I lived here once and I think you'd like it, Basie leaned in close and let them share air that was sweetened by his floral, musky scent. No, it was not an even exchange.

All these things from a man who still planned to move away forever were invaluable to Kit, who planned to stay right where he was.

"As delightful as your cooking sounds, I've decided to protect myself from the horrors of canned soup cooked in a rusty pot. If anything, bringing dinner is an act of selfish self-preservation," Kit insisted.

"The pot isn't rusty!" Basie protested, leaning closer. Then, when Kit cocked a brow, he added, "Much. Not my fault it's so damn wet here."

Kit shook his head, pushing the plate forward and presenting two forks for Basie to choose from. One had come from Kit's old home in Baltimore, while the other had a pearly marble handle—an original from Basie's own kitchen drawer. Basie took the marbled one.

"Eat your casserole, Mr. Yeats."

"Aye aye, Captain."

Basie piled a healthy serving onto his fork and gobbled it in a single bite. His whole body wilted with satisfaction, and when he let out a soft sigh, Kit could not have looked anywhere else if he tried.

"So I put some thought into what you said yesterday, about considering a place with historical importance," Kit began. "I found some options, but it was harder than I expected."

"Why? The whole east coast is one big history book," Basie asked, mouth full. "You could drop a pin on a map and *presto!*

Like magic, you're in the country's oldest sock factory."

Kit made quick work of averting his eyes.

"Now I don't want to tell you what I found."

"Oh, come on," Basie crooned, poking a finger into Kit's thigh. All of Kit's wires shorted. "You seem to have decent taste so far."

"Apparently not, since you haven't chosen any of them."

"I just want to see all you can dig up before I make up my mind!"

Kit pressed his lips together to conceal a smile. For the first few days, he worried that Basie would misinterpret his devotion towards this task; assume it was mostly a ploy to get rid of him. He couldn't know for sure that Basie had never thought this, but felt confident that the last two weeks had certainly cleared up any misconceptions.

They spent too much time lounging on the mildewy booth chairs talking about everything and nothing—sometimes they forgot to discuss research altogether. Basie was always the first to skirt their conversations away from all things related to homes and moving vans. Kit had only followed suit. He still took their task seriously, if only to spend more time with Basie.

Yet, for all of his distractions and diversions, when the topic of *Moving Away* did come up in earnest, Basie always lit up like he'd won the lottery. Like he couldn't wait to leave every blasted bit of Long Lily, Kit included, behind. It was giving Kit whiplash.

He rifled through his messenger bag, selecting the few crisp, orderly papers he had brought.

"Historical places are hard. They're either too expensive, too traditional, or their history is too..." He tossed some words around in his mind until he found the right one. "Iniquitous."

"Ah, he's an atlas *and* a dictionary. You're lucky my mom homeschooled me." Basie helped himself to another heaping bite. "Were you looking at cult towns or something? *Or!*" He jabbed his fork. "Don't tell me. Lilydale, New York. You want me to become a psychic."

Kit knocked Basie's fork with his own.

"The Lilydale psychics are very respectable, thank you," Kit scolded. He pushed bits of casserole around his corner of the dish for a long moment. "What do you think about West Virginia?"

"I've never been to West Virginia."

"You've never been anywhere."

Basie scoffed, waving his hand. "What's in West Virginia?"

"Well…" Kit snagged the appropriate sheet, laying it on the table. It was difficult to read the title across the top—the library printer was half-dead—so he read it out loud. "Berkeley Springs, home of the nation's first spa."

Wiping his mouth with the back of his wrist, Basie took the sheet, eyes darting as he skimmed the information.

"No fucking way. Forget what I said about the sock factory, I've never been to a spa."

"It's really quite cute," Kit said. "It's still in the Appalachian mountains, so it'd be familiar to you. They've got all these really incredible hiking trails; you could still walk as much as you wanted. I also looked to see if any of the electric companies are hiring. Turns out, at least three are. The spas are just an added bonus."

Basie hadn't looked up. He ran his thumb over the corner of the page, curling it in on itself.

Kit offered, "Guess what the population is?"

"How many?" Basie's voice was barely his own.

"Nine hundred."

Beside him, Basie heaved out a slow breath.

"That's fewer than Long Lily."

"It is." Kit fought the urge to grab Basie's hand to keep him from getting a paper cut, tracing his fingers over the edge of the sheet like that. "I've heard it rains a fairly normal amount there, if that makes any difference."

This drew Basie's attention.

"Why would it?"

"Seems to me that you really enjoy the rain."

"Not any more than anyone else. This place would be perfect. I could never live in a place where it rained *all* the time."

Kit paused. He studied the corner across the room where the roof was leaking. And the full buckets. And the flooding outside the window.

"Right."

Basie rolled his eyes.

"Oh, fuck off. It doesn't *always* rain here."

"It rains enough that knowing you live here practically keeps me up at night. It's only a matter of time before this roof comes right down on top of you!"

"Kit—" Basie huffed.

"I'm serious! Why live in a place that's one stiff wind away from sailing down the creek when you could stay with someone in town? At least until you're ready to move. I've lived in apartments I wouldn't wish on my worst enemy, but this place just isn't safe for you."

"As far as most of the people in town are concerned, I was

supposed to be gone months ago. I don't know any of them well enough to infringe on their kindness for that long."

"You lie all the time, Basie, and most of the time you're halfway decent at it. But you and I both know for a fact that the people in town treat you like you're their flesh and blood," he protested, sounding un-Kit-like. To everyone else, this would've sounded like genuine annoyance. To Basie, it was a reality check. "For one, Lewie would let you live with him in a heartbeat."

Basie scrubbed over his cheeks with both hands. Kit wondered if there were pricks of stubble there, or if Basie had trouble growing a beard like he did.

"He would," Basie assented. "But he's raising six out of his seven kid siblings. They barely have room in that house for all of them. I can't ask them to take me in. And I don't have anyone else."

Sometimes, Kit thought, for someone so sensible, Basie Yeats was a goddamn fool.

"You have me."

Basie looked at Kit like he was crazy, but Kit had never been more serious. Not when he moved into Wellhead. Not when he'd apologized to Basie after their train wreck of a first meeting. Not after swearing with every last inch of his being that he would help Basie find somewhere to go, because given the choice to either help or ignore Basie, Kit's choice was clear.

There'd be repercussions when Basie left for good and forgot all about him, but Kit had never felt so certain about his own self-destruction before.

"Come back to Wellhead," he pressed.

All of Basie's muscles were locked. Even though they were shoulder to shoulder, Kit could not tell if he was breathing. He was frozen, elbows leaning onto the counter, boring into Kit as if he were suspended in time.

Kit counted to thirty, waiting for Basie to answer, only to reset his internal timer when the silence persisted. He waited some more, but still, Basie said nothing.

Shame washed over Kit in a crashing wave.

How could he ask such a thing? Grief had sent Basie from the house in the first place, and that was only a couple of months ago. And in that time, only divine intervention had convinced Basie not to hate Kit anymore. The understanding between them was still on thin ice and he'd gone stomping all over it. Now they were both plummeting into icy depths, from which they might never surface.

If Basie didn't know about his ridiculous schoolboy crush, he certainly did now. Why did he have to sound so eager?

"Forget I said anything. Of course it's too soon," he rushed. He didn't know *what* exactly was too soon. Too soon for Basie to return home to his dead mother's house? Too soon for them to be sharing a space? Both? "That was really foolish of me. I'm just some stranger—"

"You're not," Basie interrupted. The low hum of his voice hit Kit like a truck. "You're not just some stranger. You're my friend and…and it's really kind of you to offer your home to me. It's just, I don't have much money to pay you for rent."

Kit frowned. "What happened to the money from when I bought the house?"

"I'm saving it all for the place in…well, wherever I move to."

Frustration churned at the top of Kit's stomach, creeping up his throat. He imagined if he told Basie he didn't have to pay rent at his own house that Basie would simply argue it wasn't his house anymore. Then they'd be right where they started.

He took a breath and tried a different approach.

"We could work something out if it really meant that much to you. I've been spending evenings working on the mural your mom was painting in the attic. You could help with that. Or—or if you didn't feel comfortable in her room, you could take care of the garden. Or the bees. There's plenty that needs upkeep."

There it was—that eagerness. Kit took another bite of the casserole to *shut his traitor mouth up*, only it was turning cold and gummy from sitting out. But if he was eating, then he wasn't talking, so he took another bite. Basie, once again, turned silent. When he scarfed another forkful of potatoes into his mouth, Kit fought the urge to tell him to warm it up in his rusty pan. Only one of them needed to suffer through room temperature casserole.

"I'll think about it," Basie said. "I've got a good feeling about Berkeley Springs. I want to research it a bit more, maybe call those electric companies on the phone to see if they'd hire me. Check out some properties for sale. But if that doesn't work out, I'll take you up on your offer."

Kit blinked. He almost asked Basie to repeat himself, but his mind was already playing the moment back on an obsessive loop.

He was going to call every electrician in Berkeley Springs and tell them that Basil Yeats had rabies and liked to kick puppies. That he pushed old ladies into traffic and swiped mint gum from the gas station every time he filled his tank. He was going to—

Alright, no he wasn't. Perhaps he'd been around Basie too long.

He had to remind himself that if Basie did stay, there was no guarantee… There was nothing promising that they… That Basie even *liked*…

Kit hoped he wasn't showing his thoughts on his face when Basie added, "There is a favor I'd like to ask you, actually."

Would you mind terribly signing this marriage license so that we can wear these matching rings I got us?

"Can I leave my things in the shed until I move? It's been a little damp here."

This was not what Kit was expecting.

Since he moved in, he'd gone back and forth—sometimes remembering the shed existed, but mostly forgetting about it entirely. He'd tried yanking the door when he first moved in, a fruitless effort, and made a mental note to call a locksmith. The questions at the estate sale came soon after. People wondering, *Got anything good in the shed?* Or *Della used to spend hours in that rickety thing. Always wondered what she kept in there.* It had been out of respect for Della, and his fragile friendship with Basie, that Kit decided to throw any awareness of the shed from his mind. He forced himself to forget about its long boards and patchy shingles. He went weeks before he actually looked past it in the yard instead of *pretending* to look past it.

Then Basie revealed he had kept the key and all the effort disappeared. Because Basie had left everything behind, even the things he didn't really want to abandon. But he'd taken the key with him.

Kit planned to grant Basie's request no matter what—not that approval was his to give. He wasn't the one with the key. But if Basie opened up the shed to store his things, the probability that

Kit would get to learn what was inside increased exponentially. That, Kit decided, was the answer he'd been looking for. Because he'd been trying to unlock Basie Yeats a thousand different ways since they met—through his misguided apologies, through his baking, through his company. But to really know Basie was to be there when he opened the shed door.

"Of course you can. You don't have to ask," Kit said.

"I couldn't just show up one day and drop all my things at your doorstep."

Kit couldn't help his shy smile. "Isn't that what I just asked you to do?"

Basie sat back, pursing his lips as he considered.

"Okay," he decided. "I'll, uh—I'll pack my bags and then drop them off tomorrow. They'll be safe there until I figure out what the hell I'm gonna do. Thanks."

"I could bring them back with me? You could save yourself a trip and just give me the key to the—"

"*No.*" Basie had never answered him so sharply before. Awkwardly, yes. Even cruelly. But never like Kit was a child about to stick his finger into an electric socket. He seemed to hear the harshness in his tone, though, because he placed the lid back on the casserole and said, "No, it's not your problem. I'll just walk over next time I'm in town."

Kit did not have to be told what this really meant, which was, *I'm going to walk over when you're not home.* He pressed his teeth together so hard his ear popped, but he smiled at Basie.

"Alright."

He'd just have to see inside the shed another time.

T HERE WAS A *MOMENT* when Kit packed up to leave: a tragedy in three acts.

Act I.

Kit, sorting through the papers he wanted to leave for Basie's perusal and deciding which ones to stuff back into his messenger bag. Basie, running dish soap and water over the forks they used, pocketing the one from his mom's collection. Kit, untying and retying his shoes so that he'd have a few extra seconds before saying goodbye. Basie, mistaking the stalling as struggling and bending to swat Kit's hands away to tie the shoes himself. Kit, forgetting how to speak. Basie, suffering a similar affliction.

Act II.

Basie's hands landing softly on Kit's, still threaded among the loose laces. Kit pausing, then turning slack. Basie turning Kit's palms so they faced the ceiling, then running the tip of his finger along the soft lines indented in his skin. Kit's breath hitching and falling apart, releasing an unsteady sigh. That same breath fanning across Basie's lips, drawing him forward as the whole earth shifted sideways. Their hands closing together, strong. Determined.

Act III.

A crack of thunder crashing near the unstable roof of the diner and Basie falling back onto the damp floor. Him, sitting there in a puddle and Kit rushing out the front door. Kit, driving away too fast for the rain and the mud. Basie, a wisp of silhouette in

Kit's rearview mirror, standing in the broken window, watching him go.

CHAPTER 14

S OMETIMES, BASIE FORGOT THAT the world around him aged.

He blamed his own immortality and Wellhead for this carelessness. Both were easy scapegoats for the egocentric way he didn't notice when the neighbor's toddlers turned to teenagers, or when some of the century old buildings in town were leveled to rubble. Sometimes, when he finally did notice something had changed, he'd ask, *How long has that been there?* If he was lucky, the answer would be *Oh, they just put that up last week.* But usually, it was: *a few years ago.* Or even: *I don't remember.* The most disorienting answer had come from Lewie, who'd said, "*As long as I've been alive, at least.*"

That's not to say Basie was stuck in the past. He could work a computer and scroll through videos on the toilet as well as anyone else. It was only that he forgot that things could get *worse* as time passed.

Take, for instance, the decrepit diner Basie had decided to squat in. If he'd paid even a little attention, he might've noticed that the sag in the diner's roof was caused by a broken branch that had cracked through the shingles. The antique wood holding the diner together was made softer by Crane's Nest's rainy weather, rotting until the beams were so brittle, they'd crumble apart with only a delicate touch.

If Basie had known about the moldered beams, he might have pushed his cot away from the leaky breach. But he didn't, so he couldn't.

It happened a week after Kit's last visit to the diner. The sky above Crane's Nest was a sea of windy thunder. It brewed a deluge of sharp rainfall that pelted the diner until finally, *finally,* the ceiling of the old Redtop Diner began to split.

There was a violent crack, a dozen bones breaking at once, then the roof came down.

Basie's eyes snapped open just in time to watch a loose beam plummeting, en route to flatten him like a mosquito. Without thinking, he threw himself off his cot, landing on the floor beneath one of the old tables. His arms wrapped around the cold metal base, holding the table up as the ceiling rained around him in a catastrophic pile of wreckage. Wooden planks, old shingles, and sharp metal hit the floor with an ear-splitting *CRASH.* Some of the debris rolled toward Basie's feet and he shrank further back under cover, his heart pounding.

When it was over, the only sound was rain hitting the tiled floor and Basie's ragged breaths. He crawled out from his tiny shelter, bare knees crunching against broken glass and toothy boards. His own steadiness surprised him as he patted blindly along the wall for the light switch. It flicked from Off to On when he found it, but sizzled and cracked in warning. The diner remained in darkness.

With a curse, Basie hobbled and hopped around, searching the rubble for whatever belongings he could find. His boots appeared first—or at least, one shoe. The other had been thrown a few feet away. He snatched both up and put them on, grimacing when they were both soaked with rain and debris. His bag appeared next, mercifully where he left it in a dry patch right by the door. The initial adrenaline of the disaster was beginning to wear off, leaving shaking hands and his choked throat in its wake, but Basie still managed to dig out his cellphone. The battery was almost dead, so whatever call he made had to count. Good thing the number was saved to speed dial.

The line rang twice, then Kit answered in a groggy voice, "Basie? It's the middle of the night. What's wrong?"

Basie pressed his lips together to steady himself.

"The roof collapsed."

"*What?*" A rustle of blankets and a pair of feet slamming out of bed. "Are you alright? Are you trapped? Have you called 911?"

"No, but I'm not hurt. Not trapped either." Basie kept his voice low, as if speaking too loudly would invite the rest of the roof to finish what it started.

"Are you sure? Because sometimes you don't realize how serious it is until the shock wears off. If you need an ambulance—"

"I don't. But I can't stay here anymore. It's—it's a mess. I'd call Lewie, but he doesn't really have any room and…"

"I'm already on my way," Kit rushed out. "I'll be there in five minutes."

Across the room, another beam snapped from the ceiling, caking the milkshake counter with a shower of drywall and debris.

"No rush," Basie answered, but Kit had hung up.

In the five minutes it took Kit to scramble from Wellhead to Crane's Nest, Basie came to the conclusion that it was better to sit outside in the storm than to tempt the diner with any more opportunities to maim him. He settled on the faded red stoop, chin to his knees, blinking away rainwater that streamed into his eyes. The lull of exhaustion and the fading adrenaline eased Basie asleep with his eyes open.

Headlights crested the hill into the parking lot and something heavy in Basie's chest calmed as if someone were lifting one of the fallen beams off his lungs. Kit left the car running, appearing first as a silhouette out of the driver's door, then emerging in all his complete, beautiful realness when he raced toward Basie.

Basie stood up just in time to catch Kit, welcoming the arms that drew him close and the face buried in his shoulder.

"I'm soaked. *And* filthy," Basie argued plainly, but it lacked feeling. As it was, his hands were stuck in the soft warmth of Kit's shirt, fingers itching to sink into the auburn curls at the nape of his neck.

Kit shook his head, holding tighter still.

"I don't mind." He drew back just enough to clasp Basie by his shoulders, using the headlights to examine him from head to foot for any injuries. His eyes drifted past Basie to look through the window at the wreckage. The skin beneath his freckles turned even paler. Basie followed his gaze to where a pile of broken boards and ceiling panels now covered the cot, jabbing in every direction. "I knew you staying here was a bad idea."

"And you can tell me all the *I told you so's* you want on the way back to Wellhead. Can we just go?"

Kit turned his troubled expression to Basie. He clenched his jaw, brushing his thumb on a patch of dirt above the heart of Basie's top lip.

"Of course," he said, distractedly. The rain had started to gather on the ends of his hair, dripping in thick pearls down his cheek. Then, he sighed, "I'm so glad you're alright," like he'd been trying to hold it back but couldn't any longer.

Basie hoped Kit couldn't see the heat blooming behind his eyes. It seemed like Kit was saying *more,* but he couldn't figure out what.

"Thanks for picking me up."

"Thanks for not getting crushed."

Basie smiled, a delicate, tired thing, then let Kit drape his arm around his shoulder and guide him to the van. The radio was playing a song Basie didn't recognize. But he still leaned his head against the window and tried to hum along.

WELLHEAD WAS OPPRESSIVELY QUIET under Kit's ownership.

Basie was used to noise. He was used to Della running the television late into the night so she could watch something while she did the dishes. He remembered hearing the crickets and the stream through the open windows and falling asleep to the strange sort of ballad that resulted when all the nocturnal noises waned together.

Now, the windows were closed. The TV was off. The sink was empty.

Maybe it was just too late for sound. Or too early at—Basie glanced at the clock and groaned—3:13AM.

Kit flicked a switch on the wall, causing dim, warm light to bleed across the kitchen table. Even though his clothes were still soaked with rainwater, Basie took a seat, stripping off his shoes and socks. He hadn't realized he'd come in only a t-shirt and his boxers until cold air drafted through the floor vents and crept across his knees. The sight was probably ludicrous—a grown man sitting like equal parts scolded child and wet rat at the table—but Kit didn't laugh or tease.

"This reminds me of the first time I ever brought a boy home to my parents," Kit said.

It was a confession, but barely—the way confessions are when the other person might already know, but the confessor needs to do the telling anyway.

As Kit stood by the sink, running a soft towel under the tap, Basie wondered what Kit was thinking, if he minded coming out to Basie like this in the kitchen. This late witching-hour dimness didn't allow Basie a very good chance to gauge Kit's thoughts. It was hard to make out all the elegant lines on the side of his face, much less whatever he was thinking behind all the polite hospitality.

Basie didn't interject, letting Kit linger in the memory. Eventually the cloth was warm enough that it steamed when he handed it to Basie. It smelled of his mother's lavender soap, but Basie accepted it with a tight smile. He had a selfish hope that Kit would come sit at the table for a while to tell the story—maybe then he could finally get a good look at his face—but Kit only moved to fill the tea kettle with water.

"My parents never did find out who he was to me," he said softly. "I didn't intentionally bring him home, either. He ended up on my doorstep because his car broke down. I don't think I've ever brought a man home, you know, officially."

Now was the time to accept the olive branch and offer his own.

"I understand," answered Basie, swiping the warmed towel up over the streaks of dirt on his legs. "The only reason my mom ever found out about my boyfriends was because Long Lily isn't a good place for keeping secrets." Something about this made Kit's back go stiff, but he kept his face turned down to watch the water rise to a boil. Basie brought his knee underneath his chin. "What was he like? I've never met any Maryland guys."

Kit let out a quiet chuckle, turning to lean against the counter.

"For starters, his name was Axe, short for Alex." A distant warmth crossed his gaze, as if he were watching something sweet from very, very far away. "And he wasn't from Maryland. He was a Jersey boy. So was I, at the time. And oh, was he abrasive. Everyone who met him was terrified of him."

Basie cocked a brow. "Really? A man named *Axe?*"

"Oh, quiet," Kit said, laughing. But Basie was stuck on the thought of Kit with someone…well, someone else. Someone like Axe, who could put the fear of God into someone with just his name alone.

"He wasn't…unkind to you, was he?" asked Basie.

"To me? Never. To everyone who even looked at him wrong, you would've thought he was Godzilla. But for all he was out-wardly intimidating, the truth was, he knew what he was pro-tecting and had a very finessed manner of doing so. That was all. He knew what he wanted too. Always said he took one look at me and made a decision right then and there. You never would have thought he was the wooing type, especially in the circumstances we were in, but I was thoroughly swept off my feet."

This sent a wave of jealousy sweeping through Basie. Even if he had the flirtatious skill to court Kit with all the grace and attention he deserved—which he didn't—immortality ensured he could never be with Kit the way Axe had. That didn't stop him from imagining a world where Kit would tell their story and say something like, "Basie swept me off my feet the very moment I saw him." If he'd known he was ruining the first lines of their story, however it would go, Basie might not have sworn at Kit the day they might. Instead, he might've said what he'd really been thinking—*I've got a good feeling about you.*

"Where did you meet Axe?" Basie said to clear away his thoughts.

Kit's lips opened, then drew closed. He considered his answer so carefully, it almost reminded Basie of himself.

"Overseas," Kit responded finally. It was clear that was as much as Basie was getting. To keep from falling into uncomfortable silence, he circled back to the start.

"You still haven't gotten to the part about your parents."

"Any good story needs a solid exposition to make the ending worthwhile," replied Kit with the most impertinent side-eye he'd ever laid on Basie. But the smile on his face only grew as he continued his story. "Axe always said it was a twist of automobile fate that brought him to my door, but I never quite believed it."

"You think he came over on purpose?"

"I *know* he did. He was very serious about us. For weeks, it was all this talk about *when could he meet my family* and *when can we get a place together?* It was complicated. I kept putting off answering him. Then one night his 'car broke down' exactly outside my house and he 'needed a place to stay.' My mother is unspeakably hospitable."

"That's something she has in common with mine," Basie said, gaze drifting to Della's portrait on the wall. "If your mom is anything like mine was, I imagine she wasn't daunted by his terrifying personality."

"Not in the least. Alex was on his best behavior. It went…" A small laugh. "Honestly, it went perfectly. It was uncomfortable at first, I really wanted my folks to like him, but there was nothing to worry about." On the stove, the kettle began to hiss out clouds of steam. Kit held the handle with a potholder, pouring into two tall mugs. "Anyways, when he came over, it was this late in the evening. My mom made him tea and we stayed up all night talking."

There was still a part of the story he was leaving out. Basie knew this instinctively, the same way he could tell the time just from the sun's shadows on the wall.

Because he couldn't help himself, Basie asked, "What happened?"

Kit set the kettle gently on the stove. "I had to move away." In the nighttime quiet, Basie could hear a tiny sniffle. "He thought I didn't love him enough to stay. But I *had* to go. It wasn't my choice. That was something he never understood. So, we ended things."

Basie didn't realize he was staring at his hands until Kit filled them with a steaming mug. The ceramic was almost too hot to touch, but the warmth was a welcome comfort. He met Kit's eyes, holding his gaze earnestly.

"Thank you for telling me."

Kit's throat bobbed on a swallow.

Then, as if jabbed with a fire poker, he set his mug on the table and grabbed the damp cloth from where it hung over Basie's arm.

"Now, how did you end up with dirt all over your neck? It's underneath your shirt and everything," he said in a rush. He touched the damp corner to the part of Basie's throat that connected with his shoulder. By then, the cloth had lost its warmth and the tepid temperature made Basie jolt. Kit pulled backwards just as quickly, expression wide with alarm.

Basie's heart hammered. He thought of what Kit knew of him. What he knew of Kit.

Slowly, he tugged his shirt over his head, letting it fall in a damp mess on the floor. The air drew thick. Kit's throat bobbed again, but he didn't look away from Basie's eyes.

"Is that better?" Basie murmured. If he spoke any louder, the words would be nothing but rasps.

Kit had no verbal answer to offer him. It was possible he was suffering from jammed, obstructed speech—the same as Basie. But as long as Basie had known him, Kit had always been a man of *doing*.

Now, he reached back out a deliberate, but confident hand, and brushed the cloth over Basie's shoulder. Gooseflesh prickled instantly, though not from the cold. Lulling under the hint of Kit's touch, Basie let himself watch the cloth move in gentle circles in the corner of his vision.

"My offer is still open, you know," Kit murmured. As he slowly disappeared from sight, Basie felt him on his shoulder blades, sweeping along the curve of his spine, and pressing into the small of his back.

It seemed like Kit wanted an answer, wanted Basie to make a

decision, but as it stood, Basie's mind was unraveled, each thought a loose thread he couldn't find the start or end of. All he could focus on was the feel of Kit's fingers through the fabric, and the base eagerness to remove the barrier.

"Did you hear me?" Kit pressed.

"Maybe," Basie heard himself say.

Then, there was breath on the shell of his ear. Then lips. Then the tip of Kit's nose in his hair.

"Stay at Wellhead with me until you leave Long Lily."

An invisible force pushed Basie backwards onto Kit's lips, letting them touch his skin. A shaky sigh escaped at the feeling of two strong hands wrapping around his chest.

Basie felt Kit's words in the base of his spine when he said, "*Stay with me.*"

It might as well have been a siren song for all Basie could try to resist.

"But—"

Basie searched his mind for whatever would come next, but no matter how hard he grasped for logic or the reasoning he had built his future on, it slipped from his fingers. Because here was Kit Elliot offering him something he'd never admitted he wanted. What else could there be?

"But?" Kit's voice barely sounded real. It was in another room and vibrating inside Basie all at once. But *what?*

Through the scattered sea of his own brain, a surprisingly reasonable thought rose to the top of his mind: if the roof *had* collapsed on top of him, did he trust his own immortality enough to spare him? Or would that have been it—the mangled parts of a small-town man who never allowed himself to have what he wanted? How ironic it would've been—to have so many extra years beyond what should've been possible, and still waste them.

But he didn't, did he? He hadn't been crushed. He hadn't died. He was here, in Wellhead Cottage with a man he wanted more than fresh Long Lily air and it wasn't a circumstance of pain like he'd expected.

He liked being here. He hadn't wanted to leave in the first place. That was the honest truth, something Basie so rarely knew the sound of.

Fingers combed through his hair. Basie felt right side up inside himself once again. When he opened his eyes, Kit was still behind him, smelling of the lavender tea waiting for them on the table. Out of the two of them, he didn't expect Kit to have the most bravery. It was time he claimed some of his own.

"Alright, I'll stay," Basie said, glancing over his shoulder. "If only to finally have a chance to get the rest of those pie plates."

A strangled noise choked from Kit, who let Basie go with a playful shove. Basie had half a mind to drag Kit to his lap, but before he could seize the chance, Kit snagged his tea mug from the table and sauntered across the room. He'd stepped out of the light, turning to a figment of shadows and slippers at the base of the stairs.

"I trust you know where everything is?"

Basie leaned back and grinned tiredly.

"You *trust* right, you old man." Kit moved up onto the first step and Basie practically leapt out of his chair. "Hold on, where are you going?"

Kit halted mid-step.

"To bed? It's almost four in the morning. I have to get up for work in two hours."

To be honest, Basie had temporarily forgotten time was a thing. The tea next to him that had been hot just a few seconds ago had gone lukewarm, which suggested that maybe it had been more than a few seconds, after all.

"Well," started Basie petulantly. "Where do you want me?" Kit's brows disappeared into his hairline. "Not like—I just mean—God, why is everything with you—" To his complete frustration, Kit's smile grew. Basie wrangled himself together and tried again, pointedly this time. "Which bedroom is empty?"

"Oh. Uh…" Kit tossed a glance up the stairs, smile dimming. By the time he turned back to Basie, it was completely gone. "Your mother's room is free. I hadn't planned to use that space until I finished the mural on her wall and it still needs a lot of work. It's been a while since I've been able to chip away at it. I've been spending most of my free time…well, you know."

"Oh," mirrored Basie. "That's fine."

"I don't mind sleeping there for the night."

"I'm not going to force you from your own bed, Kit," Basie argued. This was starting to sound more like them. Kit being too good for *his* own good, Basie trying to be reasonable and getting frustrated. He wanted to get back to the part where they were touching. The part with Kit's lips on his ear.

"It's not really *my* bed—"

"I *swear* to god if you say that bed is mine, I will walk to Crane's Nest and sleep in the rubble," Basie snapped. Kit's mouth pressed in on itself.

"Noted. Sleep wherever you'd like." Then, because it was late and because he was a little shit, he added. "*Mi casa es su casa.*" A gloating smile. "Get it?"

Basie groaned. "Yeah yeah, I fucking got it. *Buenas noches, pendejo.*" It couldn't be the last words of the night, though. Not after what they'd shared. Basie wrapped his hands around the mug, feeling as sheepish as the first time his mother took him to Catholic confession to show him what it was like. He smiled, soft. "I'm glad I'm here."

Kit softened and it felt like the whole sky opened.

"Me too," he murmured. "Goodnight, Basie."

CHAPTER 15

U P UNTIL NOW, BASIE had forgotten what his mother's room
looked like during the nighttime.

The last time he'd been like this, cowering in the dark doorway, trying to find his way around in the moonlight, he was
barely thirteen. The memories from that night were hazy, only
clear around a bitterly sore throat and the spoonfuls of honey
Della forced him to swallow. He recalled an Elizabeth Cotten
record meant to drag his feverish mind to sleep. The dusty twangs
of an old guitar plucking out a song he still hadn't forgotten the
melody of.

How strange it was to be here when Della was not. How
strange for this room to exist without her, exactly as she had left
it. His grief wasn't made of reason, and only made him feel that it
was unnatural that her belongings didn't disappear when she did.
They'd been left in their rightful spots, waiting for her to come
home. Being here made Basie another one of those expectant
things. It was an empty effort, but here he was, frozen on the
threshold, the closed door flush to his back.

On the other side of the wall, the floorboards creaked. Basie
squeezed his eyes shut and imagined Kit moving around the
room, pulling new pajamas out of the drawers and drawing

the blinds away from the open window. If he could somehow convince himself that this was *Kit's new cottage* and not *my family's home,* then maybe he could pretend that the bed was just *the guest bed* and not *another stinging reminder that my mother is gone.*

He wasn't sure how long he stood there, staring at nothing but air and moonlight, when a sweeping breeze slipped under the crack in the window, sending something on the bedside table crashing to the floor.

Basie crossed the room in a heartbeat, feeling around blindly for whatever had fallen. His fingers felt smooth wood first, then the jagged edges of fractured glass. He switched on the lamp, thawing the darkness in this tiny space between the bed and the wall.

It was a picture frame. Two pocket sized photographs were cramped beside each other under a web of cracked glass. The first was one Basie had seen a thousand times—him and his mother sitting on a bench under the willow tree just outside her window. It was the last good picture anyone had taken there thanks to a summer storm that had wiped the bench into the creek. The willow, of course, remained untouched. Basie had given his version of the picture to Lewie, because his little sister had wanted one for the fridge.

The second picture was one Basie had seen, but only through sneaking sideways glances when he thought Della wasn't looking. When she was alive, he could never appear interested in this picture. He had to pretend it didn't exist. It was a portrait of a man named Basilio, the first to avoid interest and pretend Basie didn't exist. He had forgotten that Della kept a picture of Basilio on her bedside table—like he was *family* or something.

It was impossible for him to be alive now. If Della had known what happened to her husband, she'd taken it to her grave without telling Basie.

What had he done wrong to send both of his parents fucking off to die without explanation?

His mouth suddenly ran dry. He slapped the frame back in its spot hard enough to make the cracked glass squeak against itself, and practically threw himself away from the bed and—and—

Directly in front of her wall of half-painted sunflowers.

All at once, Basie felt like he was going to be sick. He needed to get the *fuck* out of this room. Out of this house. Somehow he'd forgotten that he left this house for a *reason*—a warranted, deafening reason—and it tore the scab of his grief clean off, leaving him bleeding out in the dark.

"Hey, did the wind knock something over again? I leave the windows open to air out the paint fumes but it always seems—"

Basie jolted. He hadn't heard the door open.

"...Basie? Are you alright?"

Was he? He was breathing. That was good. It might've been coming fast and short, but breathing was good so long as you kept doing it. There were hands pressed into his eyes, too. Nails stabbing into his brow. They couldn't be Kit's. He would never hurt Basie like that. The sharp touch had to be his own. Why was his own touch so far away? Something was creeping up his throat. Bile? His heart? He wasn't sure. He forced himself to swallow it back, unwilling to cough his heart up onto his mom's floor. The taste of blood was lead in his mouth, but it was a reminder that not all of his senses had failed him.

"Basie?" Kit's voice was just behind him. "Do you want to

be alone?" The strength in Basie's legs waned. He fell to a low crouch, but shook his head once. A soft touch laid on his back where the muscles were pulled taut, and it was enough to persuade Basie's hands to stop their assault on his face and hold the tails of Kit's shirt instead.

"I think you're having an anxiety attack," Kit whispered steadily. "It'll pass. You're okay."

The tiny whimper that Basie heard from his own mouth would've humiliated him if he were in his right mind. But he couldn't think of anything past his straining heart and the ache that stretched across his whole body.

From the corner of his eye, he saw Kit dip one of his fingers into a can of paint nearby. He brought between them, and with a voice like silk said, "Blow it dry."

"W-what?" said Basie. Kit smiled softly, like Basie speaking was a good sign.

"Take a deep breath and dry the paint."

If anyone else had asked Basie to do it, he would've told them to fuck off. But this was Kit Elliot. Placing his trust in Kit was the easiest thing he could do at this moment—easier than missing his mom, easier than wanting to tear up that picture of his dad. With more honesty than Basie ever possessed, Kit told him he'd be alright, and he believed him.

Basie drew in a shaky string of air and blew. His breath came in sputters across the paint, but Kit still nodded. "Good. Again."

One after another, Basie blew breaths over the yellow patch on Kit's finger, and one after another, it got easier and smoother, until the panic had subsided. All that was left was the metallic smell of paint and a dull nausea still lingering from the strain.

When it was safe, Kit scraped the excess paint onto the lid and ran the backs of his clean fingers over Basie's cheeks. They came away wet with tears.

"I underestimated how difficult it would be for you to stay here. I'm sorry."

"Not your fault," Basie swore quietly.

"It's not yours either."

Basie's gaze darted to the empty bed and the cracked picture frame.

"You're right. It's not mine either." He worried at his bottom lip with his teeth. It still tasted of blood. "You must be one of those handsome faerie princes from that storybook, come to help the sorry son-of-a-bitch who can't seem to go one hour without needing your help."

There was a flicker of something strange on Kit's face, gone before Basie could give it more than a passing thought.

"It's nothing so noble as that," Kit said, the lines between his brow softening. "I'm just the guy who bakes the pies."

Basie scoffed weakly.

"You're selling yourself short. You're more than the guy who bakes pies," he said. "But it's really rude of you to say shit like that when I can't think clearly enough to disprove it."

Kit lowered himself and sat against the wall. Basie sat with him.

"What *are* you thinking?" Kit asked carefully. "We don't have to talk about it if you don't want to, but there's clearly something going on."

Basie's head landed against the wall with a soft *thump.*

"It's not worth saying out loud."

"I think everything you say is worth speaking out loud."

"That's because you're a goddamn angel, Kit Elliot." Another strong breeze broke into the room, as crisp and sweet as creek water. Basie wiped his nose with his arm and tilted his chin up to the ceiling, the only spot Della hadn't been able to touch.

"Everybody's got someone," he whispered. "I'm the only electrician people trust around here. I go to the store, or the diner, or someone's house to fix their shitty flickering lights, and everywhere I go, all the people have *someone.* They've got their spouses, their family and friends. I mean, even Lewie has a full house with all of his siblings. Sometimes it feels like all I have left is this house and this mural, but I don't even have those anymore. And that could never be your fault. I—" *For all the time I've been alive…* "I've never had to make a hard choice before. And maybe it's for the best that I gave this place up because I can't look at this fucking mural without getting so angry I feel like I could scream. It all boils down to this singular fact that I'm the only one in Long Lily who doesn't have a single person who cares about me."

Crickets chirped outside the window as the last words settled on the wall like a tobacco stain.

The soft pads of fingertips slipped under Basie's palm first. Skin slowly slid against skin, hand folding over hand, all of it fitting together like it was all either hand knew how to do.

"It's rude of you," Kit said sincerely, "to say something like that, even when you're not thinking clearly. Lucky for you, I *can* dispute it."

Basie knew where this was going. "You don't have to care for me out of pity."

Kit let his head loll over so he could fix Basie with a look so raw, it made Basie swallow.

"It's not pity," Kit said gently. "Has it not occurred to you that *I* don't have anyone either. If you'll recall, *I'm* the outsider. It's been a long few months trying to pretend like I belong here."

"You *do* belong here."

"Not any more than you do," Kit challenged. "You say you don't have anyone. That's the biggest load of nonsense I've ever heard. The people in this town love you because you're their own. Your best friend comes with seven siblings and I don't have to meet all of them to know they adore you. You make it so easy." He shook his head. "But who do I have if you're not my person?"

A tear tripped over Basie's lashes and down the length of his nose. How lovely Kit was in this light, haloed in golden glow from the lamp, the very edges of his hair gilded. The sun had sown more freckles on his cheeks since he'd started working outside, a constellation for the daytime. It put Basie's mind at ease to connect them from jaw to mouth, then nose to eyes where he found Kit staring back. Only, Kit was looking at his mouth.

Basie was weightless. This was a dangerous, *dangerous* line, and if he walked it a second more, he'd topple over.

"The sun will be up soon," he whispered. "You need to rest."

Kit shrugged, exhaustion smothering the motion into its smallest form. He opened his mouth, as if to insist that he could sit here all night if Basie needed him to, but Basie had taken enough from Kit tonight.

He squeezed their fingers together and slowly rose to his feet. A tingling heat shot up Basie's legs from sitting on the floor for so long, but he remained steady as he guided Kit up. It was easy in this small hour to let Kit steady himself by grazing his fingers under the hem of Basie's shirt. Even easier was Basie laying his palm flat on the back of Kit's flushed throat and guiding him out of Della Yeats' room and into the one he'd slept in for seventy-seven years.

Kit fell to the bed like a parched man falls to a spring. There was nothing of the refined Kit Elliot that Basie had come to know, only the solaced man who had finally untied himself from a well-concealed burden. Basie thought nothing could tempt Kit to rise from this nest of pillows and sheets. But when Basie took a step back, Kit caught him by the seam of his shorts.

"Wait," he rasped. "You don't have to sleep in your mother's room."

Basie, who didn't plan on going anywhere, stripped off the sleep shirt Kit had loaned him and crept around the edge of the bed and slid himself onto the remaining sliver of mattress against the wall. The utter relief of being in his own bed made all of Basie's muscles uncoil. He laid boneless on the soft surface, so comfortable, he nearly began weeping again.

An impulse rose to pull Kit by the shoulder so they could lay face to face, but Basie settled with running his hand up and down the curve of Kit's back.

"What happens in the morning?" Kit murmured, voice half-muffled by his pillow.

"It is morning."

Kit didn't take the bait.

"Did you mean it when you said you'd stay?"

"I said it, didn't I?"

"But that was…before. It's okay if you've changed your mind."

Basie leaned forward until his forehead was nestled between

Kit's shoulder blades.

"Where else would I go?" he answered simply. "I'm your problem now."

Below his touch, Kit let out a long sigh and pulled Basie's arm around his waist, cradling his hand above his heart.

"Good," he mumbled and fell to sleep.

THE ROOM WAS A basin of young sunlight when Kit stirred awake the next morning. His body was laden under the lethargic ache that comes with only a few hours of rest. He stretched an arm out, drawing in a deep, slow breath—only, there was weight on his chest. Feather-soft curls tickled under his chin.

Basie. They were laying ribs against ribs, Basie's ear nestled above the rise and fall of Kit's chest. Kit wished he'd thought to take off his own shirt to feel the warmth of Basie's body directly from his skin or the soft hair curling down his chest. At some point in the night, Basie must've stolen the quilt and buried himself firmly at Kit's side. Kit didn't mind. It was all very nice.

Carding a lazy hand through Basie's hair, it occurred to Kit that, if he could, he'd lay here forever. That wasn't possible, of course. Basie would wake eventually and Kit had to go to work. But there were a few minutes left until the rest of the world stirred awake.

Kit's eyes had just fallen closed when Basie's phone started ringing on the dresser.

He froze. His hand dropped out of Basie's hair immediately. In a poor attempt to feign sleep, he drew out each breath nice and long. But surprisingly, the sleeping beauty didn't stir.

"Basie," Kit whispered into the nest of messy hair. "Your phone is ringing." He waited for a little sigh or a tired groan, but none came. If Kit hadn't been able to feel the measured breaths Basie took in his sleep, he might've been worried.

Slipping out of the bed as delicately as possible, Kit padded on his tip toes across the room—mostly out of principle, the phone was already screaming. He read the caller ID through the sleepy blurriness of his vision, *Saint Lewie,* and swiped the green button.

"Hi Lewie," Kit said, sneaking into the hallway with a glance back at Basie, who was starfishing across the bed.

"Who is this?" Lewie demanded. "If this is Kit Elliot, I swear I'm going to be furious."

Kit scrubbed his eyes with his knuckles. "Alright, well, I can lie if you want?"

"No, don't lie. You sound like you were sleeping. Did I wake you up?" Kit had to blink a few times to get his mind to keep up with Lewie's frantic questioning.

"I was awake."

"I just said not to lie."

"And I followed directions, teacher."

"Where's Basie?"

"Out cold. You didn't wake him either."

Lewie scoffed. The volume from Kit's end faded as he spoke, like he pulled the phone away from his face. "No, Tallie. I'm on the phone with Mr. Elliot. You can make your own cereal. The Cheerios are up on the—Alright, then get the stool." Then to Kit, "I woke up to a text from Basie saying that the diner collapsed and wanted to make sure he was alright. I can't believe he had the audacity to get laid the night his roof caved in. That lucky motherfucker has a stubborn way of avoiding peril, not being there when it came down and all." He delivered the words "*get laid*" and "*motherfucker*" the way adults spell words they think children are too dumb to sound out.

"Alright, two things," stated Kit, face going hot. "Basie *was* there when his roof collapsed. He can tell you all about how he thwarted death when he wakes up. But he's fine, just a few scratches. And second, he's only here because he asked me to pick him up. Nothing more."

"Whatever you say, Casanova. Why else wouldn't he call me?"

In the background, a small child's voice yelled, "*Leeewie, I spilled the milk on the flooor!*"

"That's why," Kit answered.

"Orion can keep the kids alive when there's an emergency," Lewie objected. "For the record, Kit, I see you sidestepping the subject. I know something hap—"

The phone disappeared out of Kit's hand.

"Can I help you?" Basie drawled into the speaker, leaning his hip on the doorframe. The sight of him easy and shirtless made the base of Kit's spine a pool of electricity, the dawn light doing wonders to draw out the gold undertones of his skin and hair. Kit had practically forgotten the phone call until Basie's eyes flickered over to him as he said, "We *didn't*—" Garbled yelling echoed from the phone. Basie rolled his eyes. "I will make good on my threat to block your number. If you want to be helpful, you can help me get my things…What? Of course I'm not staying there anymore. It's a shithole that needs to be torn down…No, I'm staying at

Wellhead. Lewie…*Lewie*—For heaven's sake, *goodbye.*"

He hung up.

Basie stood there, staring at his blank screen for a few seconds, before smiling sheepishly at Kit. "Mornin'. Sorry about that."

Kit ran a hand through his own messy hair.

"Not at all. I should've been quieter. It's early yet. You can go back to sleep if you want to. Take a day off." *You had a rough night,* he wanted to add, but the peace of this morning was too soft to ruin with unpleasant memories.

"You were up just as late as I was. Why don't you call Mrs. Mallory and take a sick day?"

"Wish I could, but there's a big baking order for a wedding in Gettysburg. They want twenty pies and delivery is due tomorrow. By the time I come home tonight, I'll smell like one big apple turnover."

The smile on Basie's face was so damned tender that Kit had to shift his weight and look away. They made quite the pair, lingering in the doorway just a little too close together, talking about their plans for the day. Kit—to bake, and bake, and bake, with the promise of returning home as soon as possible. Basie—scheming the salvage and rescue mission for the things still trapped in the Crane's Nest wreckage.

"As soon as I can, I'll move my things into your mother's room," Kit said, halfway out the door to work, only to stumble to a halt against the old door frame. "Oh, I forgot! You gave me back your secret house key after the *Phone Incident.* Here, take this one."

All the portraits hanging on the walls of the entry hallway watched as Kit slipped one of the Wellhead keys off his key ring and placed it into Basie's outstretched hand. Basie's fingers closed around it, though the expression on his face was complicated.

"Have a good day at work," he said through a tight smile.

Kit paused, uneasy. Basie, he observed, always took on more than he could handle and tended to lie when asked if he was alright. Sometimes it was best to leave Basie to manage the threshold of his own hardships. Other times, it seemed that Basie was one slip away from completely crumbling apart. What if this was the final straw—being forced to stay at Wellhead because there was truly nowhere else to go?

"You're gonna be late," Basie prodded him quietly.

"Right," he forced out, letting the front door fall open. "See you at dinner."

Basie tossed him a sleepy wink, and oh, Kit was in *trouble*.

I T HAD TO BE said: Christopher Myron Elliot was a worrier of the highest degree. It was fair to assume that all of his closest friends knew this about him but underestimated the severity of his meddlesome anxiety.

The cause of today's distraction: he hadn't heard from Basie all day. For all Kit knew, Basie and Lewie were both buried under a pile of rotted wood and dangling electrical wires. The only thing giving him a semblance of peace was the knowledge that this was Long Lily—if his friends had died, he would've heard of it by now.

He'd hoped to depend on the twenty blasted pies for a distraction, but when he arrived, Lynn Mallory surprised him by having most of them baked, packaged, and ready to go. It was a terrible disaster—she sent him home *early*.

The logical thing to do would be call Basie or Lewie and simply ask how it went, like a normal person. But then he remembered Lewie's teasing. And his own pride. And Lewie Simon's uncanny way of knowing things—a dangerous force for Kit to mess with when he was being suffocated by the feeling that if he didn't get his hands on Basie Yeats soon, he'd go mad.

To quiet his mind, Kit set to work moving his things to the master bedroom, but the collection of his belongings was humble, so it took less than an hour to relocate everything. His focus would surely fail him if he tried to read or watch afternoon cable. There was only one thing that could seize the wild horse of his attention and soothe the anxiety still throbbing in his chest.

He bent to the paint cans along Della Yeats' wall and peeled them open.

Basie crossed through the unfiltered sunlight of the yard two hours later. The relief was so profound that Kit almost leaned against the wall of wet paint. He was about to push open the window and call out to Basie. Offer to help him carry his things. Make a very inappropriately timed love confession.

But his voice died as Basie crossed stiffly through the soft grass, past the buzzing bees and the freshly watered garden, to stand before the shed. He deposited the boxes in his arms on the ground, carrying too many to fit through the door.

Kit watched Basie from the window long enough for the wet paint on his nose to dry. The sequence of events should not have burned in Kit's mind the way they did, but he could not look away. Not as Basie retrieved a key from inside the pocket of his jeans. Not when the key met its match and freed the door to swing open wider and wider and wider.

Basie disappeared into the depths of the shed long enough for Kit to realize he was holding his breath waiting for him to reappear. The shadow of Basie's form shifted in the window of the shed, but Kit was too far away to make any sense of the blurry movements.

When Basie did return, he slammed the door with all his might and furiously buried the key into its lock. He did not bring any of his boxes inside.

Kit's stomach dropped.

He had half a mind to call out to Basie, see if the swelling storm brewing under his heaving chest could be quelled. That was a risky endeavor, though. Once Basie was riled up, there was no telling what he'd do or say. His rage took him out of himself. Made him a stranger.

What Kit didn't expect was Basie rushing through the patch of sunflowers in the garden to head toward the Wellhead property line. He might've stormed off without stopping, except one of the sunflowers bobbed in his way. He tore it cruelly from its stem, rending the woody stock in two. With a frustrated sneer, he clawed deep into the soft center and ripped out all the dark seeds. The petals were his next victim, torn apart and stomped into the ground in a furious haze.

"Oh, Basie…" whispered Kit, not loud enough for even the wind to hear him. Still, Basie kicked and tore and snapped and seethed at all the sunflowers until they were ravaged—a new trace of death on Wellhead property.

Basie was, Kit realized, different now than he was minutes ago.

Basie fled the yard, leaving the sunflowers bent out of shape, tangled up in each other in fierce knots. Kit stared blankly at the sunflower garden until he couldn't anymore.

Dipping his brush in the butterscotch paint on his palette, he painted the sunflowers on the wall—unscathed and vibrant. Then he worried, and worried, and worried.

CHAPTER 16

The Diary of Della Yeats,
Vol. 15. June 24th, 1944

I wish it was raining today. The sky and I have known each other a long time, but it has not yet grown into the habit of giving me what I want. And here I thought friends were supposed to cry together.

I told Basilio the news and the truth, in that order. "Sili," I said. "I'm two months pregnant. It isn't what we planned, but won't it be lovely to raise a baby in Mexico?"

He was euphoric, more joyful than I have ever seen him. So, I told him how old I was, and then I showed him the proof.

Something about the news made him fall to his knees and weep.

This is something I don't understand. If he told me he

would live forever, I'd cry tears of joy. I want to keep him forever. Does he not want that with me? I have promised him a child and a long future together. What is there to mourn? Why is <u>this</u> the news that makes him think the world is ending, when it is already halfway there?

He told me his mind does not rest. It is always in forward motion, worrying at things he should not worry over. Weeping on the floor of our bedroom, he confessed he already torments over his life and the life of his missing brother. He said it makes him bleed, and soon if he has to worry about his wife and his son living forever, he'll run completely dry.

I told him, "Love is enough to keep you awake."

"Love is enough to send me to my grave," he answered.

He is staying in Mexico. I am not.

Tomorrow, I'm getting on a plane for the first time. When I do, I will never see Basilio again. I am going to a place that a friend told me about some years ago: Long Lily. A long lily for a woman who will live a long time.

Maybe it rains more in Pennsylvania.

CHAPTER 17

BASIE COULD BARELY FEEL his fingers by the time he returned to Wellhead later that day. He'd gotten soaked through to his socks after hours of wandering around Crane's Nest, but it hadn't occurred to him just how cold he was until his fingers had started to tingle and ache. He'd forgotten that the summer rain could carry this type of chill, one with a propensity to settle deep into the marrow of your bones. The only reason he'd returned to Wellhead was to avoid amputation, because he imagined losing his hands would make his life mighty inconvenient.

It was an effort to let himself into the house. The ache in his fingers made him fumble the key ring like a fool, and when he finally got the key into the slot, he realized it had been the one for the shed the whole time. His blood began to race fast and hot out of nowhere, and he dropped the whole damn thing on the porch.

By the time he finally managed to break into his own home, Kit rushed up to him before he could even close the door. He drank in Basie's soaked clothes and tight shoulders, dipping down to Basie's raw, red hands, then back up to his eyes. With careful control, Kit schooled his expression from concern to the neutrality he always wore before his judgment reached a verdict.

"What's the matter?" asked Kit, because they were past hellos.

A whistling wind nipped at the back of Basie's neck. He couldn't remember the last time he'd been cold. He kicked the door shut.

"Can I come in?" he asked sarcastically.

"Shit, Basie, I'm not herding you out," Kit answered, though he took a few steps back. This was how Basie knew he had caught Kit off guard. Some people prepared for company by cleaning and cooking. Kit prepared his words. Without being granted the proper time, he was given to swearing. "I'm just waiting for you to tell me what's wrong."

If Basie were still the owner of this home, he would've untied his muddy boots, peeled off his wet socks, and left the whole damn mess by the door. Now, he remained glued to the welcome mat, ready to bolt away at a moment's notice.

"Nothing's wrong," Basie said, taking the towel Kit handed him. He ran it over his face and hair, wiping away the bitter taste of the lie with it. This was all starting to feel very familiar. "This will only take a second. Then I'll be out of your hair."

"Out of my hair?" Kit echoed incredulously.

"I came to ask for another favor. It's a big one, but I feel like it *needs* to be you that helps me. I mean, that's what this whole thing between us is. Us helping each other." (Though at the moment, Basie couldn't recall a single time he helped Kit with anything.)

"Alright," answered Kit slowly, leaning against the doorframe. "Count me intrigued."

Basie took a breath. It barely scratched the surface of his lungs. "Would you let me borrow the van?"

Kit straightened away from the doorjamb, arms folding over

his chest.

"The van? Why?"

"I'm moving to Berkeley Springs."

As far as announcements went, it was pathetic. Basie didn't think it made a damned difference to Kit *how* he said it, only that he *did.* Now that he had, there was no taking it back.

Kit rivaled death in stillness.

"Oh," was all he said.

"I...I decided a few hours ago—after I called those electric companies you told me about." He licked his lips and pulled out one of the informational sheets Kit had given him last week. Some of the ink was streaky where it hadn't escaped the rain, but all of Kit's notes in the margins were still intact. "They interviewed me on the phone right then and there. I only got halfway into listing my qualifications before the man interrupted me and said I got the job. He wants me to start next week."

Basie waited for Kit to say something nice, because he always did in moments like this. Except he didn't. At least, not until he remembered he was supposed to.

"That's great," he said, unconvincingly.

"They pay better than a lot of the companies here do. Something to do with the minimum wage being higher, I think," Basie added, hoping that would provide some relief. Some reassurance. He could see it didn't. "And I found a place to live. A small apartment that's the perfect size for just me. It's really nice, just like you said. Close to those hiking trails and only two hours from like, three different major cities. Oh! And there's a yard too, so I could start raising bees again."

As Basie rambled, Kit worried his teeth along his lower lip

so hard, Basie worried it would draw blood. He didn't stop when Basie had gone silent. Instead, he uncrossed his arms, then wrapped them back up again.

"*Wow,*" he breathed. "Wow, um. Okay. Wow."

"You said that already. Is that a good wow or…?"

"It's a good wow," Kit said, and it was the biggest lie Basie had ever heard. He should know. "It's just, Berkeley Springs is a bit far, isn't it?"

Basie gave a half shrug. He caught his reflection in the grandfather clock's window and cringed. It had been less of a shrug and more of an awkward convulsion.

"Less than two hours. That's why I need to borrow the van. Or— you *and* the van. Ed Nougat won't drive me that far south," he went on. "I think it could be kinda fun. A last road trip before we won't be seeing each other any—"

"No."

Now this was different. In the meager lifetime of their friendship, Basie had been the one with the No's—*No, I don't want you living in my home. No, I don't need you to apologize to me. No, I'm not planning on going out like my mom without warning. No, you can't open the shed. No, I can't move in with you.* Hearing the word out of Kit's mouth, clipped and stern, made Basie's head snap up.

Kit was…God, Kit was *glaring* at him. Before then, Basie hadn't known Kit's eyes were capable of such an act. Basie had come to rely on Kit's gaze as the only steady thing in his life, spoiled by the tenderness and kindness he'd found there. Now it was like it had never existed.

This, Basie realized, this must've been what he looked like on that very first day. Did Kit feel like this when Basie had looked him in the eye and basically told him to go fuck himself?

"I don't understand," he said, very, *very* carefully. "Why not? Did I piss you off or something?"

"No—"

"Then why won't you drive me down?"

"I just won't! Okay?" Kit exclaimed. The hands so tightly fisted into the fabric of his shirt were tossed into the air as he fled into the kitchen. Basie didn't care that he was still wearing his muddy boots—he'd done his time mopping these floors. He chased behind Kit.

"What's the matter with you?"

"What's the matter with *me*? I watched you tear up your mother's sunflowers in a violent stupor today and leave the whole garden in shambles." Basie jolted back, eyes equally wide and sharp, but Kit had no emergency brake. "Then you disappeared for hours on end, with all of your things outside by the shed—which, by the way, would've ended up soaked if I hadn't brought them in—and now you're strolling in with this *news* that's come out of *nowhere*."

"Bullshit. You knew I was planning on moving all this time because you *bought my house*." Kit stomped around one half of the dining room table, but Basie cut him off on the other side. "Hell, *you're* the one who has been picking out towns for me. Did you think that was just for fun?"

"I just think you're behaving a bit recklessly. I mean—*next week?* I thought we had a *plan,* Basie! If this is because of what happened last night, then we could've sat together and talked about it." Basie wasn't exactly sure which of last night's many events was in question. Kit didn't let him ask. "I'm not going to help you be irresponsible. I won't do it. Find another ride to West Virginia."

Around them, the walls of Wellhead creaked and moaned. Even the floorboards made eerie sounds of mourning. Basie's heart cracked along with it, in time with wooden groans and lightning flashes outside. How had everything fallen apart so quickly?

"Where do you get off judging what I do?" Basie snapped. He mussed his hair into a hornet's nest, then in the most childish impression of Kit he could manage, he said, *"I'm Kit Elliot, I killed my own fucking goldfish, but I think Basie Yeats is too simple to decide anything for himself."*

"You accepted my help! You accepted my help every day for months." Kit was fighting to keep his voice steady, but it cracked and wavered like salt on ice. Even he had his limits and Basie knew he was dancing on them with hot heels. "I thought the whole point of that was to let your friend keep you from letting your depression drive you into ludicrous life choices!"

"Last I checked, the only person allowed to parent me and judge my life choices killed herself three months ago. I have a job. I have a place to live. Tell me how that's irresponsible? It's more than *you* had when you came here. Why are you even here, anyway? We didn't ask for a damned outsider! *I* didn't ask for an outsider."

Kit's hands fell at his side.

Basie felt like the shittiest person to ever walk the earth. Probably because he was.

"Get..." Kit swallowed. "Get out, Basie."

Basie didn't think it was possible for that shitty feeling to get worse, but being kicked out of his childhood home was a harsh slap to the face. Being kicked out of his childhood home by Kit Elliot was something even worse.

"I didn't mean it," Basie said immediately, the words coming out in a flurry. "Kit, I didn't mean it. I always say shit I don't mean when I'm angry and I—"

"It's okay," Kit said. Another lie, but Basie tried to let himself believe this one. "Look, you and I can't have a productive conversation when we're angry. Visit Lewie and his siblings. Sip coffee for three hours at the diner. Walk in the rain. Doesn't matter to me. I'll—I'll cool off and explain myself when I'm feeling better." Basie opened his mouth to protest, but Kit snapped, "Just leave me alone for a while, okay?"

All at once, Basie had the unexplainable urge to hold Kit. To wrap both arms around his strong frame and press their foreheads against shoulders and ribs against ribs, just as they had been last night. He wanted to run his hand through every soft, red curl until the crease of sadness on Kit's face subsided. He wondered if Kit would want to touch him. He wondered if he'd broken this unknown thing between them for good.

"I'll go," Basie said thickly, palms up. "If you need me, I'll be at Lewie's, okay?"

The tightness drawing Kit's brows together remained stubbornly in place, but he nodded. Basie's eyes burned as he glared at the mud he'd tracked into the kitchen, then followed the trail back to the front door. Even in his foul mood, Kit walked him out, frowning as Basie stepped back into the damp, chilly air.

Basie paused on the middle porch step, then turned over his shoulder. He swallowed.

"Give me the short answer," he said above the noise of the crickets. "Why? Why won't you drive me? What about it upsets you so much?"

The breeze cooled the sharp, red ire off Kit's cheeks. Where bitterness had been, there was only regret and…something sadder. Basie recognized it from when he'd collapsed on the floor in front of his mother's empty bed. Resignation.

"There is no short answer," Kit whispered. "If you can't figure it out yourself, then there's no point in me telling you."

Unfortunately for him, Basie was more stubborn.

"Try," he pressed. "Because I have lived a really fucking long time, but I've never had someone like you in my life. You said I was your *person*. It doesn't make sense to me how you could go from being my biggest supporter to letting me go out into the world without you sending me off. And if I've done something or said something that made you want to…to give me up, then I guess—"

"*I'm* giving *you* up?" gasped Kit, like he'd been punched in the gut. "*Basie.*"

Kit marched across the porch, placed his hands on Basie's face, and kissed him.

When Basie was a boy, he used to watch the fireworks on the fourth of July from the cottage roof…

Answers were not supposed to come so quickly after a question had been asked, but all at once, Basie knew the answer to his question as if he had been born with it—as if all the things Kit was trying to tell him were the very first words he'd learned and spoken. Basie wrapped his arms around Kit's shoulders, because he had things he wanted to say too. The rough hands buried into

Kit's hair said, *Oh, I'm a fool.* His nose pressed into the apple of Kit's cheeks pleaded, *Forgive me.* Every returned kiss said words Basie could not articulate, but sounded in his mind like, *Me haces querer vivir para siempre.*

When Kit pulled back, it was because neither of them had taken breath in a very long time. Basie's chest heaved in the earthy scent of the wet ground. He didn't ever want to move.

Then, Kit swore, stumbling back. Basie echoed the curse because Kit never swore.

"I'm so sorry," Kit said. His hands shook. "Basie, I'm so sorry. But if you think I'm going to send you away like it won't absolutely kill me, then you're wrong."

An overwhelming mix of elation and misery swelled inside Basie's chest, pressing so hard on his ribs, they almost cracked. How many of Kit's needless apologies could he allow himself to accept?

This time Basie kissed him. Softer. Quieter. Kit's hands slid under the damp fabric of Basie's shirt and onto the small of his back, warm and strong.

There were no misunderstandings now.

"For what it's worth, you were right." The words fell out of Kit's mouth and onto Basie's lips in a whoosh of hot breath. "I knew the day we met that you would leave Long Lily. I just thought I knew better. Because you love this house, Basie. I know you do. And most days, I think you like me too."

"I do," Basie swore. He ran his thumb over Kit's mouth. "I meant it."

"So *stay.*"

It was like this: there was a Pre and Post-Sunflower Basie.

There was the Basie who had woken up that morning in Kit Elliot's arms and pretended to be asleep. He was the same Basie who let Kit sand down the thorns of his grief with his touches, his stories, every cup of unsweetened lavender tea. He was a Basie who, until today, had stood a chance.

And there was the Basie who had opened the shed. The Basie who trampled through the sunflowers after finding what waited for him inside, who had ripped apart the garden and watered it in his own blood and tears. He was the Basie who kissed Kit and it was *so very* nearly enough, until it wasn't.

If Kit had implored Pre-Sunflower Basie as he did now, it would've been a different answer. Another world entirely. But Basie *had* trampled the sunflowers. He was different.

He knew who he was when he spoke.

"I spent a lot of time alone in that diner. Listening to the rain. Thinking. I wondered why staying in a broken down shack was more bearable than sleeping in my own bed. Why I preferred nonperishable food to my own kitchen and all my own pots and plates. You and Lewie thought I was crazy for it. Maybe I am crazy." Now his own hands were shaking, so he grabbed Kit's. "But spending the night here helped me realize. And when I did, it was so obvious."

"What's that?"

"This house is a constant reminder that the life my mother had was a good one, but it wasn't enough to keep her here. *I* wasn't enough to keep her here. And that…that fucking hurts, Kit. She lived so long completely on her own and after such little time with me, she called it quits? I can't help but wonder why I wasn't good enough for her. Or why she didn't tell me how sad she was."

Above, the clouds parted and spilled moonlight across the irises.

"I want to let my grief go," Basie continued. "I don't want to end up like my mom did. But to do that, I need to go somewhere without the reminders. It doesn't matter how much love I have for this land, my friends, this town…You." A tear slid down Kit's cheek. "Because I do love you. Sometimes it feels like I've loved you as long as I've lived, which is pretty overwhelming because, *God,* it feels like I've lived forever."

"I know the feeling."

Basie smiled, small and sad. Kit didn't know the feeling. Not like Basie did.

"I can't stay, Kit."

Suddenly, Basie's hands were empty again. It made him want to cry.

"Okay," said Kit. "I can't drive you. I can't leave Long Lily either."

Basie ached everywhere he was alive, but he understood. They both had things they couldn't do.

"Okay."

In another life, he would've pressed his lips to Kit's cheek, squeezed his hand, set an exact time to make his last visit before hitting the road. But if Basie stayed a second longer, then he would've changed his mind—and that would've made him a liar. He was done being a liar.

"You'll say goodbye? Before you go?" Kit asked.

Oh. Okay. One last lie.

"Of course."

Then, Basie left.

T HE MORNING CAME WITH a golden crest on the mountain peaks and a crick in Basie's neck. He laid on the Simon family couch looking and feeling like a corpse at an old country wake—stiff muscles, closed eyes, hands crossed over his chest. In the blackness behind his eyelids, Basie fought against flashes of a face. Cheeks laden with freckles. A heart shaped dip above a soft mouth. Guileless eyes the color of burnt sugar. Remembering his last conversation with Kit Elliot made him wish he were *actually* dead.

Struggling to clear his mind, Basie listened to the silence, a rare guest in a house with six children. He'd imagined more noise and chaos for his going. More tears. Less of the old house creaking into its empty rooms.

Just as well. Leaving Long Lily was always supposed to be a quiet affair. Della had shown him that.

On the floor above him, the bathroom door creaked open and closed, signaling the impending waking of the house. Basie rose from the couch with a quiet sigh. He folded the guest sheets and the thin quilt with care, draping them on the plush arm of the sofa.

Then he hooked his bag over his shoulder and crept toward the door.

"Where you goin'?"

Basie spun around, finding Lewie sitting in the middle of the staircase in just his boxers and a T-shirt that read: *LL LACROSSE '09*. He leaned against the wall under the railing with an expression that would've looked like boredom to anyone else, but really indicated judgment that would've given St. Peter a run for his money.

"I'm going to see Kit," said Basie.

Lewie tapped his fingers along the banister, nodding.

"A little early for a serious conversation, ain't it?" he said.

"Goodbye isn't serious. It's casual."

Lewie let out a scoff.

"Yeah. Like anything with you and Kit is casual."

Basie shifted his weight, garnering enough wisdom to keep his mouth shut for once.

"I suppose you'll be heading out of town with Ed afterwards?" continued Lewie.

"As long as there's room in the truck."

It was Lewie's turn to sigh. For a second, Basie thought he was gearing up for another one of his scolding tirades and for once, Basie planned on having the decency to listen. But Lewie only scudded down the stairs and wrapped his arms around Basie's shoulders.

Basie felt the urge to remind Lewie that he was only going to be two hours away. That this move wasn't going to be like Della's trip to Canada.

"Send pictures of the kids?" asked Basie. "Been lookin' forward to seeing them grow up."

"Then you'll just have to visit to see for yourself," Lewie said, stepping back with a firm pat to Basie's shoulder. "Tell Kit I said hi."

Basie swallowed the lump in his throat.

"Will do," he said.

But Basie did not go to Kit. And when he broke onto the Long Lily streets, he did not turn for Wellhead to say goodbye. All at once, he understood why Kit would not drive him to Berkeley Springs.

They both had things they couldn't do.

CHAPTER 18

According to Kit Elliot, when you felt so terrible that you wanted to go from being *barely alive and well* to *never-having-existed-in-the-first-place*, the only solution was to bake. Cookies, fudgy brownies, pies from recipes passed down through generations, complicated French pastries that took years to master the art of—it didn't matter. The strategy was just to get your weepy butt in the kitchen and start mixing.

This approach had never failed him. It got him through the passing of his golden retriever when the loss felt so immense, he stopped looking out windows for fear he'd see someone else walking their dog. It eased the breakneck pace of his heart each time he did something new, like switching towns or starting a conversation with a stranger on the phone. It even filled the place of anger and tears when he'd been forced to leave Axe in Jersey—three straight months of chocolate covered Madeleines with flaky salt until his neighbors had finally started turning them down.

When Basie had kissed him on the porch steps and left him there in the humid heavy nighttime, Kit stopped all thoughts except for a single recipe: macarons. Three dozen of them.

His lips were still warm, sweet like fresh rainwater, but he ignored it as he pulled the almond flour and sugar out of his pantry.

The baking didn't do a damn thing. The memory of Basie in his arms lingered like a poltergeist. Losing a Basie who was just a friend was bad enough. Losing a Basie who loved him was another grief entirely. Especially since, for all his explanations and declarations, Basie hadn't asked Kit to go with him.

But hand whisking meringue in the middle of the night left plenty of time for crying his blessed heart out. (Only an expert could pipe seventy-four perfect macaron shells while weeping like a child, thank you very much). If he was going to think about Basie's impending departure anyway, he might as well keep his hands busy.

He was not angry or bitter. He did not fumble the recipe in his thoughtlessness or curse the fact that Basie had ever stepped foot into his life to begin with. He merely sat on the floor in front of the oven door, watched the macarons bake, and leaned his head onto both knees.

In the morning, Kit arranged the confections in a single layer in another one of Della Yeats' pie plates. The plan was simple: take the sweets as a peace offering to Basie and say one last goodbye. They would be his way of saying, *I'll be alright. Go off and have your adventure.* Something could not be a lie if you did not say it outright.

Later that day, Kit rolled his van to stop across the street in front of the Simon family house. It took a second for him to locate the house number, hidden behind a surplus of finely landscaped hedges, trees, and vines that engulfed the rest of the yard. The abundant flora disguised the sage Victorian home behind a facade of green.

Sparing a peek at his macarons to check that they survived the drive without the meringue cracking, Kit reminded himself of his plan: knock on the door, give Basie the treats, wish him the best, and bring an end to this thing between them—all without shedding a single tear. He could do it…he hoped.

Careful not to slip in any residual puddles from last night's rain, Kit carried the macaron plate in both hands all the way to the front door. In the window, the curtains parted to reveal three tiny faces and the wet snout of a black lab.

The door opened before Kit could ring the bell.

Three of the Simon siblings stared up at him, arranged in the doorway like a mismatched three leaf clover: two boys in swim trunks, and a little girl in goggles that matched her red, white, and blue one-piece. It had been a long time since Kit had interacted with this many children by himself, but he remembered advice that children were just tiny adults, and it was best to treat them as such.

He smiled kindly at them, which seemed to increase their suspicion.

"Hello, I was wondering—"

Breaking through the band of guppies, a black lab shoved into the group at the doorway. A hand snatched out and landed on the dog's harness. Instantly, the dog straightened into obedience, ears poised ready for commands.

"Who's at the door?" asked Orion Simon, one hand on the guide dog's harness and the other holding a toddler on their hip. They wore half a dozen peculiar necklaces, one entirely made of buttons that the toddler had taken to gnawing.

"Hi Rion. It's Kit," he answered. "Didn't mean to bother you when you're busy, but I'm—"

"—Looking for Basie?"

He hoped Orion wouldn't be able to hear the blush in his voice when he answered, "Yes, that's right."

It was hard to decipher the complicated twisting that came over Orion's face. Kit found that often Orion wouldn't tell you what they were thinking anyway, so it wasn't worth the effort of guessing. Hiking the baby up on their hip, they nodded back behind them.

"Back porch. Lewie just finished setting up the sprinkler after a full hour of the kids begging. Also, don't ask why Tallie's got her floaties on. Damn near killed myself trying to blow them up, so I'm not letting her take them off." They turned to head back upstairs, paused, then kept walking.

"Thank you!" Kit called after them, but they were gone.

Tiny fingers snatched Kit's free hand, tugging him through the house, past the dining room with its *long* table and the kitchen with the bursting pantry. In the living room, Kit found himself stumbling over his own feet, focused on something sitting on the end of the couch: a folded sheet and a quilt perched on top of a single pillow.

As soon as they'd crossed outside, the children released him from their death grip in favor of launching themselves feet first through the sprinkler's shower.

"Sorry I wasn't there to let you in myself," said Lewie, appearing from over the patio's edge. "The spigot was stuck and there can't be a sprinkler without running water."

"Wish I'd known, I would've brought my swim trunks," Kit

said through a grin. He scanned through the yard, only finding soft grass, misty rainbows, and enough shrieking laughter to fill the block "Basie having one of his walking days or something?"

Lewie paused halfway through sitting down on the patio's rocking chair, slapping his knees when he finally settled in. He shook his head, looking Kit up and down, the same way pitying eyes turn onto a sick, stray dog. His lips drew thin when he noticed the pie plate.

"That no good piece of shit," Lewie murmured. A dozen questions sat on the tip of Kit's tongue, but before he could ask them, Lewie nodded for Kit to sit down.

Lewie ruffled his hands through his long, dark hair. He rested his chin on his knee, clicking his tongue toward the horizon where the sun sat on top of the picket fence. Kit, on his part, could only sit and watch him. He said nothing, because starting this conversation would mean finishing it, and finishing it meant discovering the truth. Kit wasn't sure he wanted that just yet—maybe ever.

Finally, a deep sigh pushed out of Lewie's lungs. He folded his fingers together in front of him, the way all small-town men did when serious matters were at hand.

"Basie left this morning before anyone was up. Finally caught that ride with Ed he'd been preaching about." He shook his head. "Shit."

Kit was completely still.

It shouldn't have been possible. Certainly things were…*complicated* between him and Basie, but they had meant more to each other than leaving without goodbye. Even when Kit had to leave Axe, he'd bucked up the courage to break his heart with all the respect he was due. Basie was respectable too. He couldn't have just…He *wouldn't.*

"When will he be back?" Kit murmured.

Lewie knew Kit had the answer already, but he still said, "Never, probably." He swore. "Miss Della must be turning over in her grave at the way he's been acting. I'm sorry to be the one to tell you."

It was all Kit could do to fold his shaking hands together across the pie plate on his lap. He couldn't hear the kids laughing anymore.

"Must be hard for your best friend to treat you like that," Kit breathed out slowly.

"I'm sure you already know the feeling." Lewie reached over and grabbed Kit's knee. "What *happened?*"

Kit didn't know. The more he tried to remember the events of last night, the more they swirled in on each other, overlapping and rewriting the story, until none of it could be recognized anymore. Basie *had* told Kit he loved him, right? He wasn't just imagining it?

"I bet you wished you never came to this town," Lewie stated through Kit's silence.

"I don't know about that," Kit replied. This was true enough. Yesterday, he might've disagreed without a second thought. To-day, Basie was gone.

"It's funny. I was going to drive him myself, but I imagine he stuffed what he could into his bag and begged Ed to take him to the Greyhound station. Bastard saw right through me."

Kit's grip was so tight he tore through the plastic wrap over the pie tin.

"How do you mean?"

"Well, I agreed to drive him to Berkeley Springs but..." He shrugged with one shoulder. "His boxes were still at Wellhead. I was going to pick you up too."

"I see," Kit said, short and clipped. Lewie tapped his thumbs against the arms of the rocking chair.

"I'm sorry."

"What are you sorry for?"

"He's my best friend. I should've been able to figure out that he was going to leave without saying goodbye. Guess he threatened it so much that I stopped believing he had the guts to do it. But he should've taken more care with you. He didn't. So, I'm sorry."

The side of Kit's nose felt damp. He thought for a moment that maybe the kids had moved the sprinkler, but when he lifted his head, it was still far across the yard.

Oh, he thought. *I'm crying.* And once he thought that, his own spigot was released, unbinding the rest of his tears to spill freely down his face. He squeezed his eyes against the sudden memory of him and Basie, sharing food and laughing at pictures. Breathing skin on skin in the morning.

"He's doing what he thinks is best," Kit said, struggling to control his trembling speech.

"He's doing whatever is *easiest.*"

Kit sniffled. "Maybe."

It was at this moment, Lewie seemed to notice the pie plate still balanced across Kit's knees. He tugged a corner of the plastic wrap, pulling it up to get a better look at the macarons inside.

"Were these for Basie?"

Kit nodded. He poked a hole right through the center of the

cover and tore it back. The light scent of strawberry and sugar cut through the scent of hose water and grass. "They're for us now," Kit decided, wiping the sides of his face.

"His loss, then."

Rather than choosing the one closest to him, Lewie plucked the cookie from the center of the circle. A cream-petaled chrysanthemum was painted with careful strokes at the center of the pie plate, the same color as afternoon clouds.

"Did you know Della hand-painted these plates herself?" Lewie asked.

"That doesn't surprise me. Her handiwork is all over the house."

"That's why Basie was so pissed off when you wouldn't sell them to him. Don't know what he would've done with them, though. If it was me, I'd be glad my mom's prized pie plates ended up in the hands of a baker who made the best pies in Long Lily." He held up a hand when Kit began to protest. "No, I'm serious. I hear it everywhere I go. Some of your regulars at Mallory are folks who never even *liked* pie in the first place. You're a miracle worker. I knew you would be when I sold you Wellhead."

The compliment brought pink to Kit's cheeks, so he stuffed another macaron into his mouth to fill the silence. Maybe his late-night crying *did* impede the recipe, after all—the filling was a little sweet. He swallowed thickly before he answered.

"I had spent my whole life looking for somewhere to call home. Probably could've made myself fit anywhere, but sometimes you want a place to welcome you in. You know, treat you like it's been waiting for you." He scrubbed the corner of his mouth with his sleeve. "Anyhow, I'd been looking for a *long* time when I found Wellhead. It's why I told Basie I couldn't follow him."

It occurred to Kit then that there was no way he could've ever had both Wellhead and Basie. Because for Kit to have Wellhead, Basie had to leave. But if Basie had stayed, there would've been no Wellhead to move into. Nowhere else in Long Lily could suit him so well. It was not a trade he knew how to make—the man who loved him for the home he'd spent forever and a day in search of. He wasn't sure he'd made the right choice, either.

"Are you…like Basie?" asked Lewie suddenly.

Kit wasn't quite sure what Lewie meant, but the answer still felt like it should be *Yes, I am.*

"Dunno. Am I?"

Lewie studied Kit for a long moment.

"You're not an annoying No-Good-Piece-of-Shit, so I guess not. And you bake too well to be like Basie. There was a reason Della did all the baking." He smiled, stroking his fingers over the stubble on his own jaw. "You would've liked her. She was…" In the grass, one of the boys howled in delight. "She put the heart of community and family into Long Lily. Basie thought that when she died, he lost all that. It's why he forced himself to live alone in the woods where it shits cats and dogs. But he could've stayed with anyone, because the things he and Della did for this town are not easy to clear away."

"It's hard to imagine people so young could have such a strong legacy like that. I'm almost jealous."

There was another one of Lewie's assessing looks, this one longer than the last. Kit swallowed back the desire to squirm or pick up another macaron. His mouth was dry from the overload of sweetness.

"I should tell you…Last night, Basie gave me something to pass along to you. He said I should give it when he left. I thought that would be when we got back from the trip to West Virginia, but…" Kit held his breath as Lewie rummaged through his pocket. "It's sooner than I thought, I suppose. Not that it matters." He held it out. "Here, it's yours."

In the center of Lewie's palm was a key—dulled silver and plain. It had a single word scratched into its surface in choppy letters: *SHED*.

It was warm in Kit's hand, the same way it was probably always warm from sitting in Basie's pocket. Kit ran the pad of his finger across the jagged side. His face was damp again.

This key was proof that Basie had meant the things he said. Kit suspected that it would be something else too—the explanation for why he left, the core of whatever ache had been so bad he had chosen to leave his home.

"He said it's up to you whether or not to clear it out," Lewie continued. "Knowing you, though, I don't think you will."

"Do you know what's inside?"

A pause. "Yes."

Another pause.

"Keep the macarons," murmured Kit. "I've gotta go."

CHAPTER 19

T HE APARTMENT AT 42 FORECROSS AVENUE was the one place in West Virginia that could make a chronic liar finally admit the truth. It was home to everything a person could have wanted— things that should exist and did, because Berkeley Springs had gotten its start making people without a lick of magic feel calm and welcome. Things like George Washington's bathtub. Neighbors that never asked questions. Heat that cooled under the shade of the hiking trails.

And Basie Yeats, the town electrician who *desperately* wanted to go home, but couldn't.

He refused, however, to waste hard earned time and energy thinking about this fact.

There was nothing wrong with Berkeley Springs, he told himself. This was true enough. The six months he'd spent working and exploring the uncharted territory had been good. Great, even! Work was fine. His place was fine. And there was still so much he hadn't done. He was acquainted with most of his neighbors, but he was sure he hadn't met all of them.

Then, of course, there was the fact that he was trying to buy a new truck, but couldn't decide which one he wanted. Every time he thought he'd chosen the right one, a leaden doubt rumbled in his stomach that kept him from signing any papers. But once he *did*, he could go on that D.C. trip he'd been planning, see all the sights his mother visited when they were still just fields of open grass. Really, there were a whole slew of day trips and long weekends he could still experience now that his whole life wasn't caged in by the Pennsylvania trees and mountains. The West Virginia trees and mountains were much more freeing—even if they looked exactly the same.

He could absolutely spend the rest of his life here if he had to. Probably.

"How much do I owe you, Mr. Yeats?" Mr. Caughey called down the stairs to him. Basie halted, pliers frozen midair.

Best of luck to you, Mr. Yeats.

This happened too, this thing his mind did when all it could think about was Kit Elliot and only Kit Elliot. It was worse than a cassette player, because he couldn't take a hammer to it or unwind the tape. All he could do was listen and listen, until he finally admitted he enjoyed what he was hearing, even if it did make him ache down to the pits of his being.

Basie stuffed his things back into his tool belt, wiping his hands on his knees. Mr. Caughey didn't have the dustiest basement he'd ever been in, but it certainly ranked in the top ten.

"Mr. Yeats?"

Basie cleared his throat. "Yes sir?"

"How much do I owe you?" Mr. Caughey repeated.

"Oh, uh, nothing until I go to the store for the parts." *Do you always give such helpful answers?* Basie shook his head. "When the power is shooting properly to the dining room, though…About seventy-five."

"That doesn't seem like enough. You sure you don't want more?" replied Mr. Caughey. He was hunched over at the top of the basement steps, right next to the single hanging light. Basie had to squint up at him to address him properly.

First Kit's leather shoes, then the silhouette of the rest of him, tall and lovely in the cloudless sun. A sweating glass of water, a freckled thumb on his cheek wiping away streaks of dirt. A smile in the kitchen, a string of words to undo him: "You should come over more often."

"Shit," Basie mumbled.

"What was that?"

"Nothing, sir. Fifty is fine."

"You just said seventy-five."

He couldn't think straight. Why couldn't he think straight?

"This wasn't a hard fix. Whatever you have will be enough."

"That's mighty kind of you. This town is lucky it has you, Basie."

You have me. *Who do I have if you're not my person?*

Hold it together, Basie. Get your head on your shoulders, Basie.

"Heard you came from somewhere not too different from here. Where was that, again?" This was Mr. Caughey.

Come back to Wellhead.

"Long Lily, Pennsylvania." Basie said the words the same way he might've said, *Forgive me, Father, for I have sinned.* "There's plenty that's different. I like it better here."

"Well, in my opinion, there's no better place to grow old. The girls in town aren't too hard on the eyes, either." Mr. Caughey might've winked, but he was still just a silhouette in the basement doorway. Basie wanted him to move so he could go back to his apartment, lay on his bed, and turn on the white noise in his brain.

Long Lily makes me want to settle down.

"It's too late for the hardware store," said Basie. "I'll stop first thing in the morning for a new switch, then have the repairs fixed by lunchtime tomorrow. Is that alright?"

Mr. Caughey agreed, so Basie pushed politely past him on the stairs and practically vaulted himself out the front door.

The sun that greeted him was the same sun he was used to, but the last few weeks in Berkeley Springs were lacking in the reliable, pillowy clouds that usually laid over Long Lily. Where his hikes used to be spotted with cloudy shade, walking in this new town had scorched Basie's skin from tan to a warm brown.

If Kit were here, he would've turned into one big, sun-dried tomato in no time flat. He'd have to wear a massive hat to protect his cheeks, but probably still end up with more freckles on his hands. His shoulders would burn the easiest. Basie could picture Kit coming in from an hour in the garden, arms burned from the elbows down, the same color as his face. Basie would coax him into one of the dining room chairs and give him a stern talking to about sun protection while he sliced open an aloe leaf. As soon as his fingers smeared the cool gel across the red skin, Kit would sigh and make some comment about how he didn't mind a little pain. *Not if this is what he got.* Then he'd pull Basie's wrist, press his nose against the palm and—

"You alright, Basie?"

When Basie snapped out of his daydream, he was face to face with Evan Whittaker, the bulky fellow who lived directly across the street from Basie's apartment. He was perhaps the one person in Berkeley Springs whose full name Basie bothered to remember. Maybe even his only friend.

Though Basie couldn't remember walking here in the first place, he found he was standing smack dab in the middle of the town's central park. Evan was hovering over him, standing in the white gazebo, leaning over the edge. Basie could practically feel Evan's breath on his face.

Basie had always been of the silent opinion that Evan was…not *plain* exactly, but he had a way of standing that would've made it easy to lose track of him in a crowd (a small one). They usually had their conversations on their respective sidewalks, tossing their words back and forth over the pavement. Because of this, Basie was only used to seeing Evan with the entire width of Forecross Avenue between them.

Now, up close, Basie could see that Evan's beard was patchy on the chin and his nose had probably contended with a few fists.

"Well I'll be damned," said Basie. "I didn't know you ever left your front lawn."

Evan's grin grew. He leaned so far over the railing it was a wonder he didn't topple right over it.

"How else am I going to stop you from walking into traffic?" Evan replied, vaulting over the railing. He tumbled, grabbing onto Basie's arm to get his footing. "You're walking around like someone's got your remote control and there ain't a thought in your head."

"I got *too many* thoughts. That's my problem," Basie chuckled mirthlessly, starting back up the path. "Too much input. Not enough processing power."

Evan jogged to catch up with Basie, boots scuffing like he

wasn't lifting his feet enough when he moved.

"What you need is to *refuel*—fill your tank. What do you usually do to clear your mind?"

"Walk," Basie answered without a second thought.

"Well," laughed Evan, "I hate to break it to you, but that isn't working for you, man. Try again."

Basie's pace slowed. Back home, when his thoughts were a garbage disposal that wouldn't turn off, he sometimes sat with the bees, letting them crawl over his gloved hands. Other times he took Lewie to the diner for a slice of lemon meringue pie. But mostly, he called Kit.

"I walk," repeated Basie. "I don't know what to tell you. It usually works for me."

Evan slung an arm around Basie's shoulders, their legs bumping awkwardly as he tried to accelerate their disjointed walking. It was not that Basie was quick to shirk away from touch, but there was something about the familiarity of touch *here* in Berkeley Springs that made the corner of his lip curl down.

"Here's what we're gonna do. I'm taking you to the bar, I'm buying you a drink, and we're going to purge all that shit from your brain."

This was probably not possible, nor did Basie exactly *want* to purge the distracting thoughts of Kit Elliot away. But he could use a drink.

"Alright," he agreed awkwardly. "I suppose I've got time for *one* beer."

To call the Stone Tub Tavern a shack was to do it a favor. It was a little shoebox of a place, with most of its seating outdoors. Basie thought the property was sort of cozy, wrapped in a blanket of trees strung with Edison bulbs spilling just enough light onto the dry ground. The folks around him oozed their own contentment, drinking and laughing like there was nowhere better in the world to be than this little patch of open air in the mountains. Basie, on the other hand, could only focus on the humid air and how sticky the picnic table was.

Evan was just inside the tiny shack getting their drinks. Through the window, Basie could see him leaning over the counter and laughing at something the bartender had said. Piecing through his memory, Basie tried to remember a single time he'd had that effect on anyone here in West Virginia. He came up flat.

When Evan reappeared at their table, he gave the glasses a hearty swing. Beer and icy drops of condensation spilled onto Basie's arms, making him jolt back as if he'd been shocked. Evan's face twisted in a bewilderment he didn't quite have the elegance to hide, but he plopped into his seat, offering Basie one of the glasses.

"Fair warning, I'm told my taste in booze is subpar, so drink at your own risk," said Evan.

"I thought that was the whole point of coming," answered Basie. He could feel the upward curve of his mouth didn't quite reach his eye.

"I guess it all depends on how brave you are."

Under the table, Basie's knees knocked against Evan's knees—which was fine until Evan accidentally stomped on Basie's boot laces, which nearly sent Basie flying over the side of the bench trying to pull free. Stupid picnic table.

"Rough day at work?" asked Evan warily, bringing his beer to his lips.

"No," answered Basie shortly. "Why would you think that?"

"You're scowling."

Like a flicked switch, Basie relaxed his features. The simple shift brought more relief than he expected. A dull ache he hadn't noticed from clenching his jaw disappeared instantly and he could feel the muscles on his forehead smoothing out of a tight knot.

Evan nudged Basie's beer with the bottom of his glass.

"You'll feel better if you drink some of that. Bottoms up."

Basie brought the glass to his lips, if only to stop himself from making an ill-mannered, poorly timed comment about his own preferences in the bedroom. The ale was full and sweet, but the undertones of spiced hops reminded Basie too much of the beer Lewie made special trips to Harrisburg for. Basie usually went with him because he was partial to small adventures and good company. *I like the two-fifty-five air your truck has,* he'd tell Lewie. *Two windows down at fifty-five miles an hour.* The last vehicle Basie rode in, that deathtrap Greyhound, didn't have *any* air. Really, it was a miracle he didn't suffocate.

"Man, you are deep in there," Evan said, snapping a finger in front of Basie's face. "You don't have to keep everything all locked up. That's sort of the point of this whole '*Drinking with your friends*' thing. I buy you a drink, you spill your guts."

Basie still wasn't sure how he felt about calling *anyone* in Berkeley Springs his friend. Maybe he'd never truly make up his mind. But wasn't that the point? To not shoot any roots?

"Let me guess. We keep drinking until I *really* spill my guts?"

Evan's smile was crooked sideways. "I'm sure you hold your booze better than that."

"I'm sure I don't," Basie chuckled sourly.

Just as Evan opened his mouth to challenge this, Basie's phone buzzed. He might've left it, waited until it was socially acceptable to flip it over to check it. But the last time someone got within ten feet of his phone number, Orion had butt-dialed him "by accident" just to call him a little bitch.

What if there was an emergency? What if something terrible had happened to Lewie while he was on call at the fire department? What if—

Basie snatched up his phone.

"Sorry, I just have to…My best friend is a volunteer firefighter and I always worry…" He poked the screen, heart calming as the phone lit with a very calm, very normal notification from Lewie—a video. Basie tapped it before he could get a good look at the thumbnail, but when the video zoomed to full screen, he nearly dropped the damn thing into his beer.

It was Kit. He was sitting on Lewie's back porch in his usual slacks and button down, but the sleeves were rolled up and the collar was undone to the second button. He smacked a raspberry kiss onto the chubby cheek of the youngest Simon kid, baby Ethan. In Basie's estimation, there were folks who were meant to make babies smile and folks who did not have the proper programming for anyone under the age of four. Kit was decidedly the former, flurrying his fingers into Ethan's belly in a blast of tickles. Ethan shrieked in delight.

It was the cutest damn thing Basie had ever seen. He was *miserable* about it.

The camera zoomed in on the baby's face until Kit was just the gentle hands holding him up, then back out again.

"Ethan, say *Hi Basie*," Lewie's voice cooed behind the camera. "*Hi Uncle Basie.* Try it!"

For the shortest of seconds, Kit's head snapped up, terrified it seemed at the mention of his name, but then Ethan was fixing Kit with a toothy grin and his face relaxed.

"Hi baby!" Ethan squealed.

"I'm not baby! *You're* baby," Kit laughed. Ethan demonstrated his refusal of this fact by twisting his nubby fingers around the buttons of Kit's shirt, trying to yank them off. The camera panned over to Kit's face, sharpening to focus over a sunburnt nose and a pair of lips raw from chewing.

"You next Kit. Say *Hi Basie*," prodded Lewie.

Kit spared a pained look at Lewie, then looked into the camera with one of the most pitiful smiles Basie had ever seen him wear.

"Hi Basie," he said softly. "Hope you're doing well. I—Well, *we…*" He pressed his lips together, gnawing on the spot that was already rosy and raw. "Yeah. Just—Hi Basie."

Basie drew the phone closer to his face. The part of him that longed to hear Kit say something more was within arm's reach, but it was smothered out by the dread of watching the seconds run out on the phone. Just as the video came to an end and the camera's view dipped to the ground beside Lewie, Basie heard, "What? I don't have anything else to say."

Basie stared at the last, frozen frame until his eyes glazed over and he realized he was sitting inside his own mind, watching the video play over, and over, and over.

A hand shot out and snatched the phone away. Evan was pressing the play button again when Basie's body caught up enough to try to wrestle it back.

"Cut that shit out," snapped Basie.

"Relax. It's just a dude with a baby," answered Evan, spinning so Basie could no longer see the phone as he watched a second time.

Once through was bad enough, but hearing Kit's voice through the speaker a second time made Basie ache like he'd had way more than just a sip of beer.

"What? I don't have anything else to say," said Kit again.

Basie could only press his knuckles into his thighs and wait. He'd finally worked up the nerve to give Kit the key to the shed and *this* was how he reacted? Maybe he thought Basie was crazy, that everything in the shed was all an elaborate lie or a sophisticated act of delusion. Either way, it definitely didn't seem to improve Kit's opinion of Basie. It was moments like these when Basie could not come up with a single reason anyone would care about him, much less Kit Elliot, who exceeded the legal limits of *goodness*. The Kit he knew would probably tell him off for thinking something like that, but it was true. And if Kit hated Basie now for what he'd done and what he'd left behind, without having the decency to reveal it himself…well, Basie wouldn't blame him.

"I think I get it now," Evan said. Basie's eyes snapped up. He'd forgotten that he wasn't alone. Evan slid Basie's phone across the table, knocking it unpleasantly against the glass. "You're homesick."

Basie's face darkened, but Evan held up his hands in surrender before he could show his teeth. "Look man, I'm not judging you," said Evan. "Everybody's gone through it. Even me. You know I'm not from here."

As a matter of fact, Basie did not know this, but like hell if he was going to tell Evan that.

Evan spread his hands wide open on the table as if he were some cowboy saying, "*Look at me, I ain't gonna shoot you. I don't even have a gun.*" Basie peered at his calloused fingers, noting the dirt underneath his nails that sometimes matched his own.

"Maybe," began Basie, warily. "Maybe it's not homesickness. Maybe I'm just used to what I'm used to and six months isn't enough to rewrite all that in my head."

Evan took a sip of beer, swirling the foam around aimlessly as he studied Basie's expression. "I don't think you ever told me why you moved? Things hard at home?"

"Things are hard no matter where you go," answered Basie, vaguely. This was the sort of conversation he was meant to avoid, along with any other line of questioning that might deepen Basie's roots in Berkeley Springs. It was tempting while he was sitting here at an outdoor bar and drinking beer with his neighbor to forget that he was not a normal man. But maybe, if he could keep these people at arm's length, there wasn't any harm in giving them just a little truth. Just to tide them over, tide *himself* over.

"My mother passed away this year," yielded Basie. He paused, in case Evan offered the paltry condolences Basie usually received, but Evan only waited. "I suppose that's not a really sensible reason to move away."

Evan shrugged. "Plenty of people pick up and go after experiencing a loss. Was she sick?"

A familiar thickness formed in the back of Basie's throat. He swallowed. "Yes, she was."

Shifting forward, Evan folded his hands across the table. It occurred to Basie that he had made more eye contact at this table than he had in the entire six months he'd been living here.

"Listen to me, Basie," Evan said, firmly. "You just need a good distraction—that's all. You're right, it might take some time before your brain catches up with your current circumstances, but you have a decision to make. You can either mope around, walking through the town like you're looking for brains to eat. *Or,* you can have fun. Go out, take a drive, talk to people! *Get laid.* Go somewhere that isn't that giant pit in your skull." He rapped his knuckles on the side of Basie's head, revealing a tattoo of wilting flowers on the inside of his forearms.

"Eventually, that place you're from in Pennsylvania, and all the people in it, will just be a nice memory you forgot you had."

Basie sat frozen.

Because it was like this: he did not want to forget. He did not want to forget where all the odds and ends were in Wellhead Cottage. He did not want to forget how the Simon family sounded when they laughed until they were sore. He did not want to forget the diner's phone number or the wail of the tornado sirens when they were only drills.

Most of all, he did not want to forget Kit Elliot.

But the thing about Basie was that, for all the good he was, he would always be a selfish man. And selfish men spent their lives wanting. Basie wasn't sure he would be able to withstand that type of hunger.

He *wanted* to live in Long Lily. He knew that. Of course he did. He'd known from the very second he signed his apartment lease. He wanted to live in Long Lily, not because it was easiest, but because it was like his full name. Just as he would not spend his days being called a name he didn't like, he refused to live out his immortality in places that didn't bring him joy.

He wanted to make things right with Kit, too, and find a way to live in Wellhead without being choked by grief. He wanted Kit to say he loved him. He wanted to say it back. He wanted memories that were so good, he could only replace them with even better memories, until his mind was just a stockpile of evidence that proved a simple fact: no place in the world could be better than where he was.

And right now, that wasn't true for Berkeley Springs. Despite all of Evan's assurances, Basie didn't believe it ever would.

"Thank you," Basie said so slowly, the words sounded foreign to his ears. "That was surprisingly helpful advice." Maybe just not for the reasons Evan intended, but what he didn't know wouldn't hurt him.

"I'm only tellin' you what I figured out when I moved here a couple of years ago. Glad I could help."

Basie forced a tight-lipped smile. He had to figure out a way to get out of here so he could call his landlord, inform him he wouldn't be signing the new lease.

Evan reached over the sticky surface of the table and caressed his fingers over the back of Basie's palms.

"Now that you're feeling a bit better, would you want to get out of here? Maybe come back to my place?" he said.

It took everything in Basie not to snatch his hand back. Instead, he delicately removed himself from Evan's touch and hid both hands under the table, out of reach.

"That's real flattering, but, uh…No thank you. I can't."

It was Evan's turn to retreat to his side of the table. He even pulled his half-empty glass closer to his body, as if someone had drawn an invisible line through the table and getting too close to it meant peril.

"I—I'm sorry," stammered Evan. "I really thought you swung that way."

"No, I do," Basie rushed. "Shit, it's only been a few months since anyone has hit on me for real and I am already severely out of practice." Sensing the beginnings of a rant that would've centered around how he hit his romantic peak in the eighties, Basie paused, took a deep breath, and tried again. "It isn't anything to do with you. It's just…That man in the video. What'd you call him? The *dude with a baby*?"

Evan sat back, cracking his neck off to one side.

"Ah, well, that certainly answers that question."

"What question?"

"I've been wondering for weeks whether or not you were seeing someone."

"I'm not sure if I was or not," Basie admitted, wiping his hands up and down the denim of his work pants. "Looking back, it seemed like we were. But whatever it was ended when I moved."

"Tell you what," Evan said, grabbing both of their glasses—a silent message of *We're done here.* "Let me know what you think about my offer in a few months after you've had some time to move on."

He started to walk back toward the shack, but Basie called out,

"Evan, I'm not re-signing my lease tomorrow."

Evan came to a halt so quickly, some of the other drinkers paused to see what was going on.

"Why the hell not?"

"I'm moving back home." Saying it drained away the pit of dread pooling behind Basie's ribs, so he said it again. "I'm moving back to Long Lily."

Evan scoffed, shuffling on his feet so hard dust and tiny stones rolled over his toes. It made Basie remember dirt roads and a pair of shiny loafers walking to work.

"When did you decide that?" Evan shot.

Basie shrugged. "Five minutes ago?"

"You're fucking up your life if you go back there."

A memory flickered over Basie's mind. A pair of arms around him in his own bed. Hot lavender tea from a familiar mug. A tender voice cutting through the silence. *Who do I have if you're not my person?*

Basie slid out from underneath the picnic table and for the first time in forever, a grin split across his father's cheeks and his mother's mouth.

How long do you think you'll stay in Long Lily? Truthfully, this time?

"To tell you the truth," he said warmly. "I think I'll be just fine."

Because tomorrow, he would start doing immortality the right way.

Basie's apartment was dark when he slipped in through the back door, but he walked past the light switch without a second thought. He dropped his tool bag in the kitchen, found a patch of nighttime indigo light in the middle of the living room, and laid flat on the floor. Gravity and the hard floorboards released all the tension and pressure from Basie's spine. Holding up a hand, Basie studied the length of his fingers, the heel of his palm.

Tomorrow, he was going home. He didn't know how exactly—only that he'd walk if it came to it. But that was okay. He was good at walking.

Then, a thought came to his head. It lifted above the mess jumbling around in his head with such fierce clarity, Basie sat up.

It was this: Lewie Simon had an uncanny way of knowing things.

The phone in his jacket pocket buzzed, the electric paddle to his lethargic heart. Basie let out a watery laugh when Lewie's voice reached his ear.

"You ready to come home now?"

CHAPTER 20

T HE CONTENTS OF THE YEATS FAMILY SHED WERE THIS:

Forty cardboard boxes containing artifacts a person might accumulate over three hundred years of life. They were labeled by year, but not well. The items were strange enough that if you put them together in a straight line, you would not be able to come up with a recognizable sequence of events. Instead, they were objects of sentimental value—things Della had kept not because they were important to the history of the world, but because they were important to the history of *her*.

Kit opened some of the boxes to see what was inside. Some of the boxes contained very little. Knuckle bones from a game that was practically primeval. Thimbles, strangely painted ducks, and chips from porcelain plates. Other boxes were filled to the brim with exquisite gowns, carefully folded and sealed in crumbling plastic, with lace fans and perfume bottles draped across the top. It was endless! White cloth patches with red crosses stitched in the center. A pair of ivory glasses without lenses. Five Canadian dollars in silver coins. And her journals, all twenty-two of them.

Half of the boxes contained pictures, mostly of Della who had been all over the world.

But in the 1950s box, there were pictures of Basie.

In the '70s box, Basie's appearance stopped changing.
"*Oh*," Kit had breathed out. Oh. Oh. Oh.
Then, he began to laugh, or cry, or both.
What a beautiful world it was.

CHAPTER 21

From, *The Diary of Della Yeats,*
Vol. 15. July 4th, 1946

Today was Basie's second Independence Day. The first one that matters.

Through his perspective, I'm sure it went off with very little trouble. There was an issue of noise at the start of the day. This was partially because I hadn't expected the festivities to overflow past the downtown limits. But while I was dressing Basie (in the most precious stars and stripes suspenders I've ever seen!) our neighbors squealed by the house in their fancy new car. All the honking and cheering made poor Basie wet himself. Once I stuffed little cotton balls in his ears, he was fine. He even got to enjoy the marching band.

The thing is, it is so strange to celebrate the Fourth of July with Basie. All of this jubilee around him and he has no idea what it means or the cost we paid. He's a newborn, and to him, the parade is just silly men in sillier clothes making silly faces.

But to me, those men are soldiers and I know what they have seen. They are so young and that is what haunts me.

I was able to get lost in the hot dogs and sparklers and lemonade with blue food dye, when Nellie Long told me there was a man sitting on the town hall steps asking after me. She offered to walk me there. Maybe she saw his face in Basie's. I have to say, it's nice to have friends who will support you, even when you have to do something alone.

Basilio was waiting for me like he was on that street corner nine years ago, hunched on the steps, head over his knees. He wasn't searching this time. If there was anything he wanted, he already knew where to find it.

I did not sit beside him. I did not lift the veil of the stroller.

"You look older," I told him.

"You don't." And then, "You probably want to know why I'm here." He spoke in that pitiful voice he always used when he was pretending to be the world's biggest victim.

I told him I wanted to know when he was leaving. He

fixed a look on the stroller and I knew exactly what he wanted. But he still found the words to explain he wouldn't be able to rest if he died without seeing his only son. He needed to see his face once. I told him if he wanted to see Basie, he could just look in a goddamn mirror.

But still, I pulled the veil away and plucked the cotton from Basie's ears. He reacted the way he does to all strangers, by wrinkling his nose and reaching for me.

"Can I hold him?" Basilio asked and I told him he could, because I am many things, but I am not heartless.

This was the thing that changed me, seeing Basilio hold the boy we created together, murmuring to him in adoring Spanish. The rest of the parade marched by, but Basilio was there and he was holding Basie, and for a few moments, I was back in Mexico.

I do not know what he could have been thinking when he placed Basie back in the stroller. His last words to me were, "I won't be back." It didn't hurt, because I already knew it without him having to say it.

I felt dizzy for the rest of the afternoon. But it was still a good Independence Day. This year, we were all freed of something.

CHAPTER 22

I T TOOK BASIE LEAVING Long Lily for Kit to find comfort in secrets. The two unknowns he'd been carrying around no longer weighed him down like an iron anchor waiting to be raised. That slimy feeling telling him he would be lying if he didn't confess his past or his depthless love for Basie disappeared. He kept them close in his front pocket and called them what they really were: secrets, because they were just his and no one else's.

But when Basie Yeats left for West Virginia, another secret joined Kit's collection. It was the culmination of the others, two strands that had been laden with want, guilt, and shame, only to be made hurtless when the third joined their ranks.

The last unknown was this:

Every day, after he returned from an afternoon of baking pies at Mallory Farm, Kit would pull the silver key from around his neck and unlock the shed.

For an hour, he would hide away from the world to work. It was the kind of labor a person did tending the memorial of a late loved one—which is to say it wasn't really work at all. He replaced the rotting shingles, and painted over the raw plywood interior with cream colored paint until they looked like real walls. He added a softer chair by the desk and hung translucent drapes.

Sometimes he'd leave the window open, letting them pitch and swell.

But his favorite part was putting his knowledge of archival preservation to good use and making sure that the artifacts of the Yeats shed had a fighting chance of living as long as Basie would. The contents of the boxes were all but strewn in mass graves of cardboard and dust, but Kit rescued each item and restored it to the best of his ability. Old pocket watches were shined and oiled. Heirloom fountain pens were placed in plastic baggies and dishware shawled in bubble wrap. Photographs dusted, their frames restored to a bright finish. All of it was sorted in chronological order by individual year, rather than by decade.

Kit loved the work, even on days when the Long Lily sun turned the hideout into a Dutch oven. He loved it even when the photographs of Basie made Kit put his face in his hands and breathe through the tears welling on his lashes.

The redirection of his focus did not mean that the rest of Wellhead was neglected, though. Most nights, he hid away in the evenings after the sun set to work on the half-finished mural in Della's bedroom.

He meant to take his time painting, except one day he got an unexpected text message from a number he did not have the heart to delete: *I miss you.* Just those three words on a screen and Kit was up all night, painting and painting, until eventually he woke up on the floor with his face in his palette. He did not send a reply, but he typed out: *You're a coward, Basie Yeats*, then deleted it.

Elsewhere on the Wellhead grounds, the irises were thriving—always watered the right amount up to the last drop. He weeded every day, ensuring that the task could not take more than a few minutes. Otherwise, his mind would drift to a pair of callused hands on his, digging into the soil and tugging up the roots. Kit wished Basie was around to see that he'd stopped using a bee suit while scraping out the hives since Orion had started to come on Tuesday afternoons to give beekeeping lessons.

But the shed *always* came first.

Sometimes, working meant sitting at the shed's desk and reading Della's journals. It was the only way he could think of to give an immortal person who had died back their immortality, without the burden of being alive.

Kit was a man of patience, but reading the journals required more of his self-control than he expected to endure. Though Della's life was beautiful and full, he suspected his favorite part would come in the latest journals, but it would take a lot of reading before he got there.

The first mention of Basie was framed by mentions of war and fear that Kit could not ever match to his memory of Basie—a man of quiet days and a humble way for loving the place he was from. For all Basie knew lies and loneliness, fear could not touch him until he made the conscious decision to let it.

Basie's father, on the other hand, was made of fear. It was no wonder Basie wanted to run away when the people who loved him had all run away first. Kit wondered if he could hate a man he'd never met. He tried to, but the more hatred he tried to spill into his heart, the more it tasted of a salt he knew he could not stomach.

What he wanted, really, was to do better for Basie.

Basilio all but disappeared from Della's writing, and Basie filled the gaps, taking over every inch of paper with the tiniest details of his existence. He was her pride and unabashed joy, the most beautiful of anything she'd created. Reading the journals made Kit sort of feel like he was lingering on the sidelines of an entire lifetime. He wondered what Della would've written about him.

It was bittersweet when he closed in on the end of Della's journal. The journals were a way to spend time with the Basie he knew without pressing up against the boundary they'd drawn between them. Sometimes, Kit thought that the Basie in Della's journals—the Basie who did not know grief—was not all too different from the man he'd fallen in love with. If Basie had stayed, maybe he could've been that person again.

Now, Kit turned the page to the last entry and discovered why that could not be.

This last account was what Kit had found face down on the floor when he first opened the shed, right where Basie had dropped it the day he destroyed the sunflowers. At the time, it was difficult to muster up the restraint to leave this passage unread until he finished all that came before it.

Unlike the other entries, which had been addressed to no one at all, the last account was a letter. The handwriting was neater and on the lines, as if Della had taken her time in writing each individual word.

From, *The Diary of Della Yeats*, **Vol. 22. May 31st, 2022.**

Basie, Basie, Basil Yeats.

If I know you, you'll put off looking for this last entry

as long as you can. I just hope you don't wait too long. Otherwise, there isn't much I can say that will soothe the pain I'm leaving you with.

One time you asked me something I have never let go of. "What keeps the garden alive in drought?" you wondered. "What keeps the willow leaves green in the winter?" To tell you the truth, I don't know. When I first came here, I thought it must be something to do with the spiritual heart of Long Lily. Perhaps the same magnetic forces that draw moths to the moon are here in our soil, drawing immortal people like us together to make a home on equally immortal land. A community. And maybe, to some extent, that's true.

For most of my time here, I believed nothing could over-power that unyielding pull and make me bitter against my own immortality. And this is the truth: nothing has. I don't resent the way I was created or the painful memories I have because of it. I don't resent my father for giving me centuries instead of decades. I don't even resent your father for deciding that forever was just too long for him. I understand, because forever is too long for me now too. It has been.

Basie, do you remember that storybook you so enjoyed as a boy? We used to sit up in bed reading the same fairy tales over and over until you could recite the words by heart. You had some of the stories memorized before you could read and tricked me into thinking you were some kind of genius at age four.

Reading that book was my way of giving you our heritage. Those pages contain the truth of us, Basie. That we are descended from a long, long, <u>long</u> line of magical people who wanted to settle down and live much like you and I do now. The line of my family traces all the way back to a subgroup of those people who wanted to take that lifestyle off the island. While mortal people were fighting over England and the church, our ancestors were breaking off from a very strict way of staying in a singular place.

I always loved the simple way our people lived their immortality, so I decided to come to Long Lily and start that tradition here—the right way.

You might remember the faeries in your storybook were capable of great magic. I was always curious about what happened to those abilities. Only recently, I have come into the knowledge that the magic of our people is like a muscle. If you do not exercise it, you lose the strength altogether. Because our ancestors chose not to use their abilities for fear of condemnation (and subsequently, death), the newer generations—you and me—have only kept our immortality.

Here is the troubling part. Without that magic, immortal

people aren't truly immortal at all. We're just… very, very slow agers. When the time for aging does come after hundreds and hundreds of years, it costs the capability of moving and thinking. I am immortal and spoiled, so these are two things I cannot wittingly give up. You may have not noticed, Basie, but I have begun to move so slowly. There's a deep ache in my muscles that keeps me from doing what I love to do and I can't shake it. It's only going to get worse. On the outside, I'll look like I always have: thirty-seven-years young. On the inside, I will be creeping to a halt. So, I'm going to go today.

My reasons for doing this are not to hurt you or leave you alone—though I know you will be angry. But Basie, you are seventy-seven years old. You cannot spend the first, and best, half of your immortality taking care of me. You've barely been outside Long Lily. You haven't loved someone in the profound way that makes us human. You only know these mountains and a life not overly inclined toward adventure. So I have made the decision to offer you freedom. To go and see the world without worrying about leaving me behind. Find someone to take with you. Come back home to Wellhead if you truly cannot leave it for good. But don't let the Crane's Nest trees fence you in. You have too much promise for that.

I know if you and I talked about this, you'd find some way to convince me to change my mind. Except I wouldn't change my mind, so we'd spend my last days angry at one another, fighting about things neither of us could change. Am I selfish? For giving you a last memory that is so normal and unremarkable? That's what memories are for, I think. I hope you fill your mind with them.

But here is what I want even more than all of this: Answer the questions I never could. What keeps the garden thriving? What makes the willow and the bees endure through the winter? What keeps us alive? What keeps you <u>awake</u>? I'm leaving without telling you the answer so you'll stick around for a while and find out.

I love you, Basie. My sweet Basie Yeats.

Bye for now.

—Mom

(PS: The sketch for the mural in my bedroom was designed by an artist I found in a magazine. See if he'll come and finish it for me, would you? His name is Christopher Elliot. Ask him to add sunflowers.)

Kit stared at the open-faced journal until the words blurred into inky Rorschach smears.

How could he ever blame Basie for wanting to step into the world when Kit himself had already given himself over to it? How could he despise Basie's leaving when it was in pursuit of fulfilling the only will and testament that Della had left behind? It was very simple why he could not.

Kit and Basie were two halves of the same wanting, both chasing after the promise of a wholeness they'd already found.

Kit always believed he could not have both Basie and Wellhead at once; just as Basie could not have Long Lily—all the things he loved within it—and also find the meaning his mother wanted for him. Both of them had given each other up over reckless assumptions.

Only now, Kit wondered what would've happened if they had looked for their answers together.

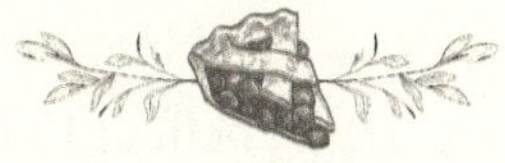

WHEN LEWIE DROVE THE truck over the Long Lily frontier, Basie turned his face to the window and let himself fall dizzy at watching the world blur. All smudgy edges and undefined shapes, Long Lily looked like a completely new dream. Basie rolled down the window and stuck his fingers through the opening. He caught cool spring air in his palm, letting each chilly burst sail his hand over invisible valleys and peaks. The side of his face felt damp, and he could feel Lewie looking at him from the corner of his eye.

"Where should I drop you off?" Lewie asked. Basie let his spread fingers fall flat against the outside wall of the truck. "Straight back to Wellhead?"

The answer should've been an immediate yes. Basie had nowhere else to go, and now that the roof had caved, squatting in

Crane's Nest was not an option. Moving back to Long Lily with the intention of taking Kit up on his offer seemed like a great idea when he was packing his things. Now, though…

"He probably hates me."

Lewie pressed his lips together like this was the answer he'd been expecting, unhelpful as it was.

"I don't think he does. He doesn't talk like he hates you."

"What I did to him was messed up. I didn't even tell him I was leaving."

"Oh, I'm well aware," Lewie chuckled mirthlessly. It did not go unnoticed to Basie that he was driving in the direction of the cottage. "Who do you think had to break the news?"

Basie groaned out a curse.

"He *definitely* hates me. I can't believe I'm planning on showing up on his doorstep like I've been lost at sea or some shit. *Hi! Sorry I kissed you then disappeared from your life without any warning. Can I still store my socks in your dresser?*" Basie's sardonic smile melted into pure horror. "Oh my god, what if he's met someone else?"

"Come on, Bas. You know he hasn't."

Logistically speaking, Basie did know this. Long Lily was not known for its overflowing surplus of queer people. And even if it was, Basie had a feeling if he couldn't move on, neither could Kit. He frowned. Was he being overconfident?

Lewie reached across the center console and mussed up Basie's hair, then clamped down on his shoulder.

"You're here to make it right. That has to count for something."

The hair on Basie's arm stood on edge as a particularly chilly breeze slipped into the truck. He angled his chin into it and closed his eyes, welcoming the raw bite. He had a spare thought that it was probably a little warmer in Berkeley Springs today than it was here.

"Okay," Basie said. "Okay. Take me home to Wellhead."

CHAPTER 23

I T WAS *EXACTLY* HOW he remembered it. The pale blue of the shutters, faded and well-loved by the sun. The irises at their peak vibrancy. Kit's van in the driveway. Empty harvest baskets sitting on the front steps, waiting to be filled. The opened shed door, swinging under a patch of shade and—

Basie's heart came to a complete stop, halting so abruptly, he wasn't sure it would ever start up again.

The shed door was *open*. Kit was home. *Kit was inside the shed.*

Lewie must've known this was going to happen, in the way he always did, because he sped off the second Basie slammed the truck door closed.

For a long moment, Basie stood there, planted in the dirt like one of his mother's irises. The only thing that nudged him past his state of suspension was the thought that if Kit came out, this would be how he found Basie—pale with terror. He deserved more. He deserved a proper hello, a proper explanation and apology. Basie would kneel on the damp ground with his hands open if he had to. He'd do a lot more than that.

Plucking together the little courage he had left, Basie crossed the yard and paused at the foot of the shed. He swallowed a large breath and—

And there was Kit—magnificent, unworldly, *beautiful* Kit Elliot.

His back was to Basie, focused deep on the workbench where he was sorting through several shoeboxes filled with photographs. His usual dress pants were cuffed above his bare feet and he was wearing one of Basie's old, moss green jackets. He was humming one of Basie's favorite songs, and hadn't heard him come through the yard.

Basie couldn't hold it a second longer.

"Kit," he whispered. It had been so long since he'd felt that name on his lips.

Kit's head lifted, but he didn't turn right away. He listened, like he was torn between blaming the wind or believing impossible things really *could* happen at Wellhead.

Then, he turned around.

Basie wondered how he could have ever left. It felt like it had been a full century. It felt like it'd been no time at all.

Kit did not speak. There was no evidence he really *saw* Basie other than his wide eyes and the wetness forming in his lashes.

This is it, Basie thought, *this is where he tells me he's through with me.*

But Kit still did not say anything. Very calmly, he pulled a picture from one of the shoeboxes and placed it in Basie's hand.

Basie's world *expanded.*

It expanded into every color he'd ever seen and every color he someday would. Louder than the Long Lily fireworks display and brighter than the whole sea of stars up close.

Because the picture was of Kit Elliot, sepia and soft in a way that was all too familiar. His eyes were smiling, though his lips were not, and he was dressed in an impeccably tailored suit. In the corner, someone had scribbled a date: *1932*.

"How old are you?" Basie asked, impossibly quiet. Kit smiled.

"One hundred and three."

Basie felt his face crumple. His chest gaped wide open. He pressed the picture against his forehead and shuddered out a sob against its musty smell.

"*God*," he said, reverent. "God, Kit."

Then Kit pulled aside the picture, tears dripping down the sides of his cheeks too.

"And you?" His voice was steadier than Basie could manage. "You're, what—seventy-seven?"

A burst of hysterical laughter exploded out of Basie. He threw his arms out to the side with a grin and said, "Seventy-seven fucking years! I'm seventy-seven years old!" It was the first time he'd ever said it so—*joyfully*. Like it was something to celebrate. "You're immortal! I can't believe it. And I'm…We're both—! I don't think I've ever been so…so…"

Kit pulled him into his arms the same second Basie began to weep. Basie clutched at him, arms tight around Kit's neck, nose buried into the familiar red curls. The scent of apple and sumac hit Basie so hard it nearly sent him to his knees.

"You've had the key to the shed for six months! Why didn't you tell me?"

"I didn't want to be the thing that dragged you home," Kit admitted, voice muffled by Basie's clothes. "You finally made up your mind."

Pulling back, Basie took Kit's face in his hands, swiping away streaks of tears with his thumb.

"I thought you would hate me," Basie whispered. He tracked Kit's warm hazel brown eyes and drank in every detail of his face. It woke all the dormant lovelorn parts of him.

"Do you think I could do anything but love you, Basie?" Kit asked, sweetly. Honestly.

A grin spread across Basie's face from which he released a torrential outpour of affection. His seventy-seven years of life were filled with so many beautiful words that would sit forever in his memory. But this confession, this simple statement of a perfect fact, was by far the loveliest.

Still, Basie had to ask, "You're not angry with me? I wouldn't blame you if you were. *I'm* angry with myself."

"I was," admitted Kit. He pressed his thumb through the crease in Basie's brow, smoothing the tension away. "But it was unfair of me to place all the blame on you. I spent so long deluding myself I would eventually convince you to stay. I went and helped you do all that research, then was surprised when you took the Greyhound."

"You asked me to stay," Basie pointed out. "You were honest every time I wasn't."

"Not about my age. I lied about that and asked you to stay for very selfish reasons, without taking into consideration the pain you were going through. I was—I was *terrible* to you, Basie."

Hearing Kit speak so poorly of himself was something Basie did not think he could endure. The only reason Kit thought he stood a chance at getting Basie to stay was because Basie had given him hope. Basie *told him* with his own mouth that he would live at Wellhead, then held Kit in his childhood bed. What else was Kit supposed to think?

No more. Basie was done with dancing around the truth. He was done letting Kit martyr himself for all of Basie's mistakes.

Shaking his head, he took a step into Kit's space, and then another, until Kit was stumbling back into the workbench. Up close like this, Basie noticed how much taller Kit was than him. Kit peered down his nose at Basie, cheeks flushed a beautiful, bright red.

Basie pushed up on his toes, grabbing Kit's shoulders, and kissed him.

Kit crumbled, letting the bench and Basie's quick arms catch him. He fell into the kiss, cradling Basie's face with both shaking hands. It seemed impossible that a person so *good* should hold him so reverently—but then, this was Wellhead.

The scent of Kit's cologne still lingered on Basie's nose when Kit pulled back, stunned. Basie smiled wistfully.

"You were never terrible. You were the reason I got out of bed in the morning."

Basie didn't know how else to say that, to him, Kit had already been absolved of everything he could've done wrong and everything that the future might bring. All because Kit had given him patience and kindness on days when Basie yelled and swore and raised his middle finger to the world. All because Kit had regarded Basie like he was something to treasure.

Now, his gaze made Basie feel like liquid gold, something beyond all value.

"I love you, Basie," he said, softly. "The morning after you left, I remembered I hadn't said it back. So now I am."

The inside of Basie's chest was pure warmth, but he still said, "I seem to recall you saying it just a few minutes ago."

Kit dropped his face into Basie's shoulder with an embarrassed groan.

"That wasn't official."

"And this one is?"

Drawing back, Kit draped his arms over Basie's shoulders.

"Signed and sealed, baby," he said, capping it with a kiss. It made them both laugh because it was the most *Basie* thing he'd ever said. Kit pushed himself up so he was sitting properly on the workbench, kicking his legs like a child on either side of Basie. Their chuckles turned into easy silence. The quiet was something Kit never turned his back to. He always seemed willing to linger in it, let it do the talking. And when it had nothing to say, he would step into it himself.

Maybe Basie could try that type of bravery for once. He ran his hands up Kit's thighs, steadying himself.

"No matter why or how it happened, I shouldn't have gone. I shouldn't have left without telling you. For that, I am really sorry, Kit."

"It's okay," said Kit, taking Basie's hands.

But Basie shook his head.

"I'm so sorry."

"*It's okay,*" Kit vowed.

And he meant it, so Basie allowed himself to believe it. Calling on that trust was as easy as lying in the grass and counting the clouds.

"There's something I don't—" Kit started carefully. He wet his lips and tried again. "When are you going back to Berkeley Springs?"

A glimmer lit in Basie's eyes.

"I'm not."

The effect on Kit was instant. "No?" he said. His lips quirked up, hopeful, and Basie was excited to tell him something good for once.

He ran his hands up and down Kit's arms. The smile on Kit's face was infectious.

"I seem to recall someone asking me to move in with him. I came back to see if the offer was still open now that I've pulled my head out of my ass."

Delighted, shameless laughter filled the tiny room. Kit pressed his nose into Basie's cheek and nodded. "*Yes!* Yes, of course the offer is still open." Then, "On one condition."

"Anything," Basie swore. "Anything you want."

Kit met Basie's gaze head on, unafraid.

"Stay for good. Don't go running off to the far corners of the world without warning. Or, if you have to…" Fingers tangled in fingers, palms squeezed tight. "Take me with you this time."

In that moment, Basie would've given Kit anything he asked for. But this was something he could deliver.

"Oh, don't you worry, Mr. Elliot. You're stuck with me. Don't laugh, I'm serious. You'll be the one speeding off to the far corners of the world just to get rid of me."

Kit turned impossibly soft.

"I'm counting on it."

Right then and there, Basie swore to protect this thing they'd created the same way Wellhead had always protected him—tirelessly, wholeheartedly, without room for error. He thought back to the words in his mother's journal. *What keeps you awake?* But Kit had given him the answer long ago. *There's more room for other things—like…well, like love.*

Basie looked between the two of them. What was there if not love and perhaps a bit of impossible magic? What better place for two impossible beings than somewhere that guarded impossible things?

They would be just fine. Eternity wasn't too long, after all.

Not willing to waste another second, Basie pulled Kit by the face and kissed him.

If someone had been standing outside the shed window, they would've seen this: Kit, jumping off the workbench, clutching Basie's waist to keep from toppling over. Basie's hands buried in the hair he loved, drawing goosebumps on the back of Kit's neck. Legs swaying together. Lips against teeth because their smiles were too wide. The combined history of Della Yeats and Kit Elliot and Basie Yeats surrounding them in half-sorted boxes. A new history beginning, a gasping cry of its very first day.

CHAPTER 24

"DID YOU KNOW THAT I was acquainted with your mother?" wondered Kit in his soft voice. There weren't chairs for both of them, so they'd taken to sitting on the soft throw rug—Basie between Kit's legs, his back against Kit's chest. It meant that Basie could still hear the man behind him, who was apparently too nervous to speak above a whisper, lest he scare Basie away.

Basie, on his part, had half a notion to never move from this spot now that Kit was carding through his hair, detangling the knots and eliciting the sweetest thrill up his spine.

"I read it in her journal. But before that, no," Basie offered. "Doesn't surprise me, I guess. She had immortal friends everywhere."

"That's the thing, it wasn't like that. She had no idea I was immortal. I'd forgotten that our paths even crossed in the first place. It makes me feel strange to think about it now."

"How do you mean?" asked Basie, playing with the hand that rested on his waist.

"I submitted the sketch for your mother's mural into my friend's humble art magazine. This was several years ago, back when I was living in…" He thought for a second. "God, Portland,

I think. Anyway, she saw it and wrote to me, asking if I might copy it for her, so she could replicate it. I suppose I expected she would do her own rendition on a canvas, which was fine with me. It was just a silly sketch to help fill the magazine. Her letter charmed me so much, I sent her the original. I remember she tried to pay me, but I ended up just returning it to the sender."

"Let me guess. She sent it back again?" deadpanned Basie.

Kit's chest shook with a quiet chuckle.

"She did. As a compromise, I donated the money to the Boys and Girls Club. I must've misplaced her letter, but I did manage to hold on to the envelope. I found it in my things when I was looking for a place to move. It's why I searched for Long Lily in the first place—it was on the return address."

Basie swiveled in Kit's hold.

"What you're saying is, my mom is the reason you're here?"

Kit shrugged. "Pretty much. I didn't remember until I read her last entry."

"Freaky," Basie mused, settling back into place. He picked up Kit's hand, tracing the pad of his finger along the heart line. "What else about you have you not told me? Like Axe. I kinda get the feeling you weren't with him recently."

If he wasn't currently wrapped around Basie, Kit might've shirked away.

"No, I was with him in 1945."

Basie ungracefully slammed Kit's hand into his lap.

"That's the year I was born!" he scowled. "I'm sorry, but I hate that."

"I had a feeling you might. Though I have to admit, I'm *very* glad you were born once that whole mess was over."

Basie frowned.

"Wait, hold on. When you said you met Axe overseas, you mean—"

"I met Axe when we were stationed in Europe, 717th Tank Battalion."

It was a grim thought, but still Basie tried to picture it: Kit no longer in his dress pants and well-fitting dress shirts, but head-to-toe olive khakis. Kit, dodging bullets and ducking from bombs, hoping that a meager helmet would protect him from the shrapnel.

It was too horrible a thought, so Basie tugged both of Kit's arms and secured them tightly around his chest.

Kit must've been able to tell the bloody tangent Basie was tumbling down because he kissed the back of Basie's head and said, "For what it's worth, I ended up being chosen for clerical support back in England. Apparently, I was much better at typing than I was at shooting."

"Good," stated Basie, holding Kit's hand to his lips. "And Axe met your parents, so he must've been okay too."

"He was," Kit said warmly. "And once we ended things, he lived a very long and happy life. I called every now and again to check in on him and his wife. He figured out my secret on his own when he was very old, but by the next time I called, he'd already forgotten."

It was more of Kit's history than Basie had ever been able to piece together on his own. He recalled Kit mentioning that he'd moved away shortly after Axe had been introduced to his parents. It wasn't uncommon for immortal people to move as soon as they started to settle down —Basie knew this as well as anyone, even if he hadn't made a habit of it himself. Moving was easier than getting tangled up in the complications of living forever among people who wouldn't. But the timing of Kit's move, along with the things his family left behind—it all seemed a little…

"Axe wasn't the reason you and your parents stopped talking, was he?" Basie asked carefully.

"No," Kit answered. "You remember your storybook. The house held faeries—that's truly what our people are called—do things a certain way. They stay in one spot and they never leave. My parents and I lived in Ireland my whole life up until the war hit. All the fighting spooked them something fierce, so we moved to New Jersey. We didn't ever plan to move from that house." Kit leaned his cheek against the curve of Basie's head. "But then I got drafted. I expected my parents to despise the idea of me traveling around the world in a blaze of patriotic glory. But in their minds, they were doing their duty by sending me off to fight. Maybe they thought all the bullets and smoke would scare me off from wanting to travel around for real."

"Let me guess, it had the opposite effect."

"I couldn't wait to go home," Kit admitted. "But I also couldn't wait to hop on the next ship back—you know, once everything was over. Only, when Axe and I got back, everything was a complete mess. One of my father's colleagues accidentally discovered our secret and was threatening to do something about it. My parents were terrified, and it was the only thing that could convince them to find a new place to move to. They wanted me to settle down near them since my aging had just begun to slow. Without asking for my input, they picked out all these places back in Ireland that were so far from civilization. Just cliffsides and fields. I knew that if I went with them, I would spend my really long life without anyone or anything at all. I couldn't stay in Jersey with Axe, but I couldn't move with my parents either. They were devastated. Told me they never, ever wanted to speak to me again."

Kit's hand started its caressing again.

"It's like your story," he went on. "Cian's people lived *like* humans, but *without* them. My parents think that if we're going to be around for such a long time, we ought to keep to ourselves. In their minds, it's safer that way. Then we can't be uprooted or disrupted by anyone who finds out our secret. It wasn't the way I wanted to live."

Basie thought back to his own preconceived notions of immortality. How if it hadn't been for his mother, he might've never shared his secret with *anyone*. But Lewie knew, and all the Simon siblings. Probably more folks than he realized knew his secret, and he hadn't been shipped off to Area 51 yet. In his estimation, wanting community wasn't a difficult ask.

"They were wrong for letting you go over that," he stated, resolutely.

"Some people are set in their ways, Basie."

"Fuck, I know that. I'm from Long Lily. We've literally been having the same crappy town festivals every year since the damn founding," he exasperated, disentangling himself from Kit's long arms. He spun and sat cross-legged so they could face each other. When he held his hands open, Kit accepted them with a hazy, little smile.

"Kit, you are the most exceptional person I know. You are smarter and wiser and more gifted than anyone I've ever met in nearly a century of living. You deserve to live the way that brings you joy, without judgment or condemnation from anyone else. And if your parents don't want to take part in that or love you for the man that you are, then…" Basie chomped down all his desire for threats and angry phone calls and long trips to give the Elliots a piece of his mind. He squeezed Kit's hands instead. "Then you are in the right place. Because you've got this town wrapped around your finger. We *love* you."

Kit brought their joined hands to his lips, lingering to kiss a tiny scar on Basie's knuckle.

"I know," he said.

Basie could see Kit spiraling down a road of unpleasant thoughts, so he prompted, "Okay, what else have I missed? We're both faeries. That's fucked up. I'd say I never believed in faeries before, but I've heard that'd make one drop dead, and I'm not trying to be a murderer."

Kit reached up to the workbench, snatching two crackers with tiny slices of cheese off his plate and handing one to Basie.

"We're only faeries in the way that most white Americans are German or Italian. Look, you don't even have any point to your ear," he argued. To prove his point, he thumbed the corner of Basie's ear.

"But you do though!" exclaimed Basie, pushing back all of Kit's hair with wide eyes. "I wouldn't have noticed if you hadn't said anything, but you've got the tiniest point on your ears. Why is it oddly attractive? I feel like I'm going insane."

Kit laughed. "Am I your very own Cian the Huntsman?"

"No, you couldn't hurt a fly," answered Basie immediately. "And I like you without the tragic ending." He dropped his face onto Kit's shoulder. "God, Kit, that could've been us if I'd been an idiot and stayed in Berkeley Springs."

"You are far from an idiot."

"That's really generous of you to say, but I lived in an abandoned diner for three months that almost killed me."

Kit's nose wrinkled at the memory.

"What was Berkeley Springs like?" he asked, changing the subject.

Truth be told, Basie hadn't thought about Berkeley Springs since he crossed the border. It wasn't that the people or the pleasant little town were forgettable. It was only that West Virginia wasn't home. There was probably someone out there who longed for Berkeley Springs the same way Basie had torn his heart out over Long Lily. But for him, he was exactly where he needed to be.

Still, he told Kit of his sad little apartment and the locals' admirable attempt to get to know him. He even told Kit about Evan asking him out and took delight when Kit grimaced.

"I turned him down. Told him I'm spoken for," Basie promised. The charming affection in Kit's eyes was a pleasant reward. "What about you? Any hot dates while I was gone?"

Kit huffed. "Oh, sure. Old man Nougat snatched me right up and showed me the town," he said flatly. "*Of course* there was no one. I was too busy in this shed eating my heart out and looking at pictures of you."

Basie grinned, leaning forward for a self-indulgent kiss.

"If I didn't know any better, I'd say you liked me."

"That so?" grinned Kit, tugging Basie flush against him. "Then let me enlighten you on just how much I *like* you."

"IF I CARRY ANOTHER suitcase down the stairs and into that van, I'm going to lay down in front of a moving tractor. A big one," complained Basie, collapsing on the porch swing. It was cooler outside than it was in the house. He tilted his face back, letting a refreshing breeze dry his sweat. Even with his eyes closed, he could hear Kit blundering out the front door, whacking their bags along the threshold.

"I hate to say it, darlin', but you've only got yourself to blame. I told you there was no reason to pack all your earthly belongings. We're only going for the weekend," Kit remarked, hoisting another one of Basie's bags up over his shoulder.

Basie cracked his eyes open.

"One: you better watch it. You're starting to sound like you live here or something."

Kit placed the bags in his hand at the top of the porch steps, then plopped down on the swing next to Basie. He swung an arm around Basie's shoulder, immediately subjecting Basie to the hell fire heat radiating off of his body. Basie almost pushed him away, feeling like his skin was going to melt off, but he liked Kit's attention and the way he smelled too much to make a fuss.

Heat aside, Basie was almost too comfortable, his head laid on Kit's shoulder. Maybe he could close his eyes and nap in his warm shade before they hit the road. They couldn't leave until the *surprise* showed up, anyway.

"Was there a two or did that list only have one thing on it?"

Kit prodded with a playful edge.

Basie bristled.

"Two: I'm the smart-ass in this relationship and I'd thank you to stay in your lane." Basie deadpanned, though he nuzzled his nose under Kit's jaw. "And three: it's been almost sixty years since I've traveled anywhere that wasn't moving or running away, so you'll have to excuse me if I don't know what the hell to bring. What if there's an emergency? I don't know what they sell in Canada."

"You absolutely do, because it's all the same stuff they sell here," Kit objected. "Also I'm curious what catastrophes you're packing for. Because if you have some gift for apocalyptic foresight you're not telling me about, kindly inform me now so I can bring enough underwear."

Crossing his arms tightly across his chest, Basie laid his head in Kit's lap, letting his leg drape over the side of the swing to rock it back and forth.

"Is it too late to cancel this trip?" Basie practically pleaded.

"Rita is expecting us."

"Well, *Rita* can shove—"

Kit smacked a hand over Basie's mouth before he could finish *that* sentence. For both of their sakes, he was striving to remain perfectly neutral about the woman who coordinated the logistics of Della's death. He was the one who went digging through the landline's history for Rita's number. The one who'd made the call and said politely, *"Hi there, my name is Kit Elliot. I'm calling on behalf of my partner, Basie Yeats. Could we take you up on your offer for a visit?"* He was also the one to hold Basie when he was shaking with rage and silent tears. The one to whisper in Basie's ear, *"You're allowed to be angry. I've got you."*

Now, Kit was the one holding Basie together when he felt someone had broken him into a million anxious pieces with a hammer.

"We'll only be gone three days," reasoned Kit, brushing some of the hair out of Basie's face. "You've packed everything you could possibly ever need, and then some, and then some *more*. I'll be right there with you the entire time. I won't leave your side until you say so."

"Do you think we're bringing enough flowers for the head-stone?" Basie asked quietly.

A fond smile warmed Kit's expression.

"Plenty."

"And you'll do the talking?"

"I'll talk her ear off if you want me too."

Basie pushed himself up onto his elbow to look Kit straight in the eyes.

"I love you," he said. "And when we get home and I remember how to be a functioning human, we'll do something that has Kit Elliot written all over it, like—I don't know, spend a day in Gettysburg and go to all the boring museums. You can even read all the plaques and I won't complain."

Kit bent over his lap to press a lingering kiss to Basie's mouth.

"How generous you are," he crooned, making Basie's cheek tint pink. "Why don't we hit the road and have it over with?"

"We can't leave until the house sitter gets here," replied Basie. It took all the strength he currently did not have to keep his features perfectly neutral. Kit, accustomed to sniffing out Basie's ulterior motives, frowned.

"House sitter? For what? The bees and the flowers that don't die? Don't tell me—Orion needed more summer service hours."

"Excuse me, those are bees and flowers that you nearly killed—"

"I keep telling you, the house was just angry you were gone. It happened again when you moved away."

"—And as a matter of fact," persisted Basie, ignoring him, "It's not Orion."

Right on cue, a Maryland U-Haul turned up the drive. It dashed on the gravel harder than most cars were brave enough to, coming to a halt at the edge of the driveway in a cloud of dust.

"Who is that?" Kit asked slowly.

Basie only grinned.

With a victorious cheer, Lara Tom hurled out of the driver's side door. Kit was on his feet in an instant, leaping over all three porch stairs and catching Lara before she could throw herself into the shrubbery trying to get to him. They were both laughing, a heaving, hysterical sound that made Basie's eyes run misty.

"What is this?" Kit cried, pulling back to hold Lara by the shoulders. He glanced up where Basie was leaning over the railing, watching. "Did you do this?" Then at Lara. "What's the truck for?"

Basie nodded at Lara. "Go ahead, you tell him."

But Lara only shook her head, her choppy hair a delightful mess around her toothy grin.

"No, I want him to figure out himself just so I can see the look on his face," she chimed. Then to Kit, she pressed, "Open the back and look in one of the boxes."

With a suspicious look in both Lara and Basie's direction, Kit circled round the back of the truck and heaved the latch up. Rushing to stand beside Lara, Basie was just in time to see Kit leap into the trailer. She threaded an arm through his elbow, squeezing excitedly.

The noon light shone enough into the trailer that Kit wasn't shrouded in dimness when he carefully pulled back the lip of one of the boxes. He peered inside, threw back the other flaps, and spun around.

"Are these—?"

"All five billion trillion of your books? Yep. Not one solider left behind," Lara said. "I even checked them all with the catalog you made. They're all there."

"Surprise!" crowed Basie, beaming so hard, he could feel his cheeks stretching. "Lara is going to watch the house while we're gone and unbox the books onto the shelves in the living room."

"They'll be all locked and loaded by the time you two get back," Lara added. "And don't get your undies in a twist. It's an early birthday present. A six month early birthday present, but a birthday present nonetheless."

Kit stared at them for a long second, eyes as wide as saucers.

"These are my books," he marveled. "The books I've spent a hundred years collecting. The books I thought I told Mr. Maris to donate."

"The books Mr. Maris donated to my tender loving care upon threat of death, yes," corrected Lara. "I can't believe you forgot I had a storage unit. I was going to tell you when I finally worked up the nerve to admit I had them…"

"But that was the night I had your phone," Basie cut in.

"The whole surprise was Basie's idea."

The proud eye contact Basie and Lara exchanged was the only nonphysical, nonverbal form of a high-five they needed. Kit looked back and forth between them, shaking his head in amazement.

Then, in a flurry of dress clothes, long limbs, and tears, Kit burst from the truck and tackled Lara in a hug. His lips smacked against her cheek, making her shrug him off. Basie was next, the thrilled recipient of a dozen kisses all over his face and the tightest hug he'd had since he first found Kit in the shed.

"I can't tell you what this means to me," Kit breathed, holding Basie's face in his hands. "How did you know?"

"I had to win over your best friend somehow," joked Basie, dimples pressing into Kit's palms. He swiped his thumb through the smears of tears glistening on Kit's face. "I just want you to have the things that make you happy."

Another laugh-hued sob bubbled out of Kit's lips. He pulled them close, one arm for each of them. The three collapsed together in a tangling mess of east coast blood and Pennsylvania air.

"I already do," he vowed.

Basie believed him, because he felt the same.

CHAPTER 25

THREE YEARS LATER

EVERY DAY WAS FULL of *moments* after that. Each was different from the one that came before. But on Saturdays, there was routine.

Basie woke like he always did, to birdsong stealing through the crack in the open window. Kit was folded against him, all of his smooth, pale skin flush against Basie's. They'd forgotten to draw the curtains before bed, so a sea of unfiltered sunlight engulfed the wall containing the completed mural. It made the yellows more yellow and stole away the guise from the greens until the flowers and the painted sky were *real.* Basie's eyes traced the illustrated stems and petals, assessing which ones had been Della's and which ones were Kit's. Sometimes it was hard to tell.

He didn't realize he was following along with his finger and tracing featherlight flowers into Kit's back, until Kit pressed a kiss to the flat bone between Basie's ribs, right over his heart.

"Why did you let me sleep in?" he rasped.

Since Basie had returned home two years ago, Kit liked to make sure their Saturday evenings were spent together. This, however, meant that he reserved the mornings for working on sorting the boxes in the shed. The work was paying off. These days, the shed looked less like a hideout and more like a tiny museum filled with the history of the world—*Basie's* world. Of course, Basie was thankful that someone would so reverently care for his mother's things, but…

"I'm a selfish bastard who likes to spend more than two minutes in bed with the man I love."

Kit kissed Basie with tight lips, always self-conscious about his morning breath, then burrowed into the crook of Basie's throat. For a moment, Basie felt he had successfully convinced his husband to stay in bed for the rest of the morning…only for Kit to slip out of bed a few seconds later.

Basie groaned, suddenly too cold for his liking.

"*Christopher*," he complained.

Kit glanced at him over his shoulder, slipping his patterned robe over himself.

"Yes, *Basil?*"

Basie scowled. "You don't *have* to go anywhere, you know. The shed will be there tomorrow and Saturdays are for lazing around."

"Are they now?"

Basie's head plopped back onto his pillow. Usually it did not take so much effort to convince Kit to come back to bed. But then, Kit was often more determined in the mornings. He leaned over Basie, laughing when he found him glaring playfully. Basie still closed his eyes, expecting another kiss, only none came. Kit swept his fingers through Basie's messy curls, and said, "Don't go anywhere, okay?"

"Whatever you say, hotshot."

He didn't have to ask him twice.

When Kit came back, he presented the strawberry pie he'd stayed up late baking the night before. He placed it on the bed between them with little regard for the bits of crust breaking off onto the comforter. Usually, he insisted on having some sort of tray to keep crumbs out of the bed. But this morning, he merely handed Basie a fork.

Before Kit could protest, Basie scooped right into the center and pushed aside the sweet filling to see which flowers were painted at the bottom of the tray. He paused—took another bite, then another, eating a tiny hole around the small bouquet of…Basie squinted. Daisies? None of Della's pie plates had daisies on them.

Upon a closer inspection, Basie saw three tiny letters signed at the bottom of the stems in familiar, swooping cursive: *K.E.Y.*

"You painted a new one?" Basie asked in a strange voice.

"One for each decade you don't age, right?"

Basie looked back at the plate, awed. He'd been eighty for four days now and it hadn't even occurred to him to keep up with his mother's old tradition. How did time fly so quickly? At this rate, he would blink and eternity would be over.

He moved the pie aside and curled himself into Kit's arms.

Outside, the numberless willow branches murmured, the bees took their rest, and the sunflowers straightened, opening up toward the endless Long Lily sun.

END

FIND OUT WHAT HAPPENS NEXT IN…
Patchwork (Tales from Long Lily, 1.5)

If you enjoyed this book and want to learn more about future Tess Carletta releases, consider leaving a review on Goodreads and joining the newsletter for extra goodies and book news.
Visit the address below or scan the QR code:
https://tesscarletta.com/#contact

A year before its publication, I thought with the utmost certainty that Kit & Basie would never get published. But thanks to those who supported and educated me, I got to prove myself wrong! The following people all contributed to the completion of this project and, ultimately, my debut as an author. I'd like to offer my sincerest, love-filled thanks to:

My parents, who have provided for me and supported all my creative endeavors, especially my growth as a writer. There was never a time when you doubted me, even when I wasn't so sure myself. I love you!

Sam, my very first editor! Your passion for queer literature is inspiring and I'm so thankful for the time and care you put into editing this book. I learned a lot from your edits, and appreciate your help in making this book much more polished than it otherwise would've been. You rock!

Brittany, my cover artist and my best friend of ten years that (as of right now) has *still* not read this book. Becoming friends with you was the birth of my first book (that will never see the light of day), a tradition of the two of us collaborating, and a lifelong friendship I am so abundantly blessed for. You being the cover artist for this book couldn't have happened any other way.

Alana, whose writing swept me off my feet the very first time

I read it. You've been a mentor and friend, encouraging me to push the limits of my creativity and write beyond the norm. Your honesty and feedback were integral for not only this book's growth, but for mine too.

Hannah, the Magician to my Raven King. You are truly one of the most talented, inspiring, and singular people I know. You poured so much love, thought, and time into giving me feedback on this book when you had much better things to worry about. You taught me all the fundamentals about revising when I had no idea where to begin.

Morgan, Jenna, and Abby, who supported this project whole-heartedly from beginning to end. And to Annie, who went the extra mile with some really helpful line edits. I really am one of the luckiest people out there, to be so unconditionally supported and loved.

My beta readers, Monica, Alexis, Irina, Annie, Deb, Ben, Michael, Alli, Kristian, Max, Rach, and one anonymous friend. You'll never know how worthwhile your comments were. Thank you for your time and for being the fresh pair of eyes on this story I so desperately needed.

Mike, who looked at a young writer he didn't know very well and still gave her one of the best pep talks a girl can get. Your words sprouted roots in my confidence and creativity, and were ultimately the reason this book ever got revised or published. You believed I could do it, so I did. Thank you!

Brett and Doug, because the theatre skills I learned under your instruction were fundamental in changing the way I look at narrative storytelling. Any writing I publish will be leagues richer than it would've been without your training in specificity, script analysis, character action, blocking, and making the most interesting choice.

My English professors, especially Brian, who knew after reading my first essay that I would be an English major. You were right! Our English department was a family of book lovers I didn't know I needed. Thank you!

Anyone who has ever read and supported my fanfiction. (Special love to Niamh, Katy, Phebs, Meg, Marybeth, and LB!) I would've quit writing years ago without the kind words of those who supported my growth as a writer, which happened almost exclusively over six years and seventy fanfiction stories. You all really are kindred spirits!

Lastly, I'd like to thank the 130 backers of the *Kit & Basie* Kickstarter, especially the following folks who gave me permission to list their names. This project would not have happened without their generous support. In no particular order, I'd like to thank: Manon, Jennifer Montgomery, Sarah Kalny, Jess Gisler, Ryan BretonNS, Cecilie Knudsen, William Powers, Felicia, André Valério, Mary Crauderueff, Natalie Jess, Ripley M., Nagore Jimenez, Allie, Aleksandra, Damian Evergreen, Brynn Kingsley, Phoenix, Abby Whitman, Elizabeth Rathburn, Jenna Rosciszewski, Meg Celidonia, Clare Weisenfluh, Sheila Rosciszewski, Rachele Heasley, Kellie, Lauren Esper, Kristian, Kayleigh Bowman, Sarah Wallace, Jessica Collins, Liv, Kimberly Rowland, Jennifer Bruce, Elijah Cowles, S.E. Sullivan, EverAfterPrint, Tess B., Tifenn, Ciarán Black, Hannah Ruiz, Nikola Prochazkova, M. Kermeen, BunnyBoyGamille, Mana Yanoska, Andrew Godecke, River Taylor, Kat Gynn, Laura Edwards, Abby, Sara Oros, Rachel Emily, Elizabeth Shewan, Nikki K,

Ricken, Emily P., Keli M, Lisa Clément-Guy, Ian, Caitlin Hodgson, Eric Daniel Saulters-Wood, Alexandra, Mel & Jay, Kathryn Schmitt, Alli DiGilio, Laura Hardner, Allison Christopher, Alana Sawchuk, Sierra Nicholes, Karen Boyer, Angelina Randazzo, Becky, Marine Lesne, Kristin Lopez, Chris Monceaux, Julia, Hannah Cecchi, Daniel Bainbridge, Nina-Marie & Paul, Rosie Pregler, Dr. Brett Johnson, Dr. Christina and Dr.Greg Brown, Abby W., Tori Kemke, and Ben K.

About the Author

Tess Carletta (she/her) is an independent author based in northern Pennsylvania. She intends to make this world a better place by filling it with happily-ever-afters and writing stories that nourish the soul. She can be found writing in all the local cozy nooks, playing RPGS, and reading in the sun with her cat, aptly named Miss Ruby the Ham Princess.